# BACK FROM THE DEAD

Peter Leonard, who has been described as 'a huge talent' (Mo Hayder) and 'razor sharp' (R. J. Ellory), is the author of four previous novels, most recently *Voices of the Dead* (2012).

*Praise for Peter Leonard*:

'Leonard has created a spectacular and deeply felt novel of history (and) revenge . . . A moving portrait of loss and identity, and one of the best books of the year.' *Catholic Herald*

'Lean and tight . . . one of those novels you don't read so much as glide through, grinning and snorting . . . You could read him all day without getting bored.' *Guardian*

'Likely the thriller of the year . . . it's the constant riffing inventiveness . . . the snap and snarl of his dialogue, the sheer clarity of action.' *Word*

'Stunning.' *Daily Mirror*

'There's the hot-plate sizzle of brilliantly written dialogue, succinct description, all you need to know about where you are in a few telling sentences, no fat at all on these words . . . tremendous stuff, really.' **** *Uncut*

# Back from the Dead

PETER LEONARD

*faber and faber*

First published in this edition in 2013
by Faber and Faber Limited
Bloomsbury House
74–77 Great Russell Street
London WC1B 3DA

Typeset by Faber and Faber Ltd
Printed and bound by CPI Group (UK) Ltd, Croydon, CR0 4YY

A CIP record for this book
is available from the British Library

ISBN 978-0-571-27151-1

FSC
www.fsc.org
MIX
Paper from
responsible sources
FSC® C101712

*For the Aisles*

# One

*Freeport, Bahamas. 1971.*

Hess heard voices, but had to listen carefully, tune into the sound before he realized they were speaking English with a British accent. He hated the British and pictured Churchill in a newsreel, pontificating after the war, the fat man with the cigar, his righteous tone more righteous after defeating Germany. Hess opened his eyes looking up at the white blades of a fan slowly rotating above him. He was in a hospital ward, an infirmary, the last bed in a big white room filled with beds, Hess on his back, a lot of activity to his left, Negro nurses moving about, checking on Negro patients. Everyone he could see had black skin. For an Aryan who believed in racial purity this was hell, God playing a cruel joke on him.

It hurt to breathe, his lungs were burning and he had a pain in his upper chest. He touched it and felt a bandage through the hospital gown. He noticed there were IVs in both of his arms, which were badly sunburned. His last recollection was floating in the ocean, hanging onto a wood plank that had drifted by, a piece of wreckage, bobbing in the water like a wine cork, for a day at least, until someone rescued him. He remembered being pulled out of the water but his memory was hazy after that.

"You're awake."

A nurse approached the bed. She had short black hair that fit her head like a cap, and the darkest skin he had ever seen, the dark chocolate color contrasting her big white teeth and crisp white uniform.

"How do you feel?" She was standing at the side of his bed, looking down at him. "My name is Camille. Are you in any pain?"

The wound in his chest itched. He scratched at it under the bandage. "What happened?"

"That's what everyone wants to know."

In a snapshot memory he saw himself lying on the black and white tiles of a kitchen floor, a hole in his chest, blood leaking out of him, feeling light-headed, sure he was going to die, Harry Levin, his executioner, standing over him. But how? He had killed Harry in Detroit, shot him point blank.

"Where am I?" Hess said.

"Freeport, sir. The Bahamas. You were delirious, near death when they brought you in. The good news, the salt water helped heal your wound. Salt's an anti-inflammatory, encourages the formation of connective tissue and blood vessels important to the healing process."

Nurse Camille took a thermometer out of an apron pocket, shook it and slid it in his mouth. "Under your tongue now. That's a good man." She held her arm up, glancing at the watch on her black wrist. "A fisherman find you floating in the channel." She pulled the thermometer out of his mouth and read it. "Temperature's down."

"How long have I been here?"

"Two days."

"What is the date?"

2

"Fifteenth of October." She paused. "What is your name, sir?"

"I don't know. Did you check my identification?"

"There was nothing on you when you were admitted. Nothing except the ring on your left hand. A policeman was by this morning. Would like a word when you're up to it. I have my rounds. I'll be back to check on you."

Nurse Camille moved to the bed next to him, attending to a gray-haired Negro man. Hess lay back staring at the fan, thinking God had spared him, brought him back to finish his work. He wanted Hess to kill more Jews. Hess thought of Eichmann saying he would leap laughing into the grave because the feeling that he had killed five million people on his conscience would be a source of extraordinary satisfaction. Hess could relate. Killing Jews had been immensely satisfying.

*

Day three. The trim dark-skinned man in a white short-sleeved shirt introduced himself as Inspector Johnson, Royal Bahamian Police. He held up his ID in a black billfold so Hess could read it. His full name was Cuffee Johnson. His ancestors had obviously been slaves that had taken their master's surname. They were originally from Africa, but where? He would have guessed Senegambia on the northwest coast where Portuguese sailors started the slave trade in the 1400s.

Inspector Johnson grabbed a chair that was against the wall, brought it over, positioned it next to the bed and sat, holding a notebook and blue plastic pen in his long black fingers. He had a wide mouth, a flat nose and dark serious eyes.

3

"Do you know your name?"

"I don't remember."

"Or where you're from?"

"No."

"Or how you got here?"

"I have a vague recollection of being pulled out of the ocean."

"You were in the water a long time, more than twenty-four hours by the condition of your skin."

"Who found me?"

"A fisherman named Ousseny. He was cruising back with a net full of mahi mahi and saw you floating. Thought you were dead. Contacted the authorities and brought you here."

"Will you thank him for me?" He was thinking maybe this fisherman could take him back to Palm Beach.

Inspector Johnson took a handkerchief out of his shirt pocket and dabbed the perspiration on his face. "Do you know who shot you?"

"I don't remember anything."

"Your clothing had labels from the Breakers Hotel in Palm Beach, Florida. Does that ring a bell?"

"I don't know."

"The Palm Beach police are looking for a missing person, a salesman from Stuttgart, Germany. Disappeared three days ago. They found his abandoned rental car. His clothing and possessions still in his hotel room. Arrived the 30th of September, went through customs in Detroit, Michigan. Was issued a three-month visa."

Hess was thinking about the key to the safe deposit box at

SunTrust Bank. It was in his briefcase in the room. If they found the key and opened the box they would know who he was.

"The man who disappeared, Mr Gerd Klaus, was staying at the Breakers. He had purchased two shirts and a pair of pants in one of the hotel shops. Does any of this sound familiar?"

Hess shook his head.

"The description of this missing person fits you. Your color hair, about six feet tall, two hundred pounds. Are you from Stuttgart, Germany?"

"I don't know."

"Do you speak German? *Sprechen sie Deutsch?*"

Hess shrugged, furrowed his brow.

"Detective Conlin from the Palm Beach police department wants to talk to you. He'll be arriving tomorrow."

Cuffee Johnson picked up the chair and placed it back against the wall.

"Where are you from, Inspector?"

"Born here on the islands, Eleuthera. Why do you ask?" He came back to the bed, staring down at Hess.

"I mean your family, your great-grandfather or his father. He was a slave, wasn't he?"

"Sierra Leone," Inspector Cuffee Johnson said.

"Are you Mende?" Hess asked, guessing his tribe.

"Limba." He closed the notebook and slid it in his shirt pocket. "But can't remember your name, uh? I'll check on you tomorrow. See if your memory come back."

*

In the morning after breakfast, Hess lay on his back while Nurse

5

Camille sponge-bathed him. He studied her face as she washed his naked body. She did not seem nervous or embarrassed, cleaning a complete stranger. Hess had never thought of Negro women in a sexual way. They were savages, animals. But being near this nurse with her high cheekbones, dark chocolate skin and voluptuous figure was arousing him. Now as she moved the sponge over his cock, it began to get hard and she glanced at him and smiled.

"Oh, look at you." She smiled. "Feeling better I see."

He could understand how the slave owners he had read about would select certain girls and have them brought to their bed. "Are you married?" Hess said.

Camille shook her head.

"Why not? A good-looking woman like you," Hess flirting with her. Would have guessed her age at thirty-five.

She smiled. "I don't find the right man." It was obviously something that was on her mind, something she thought about.

"It is only a matter of time." Hess paused. "Do you know what happened to my clothes?"

"The police have them."

Of course. He was the victim of a shooting. The clothes were evidence. "Can you get me something to wear? I do not have money here, but if you trust me I will send it to you. Inspector Johnson said I might be the missing person who was staying at the Breakers Hotel in Palm Beach, Florida, and if this is true I must be wealthy. The Breakers is a very expensive hotel."

"I believe you." She smiled. "The condition you're in though, I don't think you're going to be leaving any time soon. Can you even stand up?"

"Let's find out."

She dried him and pulled down his gown. He swung his legs over the side of the bed, sat up, feeling weak, light-headed, Nurse Camille holding on to him. He slid off the bed, feet touching the floor. He tried to stand and his knees buckled, leaning into the bed until Nurse Camille reached him, pressing her body against his, trying to hold him up. "Want to dance," Hess said, their faces inches apart.

She smiled. "I'm gonna dance you right back in the bed."

*

Day four. Detective Conlin from Palm Beach handed Hess a GERD KLAUS, MIDWEST SALES MANAGER business card and said, "This company you say you work for has never heard of you."

"I don't know what you are talking about."

"Don't you?"

Conlin was sitting next to the bed in the chair where the slave inspector had been the day before, Hess propped up on pillows, studying him. Conlin was tall and lean, with receding hair combed straight back and a sunburned nose. He wore a light blue short-sleeved shirt and a blue tie with food stains on it, khaki trousers and brown shoes that needed polish.

"What were you doing in Florida?"

"I don't know that I was."

"Sure you were," Conlin said. "Staying at the Breakers. Positively ID'd by half a dozen employees." He paused. "Selling weed? Coke? Got in over your head. Got shot, dumped in the ocean. It's a miracle you're alive."

Hess glanced up at the fan.

"You've got another problem. Fingerprints that are all over your rental vehicle match the prints on the dead security guard's car, his weapon and flashlight." Detective Conlin placed his briefcase on the bed, touching Hess' leg. "You want to tell me what happened?"

"I don't remember."

"Quit playing dumb. We know you're our guy."

Conlin opened the briefcase and brought out a fingerprint kit. Picked up Hess' left hand and inked his thumb and fingers, rolling them onto a blotter. Did the same to Hess' other hand and when he was finished he showed the prints to him. "Not bad. See there—" He pointed. "All that good ridge detail. This should be a piece of cake." Conlin placed Hess' fingerprints in the briefcase, closed the top and placed it on the floor. "Same type and caliber weapon used on the security guard, killed a high-profile realtor a few hours earlier. And guess whose prints we found?"

Hess closed his eyes for a couple seconds. He was tired and weak.

"Don't fall asleep on me, Gerd."

When he opened them Conlin was on his feet, holding the briefcase. In his discount shirt and trousers Conlin reminded Hess of a man who sold carpeting or linoleum flooring.

*

A couple days later Hess could see a policeman in the doorway at the far end of the ward, a young black man wearing the official uniform. The white tunic, blue peaked cap, and blue trousers with red stripes down the sides reminded him of a Royal Navy uniform.

Once the policemen arrived, sitting in the hall outside the ward around the clock, all of the nurses, including Camille, were less friendly, more businesslike. Nurse Camille had stopped flirting with him. She continued to check on him, take his temperature, bring him food and medicine and sponge-bathe him, but she seemed standoffish and distant. Hess was sure her sudden change in attitude was due to the fact that he was a suspect in two Palm Beach homicides. Word had undoubtedly spread.

Hess kept track of when the nurses made their rounds and when the police guard stepped outside to smoke, and when the guard walked down the hall to visit the nurses. He could hear them talking and laughing.

After the nurses made their late rounds, he would wait for the guard to walk outside, unhook the IV bag from the metal stand and carry it over his shoulder, walking around the dark ward, trying to get his legs back. At first he could only take a couple of steps before he had to go back to the bed. Now he could walk to the hall and back to his bed without feeling tired. Hess believed he had a few more days, a week at the most, before the doctor pronounced him fit, and he was transferred to the island jail.

He had been trying to think of a way to escape, somehow slip by the police guard and the nurses, when it occurred to him that the simplest, most direct route out of the hospital was right there. The window. If he could open it far enough, he could squeeze through and disappear. Hess could see cars parked lining the streets of Freeport. The hospital had been a clinic until recently, and Hess' ward was on the first floor.

*

Dr Hubert W. Sparks studied the wound in his chest. He was a Negro, fit and trim like all of them, late thirties, calm demeanor. The doctor sat him up and placed his stethoscope on Hess' chest and back and told him to breathe.

"Lungs are clear."

Hess had had water in his lungs. Now the doctor inspected the gunshot wound in his chest, poking and prodding. "Stitches can come out tomorrow," he said, studying the sutured incision.

Hess said, "Where did you attend medical school, Doctor?"

Sparks looked at him quizzically. "What's this? You want to make sure the island doctor is qualified, has the proper credentials?" He paused. "I would say a man in your position should feel fortunate you're here. Don't worry, you won't have to suffer this inferior healthcare much longer. I understand you're going to be leaving us soon."

Sooner than you think, Hess wanted to say.

# Two

"I want you to find Ernst Hess," Gerhard Braun had said when they were sitting across from each other in armchairs in the salon at Braun's estate, a room the size of a gymnasium. "He's disappeared. I would have too if an article like this had been written about me. Have you seen it?"

Braun was strange-looking: long face, big nose, eyes bulging out of their sockets, boring into him. He tossed an issue of *Der Spiegel* on the coffee table in front of Zeller.

Zeller nodded. "Quite an exposé. I have to say, I was surprised."

"About what in particular?" Braun blew a cloud of cigar smoke into the open room that drifted and disappeared.

"His alleged war crimes, although after seeing the photograph of Hess smiling in front of the mass grave, his guilt seems a foregone conclusion."

"Ernst Hess' orders were to kill Jews. He did it and did it well." Braun paused, placed his cigar in a crystal ashtray, and sipped his whisky. "His political career is finished. When, and if, Hess is caught, he will be prosecuted. But there is more to it than that."

There usually is, Zeller was thinking. He wondered what Hess had on Gerhard Braun. He knew Braun had not served the Reich in any military capacity other than supplying the

German army with weapons and ordnance. But whatever Hess had on him, Braun was concerned.

Zeller said, "Do you have any idea where he might have gone?"

"If I did I wouldn't need you."

"Any girlfriends, mistresses?"

"A model named Anke Kruger."

"Any hobbies, addictions, unusual proclivities?"

"I don't care if he has his way with goats," Braun said. "I want you to find him before the Nazi hunters and the Bundeskriminalamt do." He paused, picked up the cigar, puffing on it.

Zeller was intrigued. He sat, glancing at a Van Gogh framed on the wall—the *Portrait of Dr Gachet*. Zeller knew the painting. He had studied art at the university, tried to imagine what it was worth. "I read that it was lost during the war."

"Well evidently it has been found." Braun poured whisky from a decanter into a lowball crystal glass and handed it to him.

*

Zeller had been contacted by Horst Neubauer, an attorney representing Gerhard Braun, saying Herr Braun wanted to talk to him.

"About what?" Zeller had said.

"Herr Braun will explain everything. He will pay you five thousand Deutschmarks for your time. If you listen to his proposition and say no, the money is yours. If you agree to work for him, he will deduct it from your fee."

This is what Zeller knew about Braun. The only son of a wealthy industrialist, he had taken over the family business in

1942 at age twenty-seven after his father died of a heart attack. Braun had joined the Nazi party in 1934, believed in the cause but refused to wear a uniform, salute or click his heels. Working with Albert Speer and Ferdinand Porsche he retooled his father's factories to produce military vehicles for the Reich. Braun built tanks and tractors, and eighty-eight-millimeter anti-aircraft guns. At the high point of the war he had forty-seven factories and sixty thousand Jewish slave laborers from concentration camps, cranking out weapons. "Why kill them? Let's put them to work," Braun had said. His representatives went to the camps and handpicked the laborers they wanted.

After the war Braun was arrested by the Americans and charged with crimes against peace and crimes against humanity. He was found guilty. The judges on the tribunal sentenced him to ten years in prison on July 31, 1947. He also lost his factories, homes, art collection and money—over a hundred million Deutschmarks. Stripped of everything except his red-and-white-striped prison uniform, Braun was sent to Landsberg in Bavaria, where Hitler had written *Mein Kampf.*

That was before the Allies realized that getting Germany back on its feet required resources. They needed men like Braun, leaders to help restore industry. In 1951, John J. McCloy, high commissioner of the American occupation zone, released Braun from prison, returned forty million Deutschmarks in property and cash, and gave him control of ten of his former companies. Fifty pieces of art that had been confiscated by the Allies were also returned to him.

Zeller tilted his glass and rotated it, the whisky coating the sides. He sipped the amber liquid, tasting spice and nuts, intense citrus, lemon and orange and then hints of vanilla and roasted coffee. "Remarkable. What is it?"

"1926 Dalmore. What if this was your job, making the best aged single malt in the world? How satisfying, I would imagine."

\*

First Zeller called Fuhrman, an old friend, who worked for customs and immigration. Zeller had used him on occasion, to locate high-profile defectors. This time he asked Fuhrman to find out if Ernst Hess had been on a flight leaving Germany in the past three weeks.

"Leaving Germany for where?" Fuhrman said.

"South America." It was conceivable Hess had been in contact with former Nazis who had escaped prosecution after the war. "I would try Rio, Buenos Aires, Santiago, Lima, and maybe we'll get lucky."

"Any flight to South America would probably make a connection in Lisbon, and then fly non-stop. You're talking about a lot of flights. It's going to take time, and it's going to cost you."

A few days later Fuhrman reported back, saying he had checked the airline manifests of every flight from Germany to a South American city since September 20th. Hess' name did not appear. But Hess could have chartered a plane or chosen another mode of travel. Zeller asked Fuhrman to check with charter aircraft companies and ship lines.

\*

Next on Zeller's list was Hess' mistress, Anke Kruger. She was a former model and looked it, five ten, long blonde hair, wearing skintight blue jeans and a revealing brown tank top, breasts loose under the soft fabric. Anke lived in a posh apartment building near Leopoldstrasse in Schwabing.

"A glass of wine?" Anke said.

"Well it is five o'clock, isn't it?"

She went to the kitchen, poured two glasses of white wine, brought them to the salon, handed one to Zeller standing at the window, watching the action on the street below.

"Would you care to sit?"

"This is fine," Zeller said. "I've been driving for three hours."

"I will tell you what I know." She sat on the windowsill, long legs in black knee-high boots angled to the floor. "But it's not much."

"How long have you known Herr Hess?"

"About three years. Ernst hired me to work at a Hess AG airship exhibition. I was a model at the time. We became good friends. Later when Ernst and his wife separated we became romantically involved. We had fun, spent a lot of time together. It was serious, we talked about getting married, having children."

"When did you last see Herr Hess?" He heard a horn, glanced out the window. It was rush hour, cars creeping by on Leopoldstrasse.

"I know exactly, it was the third of October. My birthday is the fifth and Ernst was telling me he had something special planned. I could tell he was excited, but then I did not hear from him again for ten days."

"What was his excuse for missing your birthday? What did he say?"

"He had something to take care of. An emergency. He had to leave town, and apologized."

"Was this before or after the article in *Der Spiegel*?"

"At least a week before."

"Where was he calling from?"

"He didn't say. But listen to me," Anke Kruger said. "I know this man. He did not do these things they said in the magazine."

She obviously didn't know him well enough. "Is there anything you can think of that will help me find Herr Hess?"

Anke shook her head.

*

Zeller arrived at Hess AG the following morning at 9.30. Gerhard Braun, a member of Hess' board of directors, had contacted the manager, Herr Rothman, and explained the situation. Rothman was expecting Zeller, escorted him to Hess' office, and told him to take his time. If he needed anything, dial extension 12.

"I'll want to speak to Herr Hess' secretary."

"Ingrid Bookmyer. I'll ask her to stop by."

Rothman walked out and closed the door.

Zeller studied the room, which was ten meters by seven and a half, with a wall of windows that looked out at the concrete landing area. He watched a Zeppelin, skinned in silver, rise hovering above the tarmac, engineers in white shirts and dark trousers, making notes on clipboards.

He looked around. The furniture was custom-designed in light-colored wood. Hess had a big desk with a credenza behind it. On the paneled rear wall behind the conference table were six framed pictures showing the evolution of the Zeppelin, from the LZ1, photographed over Lake Constance in 1899, the Graf Zeppelin, and the Hindenburg, to smaller, sleeker, current-issue Hess AG airships. Along a sidewall, matching wooden file cabinets were lined up. There were flat files against the opposite wall, and in the middle of the room, a drafting table that displayed blueprints showing the interior skeleton of a Hess AG airship.

There was a knock on the door, it opened and a big-boned woman, early thirties, stepped in the room. "I'm Ingrid, Herr Hess' secretary." Ingrid Bookmyer, whom everyone called Booky, wearing black hornrim glasses, blonde hair tied in a bun.

"Come in and sit, won't you. My name is Albin Zeller. I have been retained by the CSU to find Herr Hess." It was an exaggeration of course but Ingrid Bookmyer would have no idea. He led her to a furniture grouping. She sat in one of the chairs and he on the couch across from her. She was all buttoned up in a dark suit, breasts bulging against the jacket, hemline of the skirt past her knees. Zeller was trying to decide if she was attractive or not. Wondering what she would look like without the glasses, with her hair down, wearing jeans and a tee-shirt.

"How long have you worked for Herr Hess?"

"Since he purchased the airship company in 1964."

"Are you close to him?"

She blushed. "What do you mean?"

"Are you friends? Does he confide in you?"

"I have worked for Herr Hess seven and a half years. I would say I know him quite well. I admire him. Ernst Hess is a brilliant man."

Ingrid Bookmyer was clearly nervous, rubbing her hands

together. Zeller now wondered if their relationship had been intimate. "Have you been to Herr Hess' apartment?"

"At times he worked from there and I would drop off test results," she said, knees together, hands flat on her thighs.

Zeller said, "When did you last speak to him?"

"Twenty-ninth of September."

"How do you remember the date?"

"I have a good memory."

"Where was he calling from?"

"Detroit, Michigan. I didn't know at the time, but he gave me the number at the hotel where he was staying. I phoned Herr Hess the next day to tell him about the death of Arno Rausch."

"And you haven't spoken to him since?"

Ingrid Bookmyer shook her head.

"You know Herr Hess is a fugitive from justice, wanted for crimes against humanity. Aid him in any way," Zeller said with more authority, "and you will be prosecuted. Do you understand?" He could see tears in her eyes, so unless she was acting he had gotten through to her. "When you hear from Herr Hess, and I believe you will, I want you to call me at this number. It is my answering service. You can contact them any time day or night." He handed her a card.

Zeller spent two more hours in the office. He found an address book in the desk. Opened it and scanned the entries. Hess, not surprising, was well connected. He recognized the names of well-known judges, politicians, scientists, doctors, industrialists. Gerhard Braun was included, as was Willy Brandt. But it was Leon Halip's name that jumped out at him for being so unexpected. Leon was the best forger on the European con-

18

tinent, a craftsman, an artist. Zeller was under the impression Halip, a Hungarian, had retired. He was sixty-two, with crippling arthritis in his hands. Zeller would have to drive to Wiesbaden and pay him a visit.

In the credenza he found a Luger, circa '37, and a box of nine-millimeter cartridges. The gun smelled as if it had recently been fired. That in itself didn't mean anything. He had probably gone to a shooting range. He might even have one at his estate. Zeller found Hess AG bank statements in a file cabinet. Hess' business account was at Deutsche Bank, listing a balance of DM270,000. Zeller checked statements going back six months and didn't see any large cash withdrawals or wire transfers. If Hess were planning to go somewhere and start over he would need money.

*

Mail was piled up on the desk in Hess' apartment, envelopes and magazines. The manager told him Herr Hess was frequently out of town, so the building concierge brought his mail to the apartment.

"Who else has a key?"

The manager said, "I have the only key, and I can assure you I monitor very closely anyone who uses it."

Zeller opened the phone bill and scanned the calls: a dozen to a number in Schleissheim he assumed was Hess' estate, several to a Munich phone number, a long-distance call to Wiesbaden, quite a few to Anke Kruger and half a dozen to a phone number in New York. He checked the address book he had brought from Hess' office and traced the number to someone named J. Mauer with an address on Park Avenue in New York City.

An envelope from Deutsche Bank listed the recent checks Hess had written, and showed a current balance of DM75,349. Again, no substantial cash withdrawals or money transfers. He found Hess' brokerage account statements in a file drawer in the desk, stocks whose current value was DM32,000. Another file held his real estate holdings. In addition to the airship company, Hess owned an office building.

In the credenza behind the desk he found a drawerful of items that, at first, made no sense: gloves, eyeglasses, bracelets, Stars of David, diamond rings, an oval locket that opened to a sepia-tone photo of a dark-haired woman, and that's when it hit him. These were probably Hess' war souvenirs. Almost thirty years had passed and still he hung on to them.

He knew Hess had been a Nazi party member, an SS officer on special assignment, touring concentration camps, picking up ideas, successful practices that could be used throughout the system. Hess had helped Adolf Eichmann organize the Wallersee Conference outside Berlin. Reinhard Heydrich had outlined the Reich's plans for the final solution to the Nazi top brass. Heydrich had to have their buy-in to succeed.

Hess had also done a brief tour with Einsatzgruppen B, a killing squad in Poland, but it had not been widely publicized. After the war, Hess had started a construction company to help rebuild the cities destroyed by Allied bombs. He was a hero, a man putting the Fatherland first. Acording to Gerhard Braun, Hess was not getting the country back on its feet because of some altruistic feeling, it was a way to get rich. He sold the

20

construction business in 1964 for seven million Deutschmarks, and bought the airship company.

*

Zeller arrived at Hess' estate in Schleissheim, thirteen kilometers north of Munich, the next morning at eleven. A butler met him at the front door and escorted him to the salon where Frau Hess, formerly Elfriede Dinker, was seated on a couch. The butler introduced him. He shook Frau Hess' hand and she invited him to sit in a big comfortable chair across from her. He had phoned ahead, made an appointment, telling her he had been hired by a group of concerned CSU party members to find Herr Hess.

"I have not seen or talked to Ernst for almost a month. I was visiting my mother in Ansbach. When I returned, he was gone," she said, sounding relieved.

Frau Hess had ruddy cheeks and blonde hair pulled back in a braided ponytail. She was quiet and formal, and nearly expressionless except for an occasional twitch that made her look like she was grinning. Her hands were folded in her lap, fingers intertwined. Zeller could now understand why Ernst had taken a mistress. There was nothing even remotely sexy about her. "Do you know where your husband is?"

She shook her head.

"Did Herr Hess talk about his war experiences?"

"Never."

"But you are aware he was a member of the Nazi party?"

"I have seen photographs of Ernst in uniform, so of course I knew he was in the military. I do not believe, as the article in

21

*Der Spiegel* stated, he murdered innocent people. Jews. To tell the truth, it seems out of character for a man given to philanthropic causes. Ernst pays for the health care of everyone working at the airship company. He is proud that he helped rebuild the country. Ernst loves Germany." She paused. "Ernst and I have been estranged for some time. We are married in name only. I am the last person he would confide in. So you see, you have come all this way for nothing."

"Is Katya at home? May I speak to her?"

"I do not want her involved in any of this. The reporters have been hounding us. Even friends have turned against her."

"Does your husband correspond with anyone in South America? Can you recall receiving mail from any South American countries?"

"What do you mean?"

"Many Nazis escaped to South America after the war." Eichmann had fled to Buenos Aires, Argentina, and Josef Mengele, the Angel of Death, had gone to Argentina before settling in Hohenhau, Paraguay.

"Why would Ernst associate with murderers? He is a respected member of the Christian Social Union." Frau Hess paused. "Is there anything else?"

Zeller noticed a hook on the bare wall behind Frau Hess, and dusty lines where a picture had hung. "I'm just curious, what did you have hanging on the wall?"

"A painting. It was Ernst's. He must have taken it with him."

"Do you know the name of the painting or who the artist is?"

"It was a Van Gogh."

"Can you describe it?"

"I never liked it and it's just as well that it's gone."

# Three

"Harry, there's a guy named Zeller here to see you," Phyllis said.

"Where's he from?"

"Didn't say. The way he talks I thought you knew him."

"He's a salesman," Harry said. "That's what they do. They make it sound like they're your friend. Probably wants to sell us a new baling press or guillotine shear. Tell him I'm busy, I've been out of town, I have to catch up." That was all true. It was his second day back after two weeks in Florida, laying on the beach and laying on top of Colette. He was tan and relaxed, trying to ease back into the work world. The scrap business and everything about it seemed absurd in his current state of mind, thinking it was time to sell the company, move on, do something else. He had a pile of transaction reports to review, trying to find the motivation to do it. Wasn't in the mood to talk to a salesman, listen to his pitch.

"I told him, Harry. He said he'd wait in the lobby."

Harry heard a dog bark.

"I had to bring Lily with me today," Phyllis said. "Her has a tuminache. She'll be good though, won't you?" The dog growled. "Yes, her will."

Whoever the guy was he'd get tired of sitting there. Phyllis had referred to it as the lobby, but in fact it was a claustrophobic six-by-eight-foot space with off-white cinderblock walls, one featuring a framed watercolor of a ship docked at sunset an old girlfriend had bought for him at an art fair in Traverse City. There were also two uncomfortable, chrome-framed teal naugahyde chairs, circa '63, that had been in Harry's basement.

He was trying to concentrate on the reports when the phone rang twenty minutes later. "Harry, he's still here."

"Close your window, ignore him." There was a sill with a double glass window on the wall next to Phyllis' desk. One side slid open so Phyllis could talk to whoever came in. Harry was going to say, you want to get rid of the guy, take Lily out there, have her piss on his leg, but Phyllis the dog-lover would've taken offense.

An hour later Phyllis buzzed him on the intercom. "All clear, Harry. He left." It was 4.15. "I'm going to leave a few minutes early, you don't mind. I want to take Lily to the vet on the way home."

At 4.30 Harry decided to call it a day, too. He was going to the bank in the morning right from his house, withdraw twenty-five grand to buy scrap, keep the business going. He took the .357 Colt out of the Mosler safe that was bolted to the floor behind his desk. Held the gun, pushed the latch forward and the cylinder popped open. There were three spent shell casings. Two had gone through the French door of the Frankels' master bedroom in Palm Beach, through the Italian armoire, the stucco inner wall and brick outer wall, and were probably somewhere in the Atlantic ocean. The third round had blown Hess off his feet and ended his life.

He tapped the shells out, grasped the cylinder with his right hand and fed three Remington 125-grain .357 cartridges into the empty chambers. Swung the cylinder closed with his left hand and heard it click.

When he got outside Harry threw the spent shell casings onto the mountain of scrap metal behind the building, and watched the last semi rumble out of the yard. His crew, through for the day, were putting equipment back in the warehouse.

Phyllis had hired a Vietnam vet named Archie Damman to work the scale after Jerry was killed. It wasn't a done deal, but Harry liked what he saw. This guy Damman put in the hours and seemed to know what he was doing.

He thought about Colette as he cruised through Hamtramck on his way to the freeway, couldn't wait to see her. She had driven back from Florida with him, and made the trip fun. He enjoyed spending time with her, had gotten used to having her around, and missed her when he went back to work. This was new for Harry. He'd thought about it, analyzed it and decided he'd had trouble with previous relationships because everyone he'd been close to had been killed. He'd dated a lot of girls in the eighteen years since Anna had died, but most of the relationships had lasted less than a month.

Harry didn't know what was going to happen with Colette. Her career was in Germany and he'd been kicked out of the country, and they had only been together for a couple weeks, but he sure liked her. She was going back to Munich in a few days and that would be their first real test.

On the way home Harry stopped at the cemetery and stood in front of Sara's gravestone. He hadn't been here since she'd been buried almost seven weeks ago. He still couldn't believe it, but there was her name etched in black marble.

Sara A. Levin 1953–1971

It wasn't supposed to happen this way. Sara should've been standing here looking at Harry's grave. He picked up some twigs and leaves on the ground and put them in his coat pocket. "How're you doing, honey? You doing all right?" He paused, feeling self-conscious. Was this crazy, talking to Sara like this? No, Harry said to himself. It's okay. "I met somebody, a girl named Colette. I think you'd like her." He paused. "I miss you."

*

Colette was on the couch in Harry's den, having her lunch, chicken salad on lettuce and tomato, watching a soap opera called *General Hospital*, when she heard the doorbell, stood up still watching the television, looked out the front window and saw a white van parked in the driveway. It said *Acme Carpet Cleaning* on the side in brown letters. The doorbell rang again. Harry didn't mention anything about having his carpets cleaned. Maybe they had the wrong address.

From the back hall Colette could see a man in a red cap through the glass panes in the door. He saw her and waved but she sensed that something was wrong. Colette moved into the kitchen, picked up the phone and dialed Harry's office number. She heard the side door open, and the sound of footsteps. Heard Harry's secretary say, "S&H Scrap Metal Recyclers, how may I direct your call?" The phone was taken from her and replaced in the cradle. There were two of them. They picked her up, carried her into the living room and rolled her up in one of Harry's antique rugs, legs pressed together, arms pinned to her sides. She couldn't move, could barely breathe, started to panic.

They never said a word, picked her up and carried her outside. She could feel a cool breeze blow through the open ends of the rug and it calmed her a little. They slid her in the back of the van and closed the doors. Colette heard them get in the front, heard the engine start and felt the van move, backing down the driveway. All she could think—it had to be retaliation for the article she had written about Hess. But how would anyone know she was staying with Harry? She didn't tell her editor, didn't even tell her mother.

Colette was on her side. She could smell dye on the fabric and taste the dust. She sneezed a couple times. Her nose itched. She bent her head forward and rubbed it against the coarse fabric. She smelled cigarette smoke, and felt the sway of the truck and felt herself sliding. Heard the twangy chords of country music on the radio, and the sounds of traffic outside the van. They were moving at a steady speed now.

She tried to take her mind off what was happening, pictured herself skiing with her mother in Courmayeur, the Italian side of Mont Blanc, going down the mountain, skis buried in deep powder, leaning back, her mother slaloming down the mountain in front of her like a teenager.

Colette heard cars passing the van going in the opposite direction and then the whining sound of tires on asphalt. The van slowed and made a left turn and a right and came to a stop. The rear doors opened and she was lifted out and carried, felt the rug tilt up as they went up a couple steps, entered a room and put her down. Then she was spinning as they unrolled the rug. Colette, dizzy, trying to focus, seeing white walls and a brick fireplace. She was on the dusty wood floor, in a house, shades covering the windows. The two men were dark shapes in the dark room, the sour smell of sweat and cigarette smoke clinging to them. "*Sprechen sie Deutsch*?"

"No, we don't *sprechen sie* no *Deutsch*," the one wearing a red cap said. He spoke with a southern accent.

"What do you want?"

The one in the cap moved behind her, holding her biceps. The second one picked up her legs. "We'll let you know," he said.

"Ain't suppose to talk at her," the one in the cap said.

"Don't worry about it, okay? Just pick her up."

The one behind her had his wrists under her armpits now, hands holding her breasts.

"Well lookit her, will you? Don't like nobody touching her sweater pups," the one in the cap said.

"Pup's ass, Squirrel, them's full grown."

Colette started to twist and kick.

"We got us a little cougar, ain't we?" the man behind her said. "Full of piss and vinegar. I'm going to drop you on your head you don't stop squirming."

Colette went slack and they carried her along a hallway, through a door, down a narrow staircase into the cellar, tied her tight to a chair, arms behind her back, her legs bound to the chair legs. When her eyes adjusted she saw the furnace and hot-water tank on the other side of the empty room that had unpainted block walls and high windows on both sides covered with newsprint.

"Don't y'all go nowhere," the one wearing the cap said. The gamey smell of him made her sick. He touched her breasts, hands hard and rough. "I be back for some of your sweet, sweet cooze."

Colette watched them walk up the stairs, already uncomfortable, arms and shoulders aching.

*

She must've dozed off. The sun had moved over the house and the light was brighter coming through the papered windows on the west side of the room. She heard footsteps on the stairs and saw the one in the cap appear and move toward her, grinning. Colette could smell him before he reached her, an odor so foul she had to breathe through her mouth. He walked around behind the chair, placed his hands on her shoulders and started to massage her.

"All them German girls stacked like you?"

He reached over and pulled the top of her blouse open. Two buttons popped off and hit the floor. Colette felt her pulse race. He dug down and pulled her breasts out of the cups of her bra, squeezing them with callused hands.

Colette screamed, hoping the other man would hear her and come down.

He put his greasy hand over her mouth, pawing her with hard thick fingers. She tried to bite him and he slapped her across the face with an open hand.

"What the hell you doin' down there, Squirrel?" the other man said from the top of the stairs. Colette heard him come halfway down.

"Nothin'."

"Get up here."

Squirrel leaned in with his face close to hers. His breath had a bacterial reek that made her gag.

"I'll be back," he said and walked up the stairs.

*

Colette had fallen asleep and woke to the sound of footsteps on the stairs. The light in the windows was fading. She felt herself start to wind up again, thinking Squirrel was coming back for her. But it wasn't him. A tall man in a black leather jacket appeared with a folded lawn chair. He opened it and sat a few feet from her.

"You are from Munich, I understand."

Colette stared at him.

"Would you like to come upstairs, have something to eat and drink, use the toilet? You have been down here a long time. All you have to do is tell me what I want to know." He paused for a beat and said, "Where is Ernst Hess?"

*

Harry pulled in the driveway, parked and went in the side door. He expected to see Colette in the kitchen, starting dinner. She was going to make sauerbraten, potato dumplings and red cabbage, an authentic German meal. He'd been thinking about it all day and he was hungry. Colette was a terrific cook, and that was another benefit of living with her. He threw his keys on the counter, hit the message button on the answering machine. Another one from Galina.

"Harry, you going to call me one of these days?"

No, he said to himself. Walked into the foyer, glanced in the den and moved into the living room. Someone was sitting in

30

his leather chair, legs crossed on the ottoman. The man had dark shoulder-length hair and wore black jeans, a white shirt and a black leather jacket.

"I don't think you're a burglar," Harry said, "or you'd be looking for the silver, so tell me what you're doing in my house?"

"I stopped by your office. We could have handled it there, but you were too busy to see me," he said with an accent that sounded like he was from Berlin.

"You buying or selling?"

"I am trading."

"For what?" Although Harry had a pretty good idea.

"Where is Ernst Hess?"

"I'd try his estate in Schleissheim or his apartment in Munich. Maybe start by talking to his family and business associates?"

"I know he came here to see you."

"Where's Colette?"

"Safe for now. Tell me about Herr Hess."

Harry pulled the Colt from under his shirt and aimed it at him. "I'll tell you what. You want to trade, I'll trade Colette for you. We can start there, see how it goes."

"Put the gun away. You are not going to shoot me or you will never find her."

The guy got up and came toward him. He was tall, six two, six three, and looked like he was in shape. Harry pulled the hammer back with his thumb. "First one's going to blow out your knee cap. You better hope there isn't a second one."

That seemed to persuade him. The German froze.

"I'm going to give you another chance. Where's Colette?"

"Not far from here."

"Let's go see how she's doing."

"I have to call, tell them we are coming."

"How many are there?"

"Two."

"We're going to surprise them," Harry said. "And if they've done anything to Colette, you're the first one I'm going to shoot. Believe that if you believe anything. Take off your coat, throw it over here and turn around." He did and Harry checked the two outside pockets of the jacket, found a parking receipt, and a pair of handcuffs. There was also a piece of notepaper that had an address on Crooks Road in Troy and a phone number. "This where they have Colette?"

In the other pocket he found car keys and a small semiautomatic. He ejected the magazine and put it in his pocket. The German had his back to Harry, looking over his shoulder.

"Take off your clothes. I want to see what else you've got."

The German stripped down to his briefs and tossed everything on the floor at Harry's feet. Harry picked up the man's pants and checked the pockets, found the key to the handcuffs and his wallet. Opened it, name Albin Zeller from Munich on the driver's license. "You a Nazi, too, Albin?" Harry said.

Zeller, with his back to him, didn't say anything. He was less threatening now in his underwear, thin legs, pale skin that had never been in the sun.

"Why are you looking for Hess?"

He didn't respond.

"You break in, say you want to talk, but you don't say anything." Hess was a wealthy man and a member of the Christian Social Union, an important political figure in Germany. Harry could understand why there were people who wanted him found. Hess must have told someone his plans. Otherwise how would Zeller have been able to follow his trail to Detroit? Harry threw him the handcuffs. "Put them on."

Zeller turned, caught them, clamped them on his wrists.

"Where's your car?"

"On the street."

That wasn't going to work, walking a handcuffed Nazi in his undies out to the car at gunpoint. "All right, let's go. We'll take mine."

"They are expecting a phone call."

"Well they're going to be surprised then, aren't they?"

"What about my clothes?"

"You're not going to need them."

"You drive up to the house they will kill her," Zeller said.

"Then we won't drive up to the house."

Harry was parked in the driveway by the side door. It was 5.30 and almost dark. He led Zeller out, popped the trunk, took his eye off the German for a second and Zeller took off, hurdled the neighbor's fence like a track star and disappeared. Harry started after him and stopped. Went back to the car, closed the trunk and drove to Troy to find Colette.

# Four

At 1.27 a.m., Hess saw the Bahamian policeman walk by the door, going outside to smoke. He pulled the IV out of his arm, slid out of bed, crossed the room, the ward quiet, patients asleep. Light from the moon was coming in the window next to his bed, illuminating part of the ward. At the door he glanced to the right and saw the policeman at the end of the hall. He looked the other way: no one was at the nurses' station. He went back through the room to the window next to his bed, opened it and punched out the screen.

"What do you think you're doing?"

Hess turned and saw Paulette, one of the night nurses, coming toward him across the ward. She must have been in the toilet room.

"Have you lost your mind, man? Get back in da bed."

She reached him, hands on his arm and shoulder, trying to pull him away from the window. "Come on now, we don't want no trouble."

Hess pivoted and went for her throat, taking the 110-pound woman down on the hard tile floor. She thrashed and fought, legs kicking, fingers trying to scratch his face. He had never strangled anyone. It required more effort than he realized. He kept his weight on her and the pressure on her neck and gradually she stopped fighting, eyes bulging, and went limp. Hess was breathing hard, exhausted from the effort, sweated through the hospital gown. He glanced toward the doorway, heard footsteps coming along the hall, picked up Paulette, put her in his bed and covered her with the sheet and blanket.

He brought a chair over, stood on it and slid his feet through the window, sitting on the sill, turned on his stomach and lowered his legs until his feet touched the ground. Barefoot and naked under the gown, Hess crossed the street, feeling weak, and moved past dark storefronts in downtown Freeport. He saw two figures approach, slim Negros in white shirts, skin blending with the darkness.

"What we have here?" the first one said.

"We take your money," the second one said, waving a knife at him theatrically.

Hess looked at them and smiled.

"Man what you wearing?"

"Look like he escape from the hospital," the second one said.

Hess picked up the front of his hospital gown, flashed them and laughed.

"Keep away from him," the first one said, stepping back. "Crazy old bugger, man's a mental case."

They moved past him down the street, Hess watching until they disappeared. He walked along the storefronts, stopping in front of Morley's, a men's store, bright-colored island attire on headless mannikins in the window. He continued walking to the end of the streets, went right and right again, moving down an alley behind the stores.

Morley's had a solid rear door with deadbolts top and bottom. There was a window behind closed shutters. He saw headlights coming toward him, ducked behind a big blue trash bin, watching as a police car crept by, its spotlight sweeping across the buildings.

When the police car was out of sight Hess went back to Morley's and dug his fingers into the shutter slats, pulling the sides open. The window was latched, so he broke a center pane in the upper half with his elbow. The glass cracked and shattered. Hess reached in, turned the clasp, slid up the bottom half of the window and climbed in the room. Then he pulled the shutters closed and locked the window.

It was a tailor shop, three sewing machines on worktables, bolts of cloth stacked on deep shelves. He walked into the store and looked around, checking the racks of trousers and jackets, and shirts folded and stacked on wooden shelves. He tried on a pair of white-cuffed trousers that bunched at his feet. He pulled the waist up higher on his stomach and they fit better, still too long but acceptable. Hess slipped a white short-sleeved sport shirt over his head and tucked it into the trousers. He chose a black leather belt from the belt rack, size thirty-eight. And a light blue sport jacket, size forty-four. The collar needed work and the sleeves were half an inch too long. Hess liked to show a little linen, although with short sleeves what did it matter? He posed in front of a full-length mirror, decided the white trousers were too much and swapped them for a pair of light gray trousers that were cut the same way. He took off the blue jacket and tried on a yellow one, decided it was too loud and went back to blue. He selected black espadrilles for stylish comfort, and a tan Bailey straw with a black band. The transformation was remarkable, Hess changing from ward patient to prosperous island gentleman.

He opened the cash register behind the counter and took

150 Bahamian dollars. The manager's office had a couch. He removed the hat and jacket, lay down, exhausted, and closed his eyes, listening to the sound of police sirens in the distance.

In the morning he felt better. He scanned the street from the front window, unlocked the front door, walked out of the shop and down the street, hailed a passing taxi, and rode to Lucaya.

Hess sat at an outdoor cafe overlooking the marina, sipping coffee, watching clouds drift in over the glistening turquoise water that turned a darker shade of blue further out. He watched Bahamian police in their distinctive uniforms patrolling around the docks, checking boats, talking to owners. When the police were gone he paid his check and walked down to the marina. There were half a dozen yachts with Florida registry. Two, he noticed, were from Palm Beach. He was admiring a big Hatteras from Fort Lauderdale named *Knotty Buoy* when a dark-haired guy in sunglasses walked out on the aft deck with a flute of champagne in his hand.

"Just looking at your boat," Hess said. "I hope you don't mind."

"You a sailor?"

"Once a sailor always a sailor," Hess said, going back to his southern accent. "My last one was a '68 Trojan."

The Hatteras owner smiled. "Last of the wooden boats. Nothing prettier than that polished teakwood deck and hull. All teak inside too. You have the thirty-eight or the forty-two?"

"Forty-two. Twin diesels cranking out six hundred forty horsepower."

"Do twenty-four knots I'll bet. Still own her?"

"Sold it when I moved to Atlanta," Hess said, total fabrication.

"Why the hell'd you do that?"

"It's a long boring story," Hess said.

"Come aboard. I'll show you around."

Hess went over the transom and climbed down the steps to the aft deck.

The man came toward him, arm outstretched. "How you doing? Tony Brank at your service."

Brank was short and muscular, shirt unbuttoned to his navel, gold chain around his neck, long hair pulled back in a ponytail. Forty-five. "Emile Landau," Hess said, shaking his hand. "Brank. That's an unusual name. What nationality are you?" Wondering if he was a Jew.

"Eye-talian. Brancaleone originally," he said, pronouncing it with Italian flair. "I needed something shorter, snappier."

Hess could hear police sirens. "What's going on?"

"Some crazy bastard killed a nurse in the hospital last night. Police are looking for him. Searching every boat. You're not the guy, are you?" Brank frowned, and then broke into a grin. "Just fucking with you, partner. Come on in."

Hess followed him into the cabin and through a salon that had a sectional couch on one side facing a built-in television. The couch was covered in zebra-skin fabric, the lampshades in leopard. The ersatz Serengeti decor puzzled him. At the opposite end of the salon was the pilot station, with a set of controls to steer the boat, compass, Loran. Brank led him down a couple of steps to the galley, the room done in teak with Formica countertops. He could see the neck of a champagne bottle sticking out of a silver ice bucket.

"Champagne?" Tony Brank said. "It's Taittinger's."

"How can I refuse?" Hess said, smiling.

38

Brank opened a cupboard door, reached in and brought out a flute, filled it halfway with champagne, bubbles rising to the rim of the glass, and handed it to him. He poured more in his own flute, held it up and said, "To salty dogs."

Hess toasted him and sipped the champagne, tasting the fruity chardonnay grapes.

"What do you do, Emile?"

"I'm a builder," Hess said. "Homes. Office buildings. Whatever you need built. What about you?"

"Erotic films," Brank said, tracing the comb lines in his hair with his fingertips. "See *Twat's Up, Doc?*"

"No, but it sounds familiar," Hess said, no idea what he was talking about.

"Christ, I hope so. Longest-running adult film of all time. Twelve million in domestic grosses, twenty worldwide. Orientals ate it up. No pun intended. Bought this boat with the proceeds."

A blonde in a nightgown walked into the galley behind Brank, yawning and rubbing her eyes. "Tony, will you keep it down? I'm trying to get some fucking sleep." She paused, fixing puffy eyes on the Taittinger bottle. "You're not drinking champagne, are you? What the hell time is it?"

"Babe, say hello to Emile Landau."

She glanced at Hess and looked away. "I'm not saying hi to anyone the way I look." She turned and walked out of the room, hips swaying, the looks and natural glamour of an actress or model.

"Anything with tits or batteries," Brank said, "eventually's going to give you trouble. My wife, Denise. Recognize her?"

Hess shrugged.

Brank grinned. "Star of *Deep Six*." He drank some champagne. "Helluva picture." He scratched the hair on his chest like a caveman. "She was an auto-parts model posing in a two-piece, holding a suspended crankshaft like a big steel dick when I met her. Discovered her, really. High-school dropout from Bay City, Michigan with a body that wouldn't quit. I'm looking at her bazooms and I go, 'Kiddo, I'm going to make you a star.' She looks at me, giggles and goes, 'Okay.' Rest is history." Brank grinned thinking about it, finished his champagne, belched and went up the steps to the salon. Stopped, looked back and said, "I want to show you something."

Hess followed him outside and up a wide, slightly curved aluminum ladder with white plastic steps to the flying bridge, trying to hold the champagne glass without dropping it. There was a white plastic chair bolted to the deck behind a sleek control panel, steering wheel and throttles, windscreen that wrapped around the front, canvas Bimini top pulled taut above them. Behind them there was a dinghy on the overhang of the aft deck.

"Got twin Detroit diesels pooling seven hundred fifty horses. Had them tweaked to do twenty-six knots."

"A boat this big? I'd have to see it to believe it," Hess said, challenging him.

Brank smiled now. "Oh, I get it. You're from Missouri, huh? Okay," he said, starting the engines. "Want to see for yourself, huh?"

Hess could hear the rumble of the exhaust pipes stirring up the water.

"Think you can release the dock lines?"

From the captain's chair on the flying bridge Brank steered the Hatteras, zigzagging through the marina, Hess sitting next

40

to him on a built-in bench made of fiberglass, sipping champagne. Just past the seawall Brank gunned the throttle and they took off into open sea, picking up speed, hull rising, slicing through whitecaps, cruising in deep water within a few minutes, flat blue ocean stretching to the horizon.

Brank, hands on the steering wheel, said, "Check this out."

Hess got to his feet and stood behind Brank, glancing at the speedometer. They were flying through the water at twenty-six knots.

"What I tell you?" Brank said, grinning.

They cruised until the land behind them had disappeared, Brank glancing at him, a bemused look on his face. "What do you think?" Yelling over the sound of the wind.

"What's that?" Hess said, pointing at the horizon.

"An island."

"Which one is it?"

"No idea. There are like seven hundred of them. I was going to pull over for a while, maybe take a swim. I've got suits, you want to join me."

Hess said, "I have to go below for a minute."

"Head's on the other side of the galley, down the steps on the left," Brank said. "You're not getting seasick on me, are you?"

Hess shook his head, although he did feel queasy, still not himself.

"See Denise, tell her to make us some lunch."

*

Hess saw the ship-to-shore radio on the counter next to the cabin controls. He went down the steps into the galley, opening

41

drawers and cabinets, found a flare gun, a Buck knife, a Smith & Wesson revolver. Broke the gun open, saw it was loaded, and put it back.

"What you looking for?" Denise said, walking in the room behind him.

He glanced over his shoulder at her in a bright orange bikini, blonde shoulder-length hair combed straight and tucked behind her ears, face looking flawless under a fresh layer of makeup. He stared at her heavy breasts bursting out of the small bikini top.

"A Band-Aid," Hess said, thinking of an excuse. He closed the drawer.

"Over here." She came up next to him, opened a cabinet door and took out a box. "You have a boo-boo? Let's see."

Earlier, Hess had nicked his index finger on the stairs, climbing to the flying bridge. There was a small mark where the skin had been cut. He showed it to her.

"That's it? You big baby." She opened the box, took out a Band-Aid, removed the wrapper and rolled it around his finger. "How's that? Big baby feel better?" she said. "Sorry about earlier. I was tired and crabby as if you couldn't tell. I'm Denise."

She offered an elegant red-nail-painted, long-fingered hand. Hess took it and brought it to his mouth, kissed it delicately, and said, "Emile, and the pleasure is all mine."

"Well you're just a gentleman's gentleman, aren't you?"

"Tony said if I see you, ask you to make lunch."

"Aye, aye," she said, saluting. "Better go talk to the captain, see what he's got in mind."

He watched her hips on long tan legs sway up the stairs to the salon. Now he opened the drawer, picked up the revolver and slid it in his jacket pocket. He took the Buck knife, went up to the pilot station, cut the receiver cord on the radio, and went back on deck.

# Five

Rausch had been killed in a bizarre shooting by Colette Rizik at her mother's residence in Bergheim, Austria. Colette, the *Der Spiegel* journalist, claimed self-defense. Zeller found it difficult to believe that a woman, an amateur with no combat training, had out-gunned a former soldier and firearms expert.

Arno Rausch had lived with his mother in a pre-war apartment building near the English Gardens until the old lady had a stroke and was moved to a nursing home in Hanover where she died in '67. Herr Braun had said no one, to his knowledge, had set foot in the apartment since Rausch was killed, so whatever clues were to be found were evidently still there. The apartment was dark and stuffy, drapes closed, dim light shrouding heavy overstuffed furniture from the thirties. He opened the drapes and now it looked like someone's grandmother lived there, not a fifty-year-old man, Zeller scanning bookshelves filled with Hummel figurines and antique plates. And a wall covered with cuckoo clocks that had all stopped working. Why on earth would Rausch have kept the apartment like this? Even the mother's bedroom appeared untouched, clothes hanging in the closet, grey hair webbed in brushes and combs in the bathroom as if she had been grooming that very day.

The apartment, cluttered with old-world bric-a-brac, was an

odd contrast to the squared-away neatness of Rausch's room with its framed military insignias and weapons: pistols, rifles, shotgun, sub-machine gun and assorted combat knives. Rausch, it appeared, was a big German momma's boy, who, if provoked, might be able to single-handedly take out a platoon.

Zeller had found cardboard boxes stacked in the closet. He carried them out, and set them on the floor in the salon. The boxes were filled with files on former Nazis, prominent citizens still living in Germany, police officers, politicians, judges. There were profiles and photographs in each of the folders, Zeller wondering why Rausch would have this information—until he dug a little deeper and discovered the boxes were the property of a Jewish organization known as the ZOB that helped German authorities find and prosecute war criminals.

There was a file on Ernst Hess, profiling his life, Nazi party affiliation, SS number and alleged war crimes, including several photographs of Hess in an SS uniform, posing in front of a pit filled with dead Jews. Similar pictures had been featured in the article about Hess published in *Der Spiegel*.

There was an audio cassette in the folder that said *Cantor Interview* on the label in black marker. He slid the tape in his pocket, took the ZOB file on Hess and walked out of the apartment. He went back to his car and drove to the autobahn.

Zeller listened to the tape on the way to Wiesbaden. The interview was really a conversation between Lisa Martz of the ZOB and a Holocaust survivor named Joyce Cantor. Joyce, now an American citizen, was visiting Munich for the first time since the war, and bumped into a former Nazi in broad daylight on Maximilianstrasse. The Nazi had been responsible for murdering hundreds of Jews in the forest outside Dachau concentration camp in April, 1943.

Her story was corroborated by a second survivor, Harry Levin, who had positively identified the Nazi as Ernst Hess. Although no names were mentioned, these eyewitness accounts were the basis of the article about Hess in *Der Spiegel*. The article appeared October 12th. But Hess had already disappeared a couple weeks earlier. He must have known he was going to be prosecuted.

Zeller arrived in Wiesbaden at 5.17 p.m. Parked and got out at Kaiser-Friedrich-Platz, saw the neo-Gothic spires of the Marktkirche and made his way through the marketplace. Vendors were starting to close up for the day, breaking down their stalls, packing their goods in vans and trucks.

He crossed the street, entered a building he hadn't been to since his time with the Stasi, rode the elevator to the fourth floor and walked to the end of the hall. Zeller knocked on the door.

"We're closed," a voice said from inside.

He turned the handle, surprised it was unlocked, opened the door and went in. "That's no way to talk to a former client."

Leon Halip, sitting in a leather swivel chair, was studying an image on an angled drafting table, high-beam gooseneck lamp providing illumination. He looked over the top of his eyeglasses at Zeller, massaging swollen fingers, one hand rubbing the other. Next to him a dark-haired teenager was trimming the border around a photograph with an X-Acto blade. Leon Halip at sixty-two looked like an old man, blinking and squinting, trying to focus on him.

"Former client, uh? So former I do not recognize you."

46

"Friedrich Benz." It was the name on the forged documents Leon had made for him years earlier when he left the Stasi.

Leon smiled and nodded. "Ah, yes, Herr Benz. August 1963, if I'm not mistaken. Of course I remember you."

"I heard you were no longer in the trade," Zeller said. "But you appear hard at work, and I see you have an apprentice."

"I still have an eye, is the hands that no longer function." His arthritic knuckles looked like red grapes, swollen and painful. "My grandson is learning the profession."

The kid resumed his task, running the blade along the edge of a metal ruler.

Leon Halip, with a heavy Hungarian accent, said, "You think I am out of the business, so why are you here?"

"What name did you use on Ernst Hess' passport?"

"I have no idea what you're talking about."

The grandson glanced at Leon like he wanted to correct him, but didn't say anything.

"Interesting you can remember me from eight years ago, but not Ernst Hess from less than one month."

"It is impossible to remember something that did not happen, Herr Benz."

Zeller drew the Makarov from the side pocket of his leather jacket, aimed it at the kid. "Now you see I'm serious."

"You point a gun at my grandson. You don't think I would tell you if I knew?"

Zeller took the suppressor out of his coat pocket and screwed it on the end of the barrel.

"Gerd Klaus," the old man said.

"You're sure?"

Leon Halip kept his eyes on Zeller and nodded.

"When was he here?"

"Twenty-eighth of September," he said, pulling on the end of his mustache.

"Where was he going?"

"We don't get involved beyond the papers. You should know that."

Zeller raised the Makarov and shot the boy first and then turned the gun on Halip and squeezed the trigger.

*

"Klaus flew Stuttgart–London–Detroit the twenty-ninth of September, arriving in the morning of the thirtieth," customs agent Fuhrman said by phone. "Five days later he took a flight from Detroit to West Palm Beach, arriving the fifth of October."

"Anything else?" Zeller said.

"From what I can see that was the last commercial flight Herr Klaus has taken."

Zeller was now convinced that Hess leaving the country had nothing to do with the *Der Spiegel* article. He was going after the Holocaust survivors. Taking out the witnesses would dilute the prosecution's case. That's why he had not withdrawn or transferred any large sums of money. He had been planning to come back, but something had happened.

# Six

"We'll stop here for lunch," Brank said.

The Hatteras was in turquoise water about five meters deep when they dropped anchor near a small deserted island with a white sand beach. Brank took off his shirt and folded it over the back of a chair on the aft deck. The blue shorts he was wearing were swim trunks. Brank raised bent arms, flexed his biceps and grinned. He was a hairy little ape wearing a gold chain with a gold horn on it, the *mano cornuto*, worn by superstitious Italians to ward off cuckoldry. And he was married to an erotic film star. It couldn't have been more incongruous. Brank strode across the deck, climbed up on the transom, arced his arms and hands over his head, and dove into the ocean, swimming under water and then surfacing, floating on his back. "You've got to come in. It's wonderful," he said, kicking along the side of the yacht, grinning at Hess. Ernst was thinking he should fire up the engines and speed off with the erotic film star, leave Brank frolicking in the water.

Brank swam for ten minutes, climbed back in the boat, sucked in his stomach, dried off with a towel and went inside. Denise came out and set the small round table on the aft deck. First she put down a white tablecloth and then brought out napkins and silver, plates of shrimp salad with sliced tomatoes and grapes, and a bowl of apples.

The apples reminded Hess of *shpil*, a game the SS had played on the Jews of Miedzyrzec. He had been sent to Poland, arriving May 1, 1943. The next day all of the Jews in the Miedzyrzec Podlaski ghetto had been rounded up for deportation, and forced to squat in the marketplace for hours on a hot day. Hess thought of a way to relieve the boredom and entertain his men. He told guards to toss apples into the crowd. Any Jew hit was pulled out and beaten to death or shot. It was high drama. The Jews were terrified and the SS guards were having a wonderful time. Whenever a Jew was hit the guards erupted with laughter. The game went on all afternoon and continued at the train station. The dead bodies were then loaded into freight cars with the prisoners going to Treblinka.

*

Brank came out with a bottle of Blue Nun and three stemmed glasses, wet hair combed back, beach towel wrapped around his waist, no shirt. "You're going to love this. Famous som-al-yer in Boca turned me on to it."

He set a glass at each of their places and poured the wine. Hess was familiar with it, a mediocre Liebfraumilch he would have refused to drink in any other situation.

"Tony tells me you're an actress," Hess said to Denise, trying to shift the conversation into gear.

"And a good one," Brank said. "Still is." He winked at her.

"I quit when Tony proposed."

"How long have you two been married?"

"Seven years," Brank said. He raised his wine glass. "To seven more."

They clinked glasses, sipped their wine and ate the shrimp salad that Hess had to admit was delicious. When they were finished Denise cleared the table. Brank and Hess smoked cigarettes and finished their wine.

"Where is Florida from here?"

"You kidding? That way." Brank pointed at the horizon. "Due west about sixty miles. Latitude twenty-six degrees north, longitude eighty degrees west."

Of course, Hess was thinking, follow the angle of the sun. Easy to do on a nice clear day like this. "Don't you use the Loran?"

"Yeah, but you still have to chart your course. I thought you were a sailor."

At one time Hess had an Italian yacht he kept in Nice. "I have a captain."

"A captain? You pussy." Brank grinned. "Kidding you, partner. Say, I never asked. What're you doing in Freeport?"

Hess didn't answer because Denise came back on deck in the orange bikini, breasts bouncing in the skimpy top, long legs, flat stomach, barefoot, carrying a striped towel.

"Ready?" Denise said.

"We're going to explore the island," Brank said.

"Come with us," Denise said, throwing her towel on the chair next to Hess.

"No, I'll stay here and relax, if you don't mind. Maybe take a nap."

"You don't know what you're missing," Brank said.

Denise climbed the stairs to the top of the transom and

jumped. Hess heard the splash when she hit, got up and stood on the port side of the Hatteras, watching Denise floating on her back in the turquoise water. Brank removed his towel skirt, ran to the stern and dove over the transom, swam to Denise and the two of them held onto each other, treading water before swimming for the island. They made it to the beach, got out and started walking, stopping occasionally to pick up shells. When they were out of sight, Hess went to the bow, raised the anchor and felt the yacht start to drift.

He climbed the ladder to the flying bridge, glanced in the direction of the island. From this higher vantage point he could see Brank and Denise strolling, holding hands like young lovers, coming back toward the stretch of beach closest to the boat. Hess sat at the controls, started the engines, heard the rumble of the exhaust, looked back, saw Brank running, Denise trailing behind him.

Brank was in the water halfway to the yacht when Hess opened up the twin throttles and took off, the Hatteras picking up speed, and within a few minutes the island was fading in the distance. Hess went below and punched new coordinates into the Loran, and put the yacht on autopilot. His chest itched from the gunshot wound. He rubbed it and tried to relax.

Three hours later he passed a freighter creeping along the horizon, and a couple of fishing boats before he saw the Florida coastline, Hess using a telescope in the salon to identify the twin spires of the Breakers Hotel, confirming it was Palm Beach.

When he was five hundred meters from shore, Hess turned off the engines and lowered the boat, cranking it over the port side to the water. He went down the stairs, crossed the deck and stepped over the side into the dinghy. He started the outboard motor, unhooked the davit lines and cruised toward shore.

# Seven

Kraut's name was Albin Zeller. They said they'd meet him at a farmhouse on Crooks Road in Troy, the meeting arranged by Russell Gear of the American Nazi Party. Dink drove by in the pickup, Squirrel in the passenger seat, drinkin' cans of Pabst like they going to shutter the brewery, saw the white clapboard house set back from the road, cornfields surrounding it on three sides, barn in back, quiet and secluded for their purposes.

Dink pulled over on the shoulder, waited for a couple cars to pass, and did a U-turn. He went back to the farmhouse and parked behind a green Camaro on the gravel drive. Saw a dark-haired guy come out the side door and stand at the top of the concrete steps. Dink glanced at himself in the rearview, brown hair comin' out from under the Cat Diesel cap, hanging on either side of his face to his jawline, word *evil* tattooed on both eyelids. Lower lip stuck out, swollen with tobacco. He spit out the window. "You just drink your beer, let me do the talking," Dink said, turning toward his sidekick, whose face was partially hidden by the brim of a Red Man cap.

Squirrel met his gaze but didn't say anything. He wasn't much of a talker.

They got out of the truck and moved toward the house, Squirrel, stomach hanging over his belt in a tee-shirt that said *The Devil Made Me Do It* in white type on the front, greasy brown hair under the cap, carrying three cans of Pabst Blue Ribbon in a plastic tightener. Only guy Dink knew could drink all day and still function.

"How y'all doing today? You must be Mr Zeller. I'm Dink Boone, and this scarry-lookin' east Tennessee redneck is Aubrey Ponder, answers to Squirrel."

"You were supposed to be here thirty minutes ago," Zeller said, German accent, sounding pissed.

"Yeah, well, what can I tell you?" Dink said, not explaining or giving the Kraut an excuse. He spit tobacco juice, a brown gob that splashed on the gravel stones at his feet.

Squirrel pulled a beer out of its plastic ring, popped the top and took a pull. "Gonna tell us what you need done, or what?"

Zeller held the door open for them and they filed past him in the kitchen, and sat at an oval Formica table with chrome trim, the yellow finish worn off in places. Dink's momma had served his favorite dish, grits, pork scraps and trimmings, on one just like it.

"We was up this way not too long ago ended up stayin'. US Court of Appeals upheld a district court order calling for busing as a way to achieve racial balance." Dink met Zeller's gaze. "Ever heard of a bigger crock of shit in yer life? They start busing white kids to nigger schools. We come up to burn the buses and beat hell out of the niggers. I talked to a boy was involved. Kid said, 'Blacks is different. They have different personalities and all that.' I said, 'No shit, Sherlock.' One white momma chained herself to a bus rather than see her child put through that charade of integration. I know we're not here to talk about that. But you bein' from the Fatherland and all, I'm sure you can relate."

Zeller told them about this German honey—*fraulein*, Dink thought he said—stayin' locally with some Jew. Told them what he needed done.

"So we go to the house, get her, bring her here, right? Then what?"

"I will interrogate her," Zeller said, sounding like Colonel Klink on *Hogan's Heroes*.

Dink said, "What if she don't feel like talkin'?"

"Don't concern yourself."

Dink said, "What do you want to find out?"

"Bring her here," Zeller said. "That is all."

"She don't tell you what you want to hear, give her to us," Squirrel said, grinning, showing tobacco-stained teeth.

"I will handle it," Zeller said, elbows on the table, turning a ring on one of his fingers with the opposite hand.

Dink said, "Where you from in Germany?"

"Berlin."

"That's where the wall is at, ain't it?" Dink said. "What's it look like?"

"What do you think?"

The Kraut was lookin' at Dink like he'd just chugged a quart of bourbon.

"Hey, Herr Zeller, know how to stop a dog from humping your leg? Pick it up and suck its dick," Dink said, holding back the grin that was trying to bust out.

Zeller gave him a sour look.

Squirrel drained his beer, pulled another out of the plastic tightener and popped it open. Glanced at Zeller and said, "Last one, want it?"

Zeller shook his head, reached in his shirt pocket and

handed Dink a piece of paper with a name and address on it, Harry Levin in Huntington Woods. Yeah, he knew where it was at.

It was Dink's idea to steal the carpet-cleaning truck, show up like tradesmen, pull in the driveway, ring the bell. How y'all doin'? We're here to clean your carpeting. What do you mean, you don't know anything about it? Look here. Says so right on the form. They'd boosted the truck from a lot over on Eight Mile Road, hot-wired her and drove back to the farmhouse.

*

It was early evening, sky overcast, getting dark as Harry passed the mall and the treeless subdivisions of Troy, the lots big and open now, farms here and there. He slowed the Mercedes, trying to see an address, get an idea if he was going the right way, read numbers on a mailbox and saw he was close. A couple minutes later he passed it, a white two-storey house with a wide porch in front.

Harry pulled over on the other side of the road, turned off the lights, got out of the car, closed the door and crossed the road, moving along a line of elm trees. No traffic. Slight breeze blowing, the smell of wood smoke in the fall air. He stood behind a tree, watching the house, lights on the first floor, Ford pickup parked in the driveway. The screen door swung open and a man in overalls walked out on the porch, glanced toward the road and spit. Now another man wearing a red cap came out, placed his beer can on top of the railing, moved down the steps and urinated on the lawn.

When they went back inside Harry drew the .357, moved

past the house, and walked along the edge of the cornfield to the barn. Opened the door and went in. There was a white van that said *Acme Carpet Cleaning* on the side, looking out of place next to the farm equipment. He checked the rooms, went up to the loft, no sign of Colette or anyone else.

Harry moved out of the barn, crouching behind the green pickup parked next to the house. He waited, listened, didn't hear anything, moved around the back of the truck. There was a rebel flag on the tailgate. He moved to the house, opened the side door and stepped into the kitchen. Heard a TV on in another room and laughter. Walked through the dining room, saw the two guys sitting on a couch, watching *The Beverly Hillbillies*.

Elly May: I wonder why they got two sets of steps.
Jethro: That's easy! One's for going up, and the other's for going down!
Elly May: Oh.

They laughed with the laugh track.

Harry went back to the kitchen, opened a door that led to the basement, turned on the light and went down the stairs, saw Colette gagged and tied to a chair in the middle of a damp cinderblock room.

He could see tears in her eyes as he got closer, blouse ripped open halfway down her chest. Harry slid the gun in his pocket, and undid the bandana that was tied across her mouth and knotted behind her head. Held her face in his hands. "Don't say a word," he whispered. "They're upstairs." He untied the ropes, helped her up and she put her arms around his neck, clinging to him. "It's going to be okay. We're going to walk out of here."

They went up the stairs, Harry leading the way, holding the big Colt in front of him with two hands, Colette hanging onto him from behind. The door was open a crack. He heard someone come in the kitchen. Heard the refrigerator open and close. Heard a bottle cap hit the floor. Then someone said, "Check on her?" in a heavy southern accent.

"Where you think she's gonna go?"

Harry wondered what Zeller's connection was with these rednecks.

"Why don't you go down, have a look see just to be sure."

"You mean to relieve your concern?"

"Here's the way it is. We split the chores. I checked on her last time. So now it's your turn. Get it?"

"Tell you what, when the TV show's over I will do just that."

"And keep your goddamn hands off her."

Harry heard them walk out of the kitchen, apparently agreeing to suspend hostilities for the time being. He took Colette the rest of the way up and they went out the kitchen door, eased it closed and stepped into the yard.

*

"What'd they do to you?" Harry said when they were in the car, looking across the seats at each other.

"Scared me, Harry."

He could see her cheek was bruised and swollen, and felt rage come on like a switch had been flipped inside him. Colette reached over, grabbed his hand and squeezed it.

"It's all right now," Harry said. "It's over." He started the Mercedes and did a U-turn, accelerating past the farmhouse.

"There is another one, a German. He came down to the cellar and asked questions about Hess. Did I know where he was? I told him I didn't know anything, and he gave up but I could see he was frustrated and knew he wasn't finished."

"Why didn't you just tell him?"

"And then what, Harry? You think he was going to give me a ride back to your house like nothing happened?" Colette leaned over and put her hand flat against his chest. "I thought I was dreaming when I saw you." She grabbed his hand again and held it in both of hers. "These men looking for Hess are going to keep looking. They think he's alive. And they're not going to stop until they prove otherwise. Maybe he has something on other former Nazis. More photos. More evidence of politically connected Germans who murdered Jews during the war. It could be another story. Maybe even a book."

"If you live to tell about it."

"Well, I can't just let it go, Harry. This is what I do."

Even in the dark interior he could read her expression, see she'd made up her mind.

He drove back to his house, and kept going. Zeller's car was gone. Of course it was gone. Harry had taken Zeller's gun, but left his clothes and keys in the house. He debated whether to call the police, tell them someone broke in. Tell them Colette had been kidnapped. But he decided against it. What was he going to say? A German heavy came to Detroit looking for Ernst Hess, a former Nazi accused of committing crimes against humanity in a war that ended twenty-six years ago. "Was anyone hurt?" he could hear the cop asking. "Was anything stolen?" "Just the Tab-

60

riz. It's a rug", Harry could hear himself saying, and the cop looking at him like he was nuts.

Harry took Colette to Club Berkley for dinner. She was starving. They ate steak pan-seared in garlic butter, the house specialty, French fries, and washed it all down with bottles of Heineken. After, they checked into a no-frills motel on Woodward Avenue. Harry didn't want to risk going home, have to deal with Zeller and the rednecks again tonight. He needed time to think, figure out what to do.

*

Dink thought he heard someone in the kitchen. Grabbed the .45, turned, leveled it and saw Zeller. "Jiminy goddamn Christmas, where in the hell you been at?"

"Where is she?" Zeller said.

"That a trick question?" Squirrel said.

"Go down and see for yourself," Zeller said, hands on his hips. "She's gone because you are here watching television, not paying attention."

Dink was kind of embarrassed. "I tell you to go check on her, or what?" he said, throwing Squirrel under the bus.

"Well she didn't untie herself," Squirrel said. "I'll tell you that."

He had a point. That crazy-ass redneck knew how to tie a knot. For sure.

Zeller said, "It was Harry Levin."

"How'd he know where she was at?" Dink said, gaze holding on the German.

"He had a gun," Zeller said.

"So'd you, I thought," Dink said.

"Whyn't you take it from him?" Squirrel said to Zeller.

"'Cause he ain't Superman. What's next on the agenda, *mein Herr*?" Dink said, looking at Zeller. "I think maybe you should fill us in. Looks like you're in over your head, might could use some help."

# Eight

When he was within ten meters of the beach Hess turned off the engine and coasted to shore. The bottom hit sand in shallow water and the boat came to a stop. Hess stepped into the ocean halfway to his knees, dislodged the dinghy, and let the current take it back out to sea. Further out, the Hatteras looked like it was drifting with the tide.

He was on a private beach, deserted in the early evening. Hess walked toward South Ocean Boulevard, wet espadrilles and trouser cuffs getting caked with sand. There was a huge Mediterranean villa straight ahead on the other side of the road, and to his right a beach house that matched the villa's Italian shade of umber.

Hess had Brank's watch, wallet, credit cards and $1,500 in cash. He also had Brank's Smith & Wesson .38. The sun was fading, casting streaks of red behind the oceanfront estates as he walked the beach side of the road, saw the sign for Via Bellania and knew he was only a couple miles south of Worth Avenue.

He kept going, walked with purpose, arriving at Gulfstream Road at 6.40 p.m., and entered a seafood restaurant, went through the bar and dining room to the telephone that was in a hall leading to the restrooms. Hess opened the Yellow Pages, selected a taxi service, phoned and asked to be picked up at Charley's Seafood. It would be fifteen minutes, so Hess found a seat at the crowded bar and ordered a Macallan's neat.

"You look familiar," the woman sitting to his left said. "You're a character actor, aren't you? Or maybe just a character." She smiled, gliding her fingers up and down the stem of the martini glass.

"You must have me confused with someone else," he said, glancing at her.

"What do you do?"

Hess studied her, a plain-looking brunette without a lot to work with, and yet, there was something appealing about her.

"I produce erotic films," Hess said.

"So you're not in front of the camera, you're behind it," she said, picking up her martini glass, taking her time before bringing it to her mouth, sipping the drink. "Dirty movies, huh?"

"I prefer to think of it as art."

"Of course." She speared an olive with a plastic sword and put it in her mouth, chewing slowly, savoring it.

"What are some of your movies?"

"Have you seen *Twat's Up, Doc?*"

"No, but I've heard of it." She shook her head and smiled. "You did that?"

"Largest-grossing erotic film of all time," Hess said.

"Don't take this the wrong way, but you sure don't look like the type."

"Public perception is it's a sleazy business."

"Exactly, and you don't look sleazy."

She had good teeth and skin, and an outgoing personality. Late thirties, maybe forty.

"What's another one?"

64

"*Deep Six*. It was my ex, Denise's, film debut."

"Your ex was a porn star?"

Hess nodded, picked up his drink and took a sip.

"What's that like? I mean watching her doing it with all those studs."

"Why do you think I'm divorced?"

A valet in a red vest came in the bar and said something to the bartender. "Somebody call a cab?" the bartender said, heavy New York accent.

Hess drank his single malt in a couple swallows, put the glass down on the bar top, and a $20 bill next to it. "I have to go," he said to the brunette.

"I'll give you a ride," she said.

"Cab?" the bartender tried again. "Anyone?"

"I have a car right outside. I'm Lynn, by the way," she said, offering Hess her hand. "Lynn Risdon."

"Tony Brank," he said, taking her hand in his.

"You don't look like a Tony." She finished the martini and placed it on the bar top. Hess raised his hand and the bartender moved toward him.

"Another round?"

Hess nodded.

"You get remarried?" Lynn said. "I don't really care, but I guess it's better if you didn't."

"Still single," Hess said. "Until the right woman comes along." He thought about Anke, his mistress. She had become demanding like a wife. Wanted a commitment, wanted children. That relationship was over as well, and Hess was relieved. "What about you?"

"Divorced," Lynn said. "Best thing that ever happened to me."

*

An hour and three martinis later, Hess escorted Lynn Risdon to the parking lot. She was drunk. He could feel her weight, the sloppiness of her stride as she clung to him. He had watched her transform to annoying from interesting, the alcohol making her stupid and clumsy. "Where's your car?"

"It's got to be around here somewhere," she said, slurring her words, glassy eyes scanning the lot. "There tis." She pointed at a white Ford Mustang.

Hess said. "Where do you live?"

"On Seabreeze."

He had passed the street a number of times, remembered it was just north of Worth Avenue.

"Anyone in the house?"

"Whaaat?"

"Do you live with someone?"

"Nooo . . . I told you, I'm divorced."

"You better let me drive," Hess said. "You can't even stand up."

"I drive sitting down," Lynn said and laughed. She reached a hand into her purse, feeling around. It took a few minutes to find the keys, half a dozen on a silver ring. She handed them to Hess. He unlocked and opened the door, sat her in the front passenger seat, leaned in, brushed her cheek with his, buckling the seat belt around her.

She touched his face and said, "Is Mr Scruffy growing a beard?"

He closed the door and walked around the car and got in. "What is your address?"

"Whaaat?" She was angled in the seat, leaning back against the door, eyes closed.

He reached over on the floor in front of her, picked up the purse, opened it, found her wallet and driver's license. He drove to Seabreeze Avenue, checking addresses. Lynn lived in a single-storey house hidden behind a sculpted wall of hedge four blocks from the ocean. Hess parked on the circular drive. The front porch light was on and there was a light on inside.

He got out, went to the front door, tried several keys until he found the right one, and opened it. Went back to the car, picked Lynn up and brought her into the house and bumped the door closed with his hip. He heard voices in another room, sat Lynn on a couch in the salon, and went to investigate. A television was on in the kitchen. He turned it off.

Adjoining the kitchen was a utility room with a washing machine and dryer. On the opposite wall built-in shelves held tools, cleaning supplies, an assortment of items, including a coil of rope which he grabbed, and a knife. Hess walked though the house. There were two bedrooms off the salon, one obviously lived in, disheveled, and the other spotless. He went back in the salon. Lynn was stretched out, sleeping on the couch. Hess bent and picked her up, carried her to her bedroom, and laid her across the double bed. He cut lengths of rope and tied her ankles and wrists while she slept.

Hess had been in the same clothes now for twenty hours.

He went into the master bathroom, undressed, turned on the shower and stood under the hot water.

He dried himself with a pink bath towel, and wrapped it around his waist. Found a razor and shaving cream in the cabinet under the sink, and shaved in front of the fogged-up mirror he had to keep wiping clean with a towel.

He dressed, feeling better, checked on Lynn, still asleep. Went to the kitchen, opened the refrigerator, found sliced turkey in the meat drawer and made a turkey sandwich with Dijon mustard. He poured a glass of milk, sat at the table and watched TV, a program called *McMillan & Wife*, starring Rock Hudson. When he finished the sandwich, Hess turned off the TV and went to the guest room, stretched out on the bed and fell asleep.

*

Lynn Risdon's head was pounding and her mouth was dry from the vodka. She'd have to slow down, take it easy for a while. She was drinking too much, getting drunk almost every night. She was on her side, couldn't move her arms. They were tied behind her back, and her legs were tied together at the ankles. What was going on? Was the erotic film producer into S&M? At first she thought it was a dream. But her eyes were open staring at the red numerals on the clock in her dark bedroom. She remembered being at the restaurant, sitting at the bar drinking a martini. Talking to the guy. What was his name? Brank, that was it. They'd had several drinks, having a good time. Remembered offering him a ride home, the events of the night a little hazy after that. Lynn couldn't remember how she got home. Did she drive? Or maybe he did. Then, in a flash of memory she saw herself hanging onto him leaving the restaurant. But he was a good sport, didn't seem to mind. She'd picked up other men in bars, and brought them home, had sex and never heard from them again. Lynn liked being in control, liked initiating things. Guys picked up girls all the time. Why couldn't girls pick up guys? It was 1971 after all.

Now as her eyes adjusted she could see rope binding her ankles and wrists. Why would he do that? Why would he leave her like this? She was going to fuck his brains out. It didn't make sense. She swung her legs over the side of the bed and tried to sit up. Now what? She couldn't walk, couldn't crawl. Lynn looked at the phone on the bedside table and slid along the bed on her knees, knocked the receiver off the cradle, and it went over the side of the table and landed on the floor. She pressed the o button with her chin, heard the operator's voice say, "How may I direct your call?" and went down on the carpet, trying to get closer to the phone.

"I'm in my house, tied up. Call the police?"

"Where are you calling from?"

"Palm Beach."

"What's the address?"

He came in the room, standing over her, picked up the receiver, put it back and ripped the cord out of the wall. He picked her up and dropped her on the bed. It was the porno-movie guy from the bar.

"What're you doing?" Lynn was afraid now. "What's with the rope? You into bondage? I'll try anything once. What the hell. It might be fun."

He pushed her on her back, arms under her.

"Stop it. You're hurting me."

He reached for the pillow. She thought he was going to put it under her head.

"How'd we get here? You must've driven, right?" she said, trying to reconnect with him, but he didn't respond. And now he put the pillow over her face, pressing down and she couldn't breathe. Fought to get out from under him with everything she had, but he was sitting on her. Lynn thought about Larry, her ex, wondering why she'd wasted twenty years of her life with him. She pictured his face when he found out she was dead and he wouldn't have to pay alimony. She thought about her parents and her brother, Chris. Would anyone miss her when she was gone? And then she was floating, looking down at herself, Brank, the porno-movie guy still holding the pillow over her face. He didn't know yet.

*

Hess felt her body go slack but kept pressing the pillow on her face, watching the minute hand on the clock go around three more times, and let up, lifted the pillow and saw her eyes staring at him, an expression of fear or panic frozen on her face. He pulled the side of the bedspread up and covered her. He would have to figure out what to do with the body, but not now. Hess was tired. He went back in the guest room, laid down on the bed and fell asleep.

In the morning, Hess had two soft-boiled eggs and toast for breakfast, watched the news on the small TV in the kitchen. One story in particular piqued his interest. A somber female reporter was broadcasting live from a marina. "Last night the US Coast Guard discovered an abandoned yacht half a mile off the Palm Beach coast. The names of the yacht owner and his wife are being withheld by authorities, pending a police investigation."

Now the camera pulled back and Hess could see the white fiberglass hull of Brank's Hatteras behind her. The reporter gave her name and the name of the TV station and signed off.

At 8.45, Hess drove Lynn Risdon's car to the SunTrust Bank on Royal Poinciana Way, waited in the parking lot until the doors opened. Dana Kovarek, the assistant manager who had rented Hess the safe deposit box a week earlier, did a double-take when Ernst walked into his office and said, "Dana, remember me? Gerd Klaus. I want to open my box."

"I remember, but it can't be. You died. I saw the death certificate."

"Do I look dead?"

Kovarek was nervous, eyes darting around. "Your daughter came with the key, a death certificate and a court order claiming she was your rightful heiress. Don't you remember, I explained the terms, conditions and procedures associated with having control over your safe deposit box," Kovarek said, sounding defensive. "We talked about relatives of the deceased and their right to claim the contents of the box."

Hess had no recollection of them discussing what would happen if he died.

Kovarek said, "Your daughter had to open it to get burial information, the deed to your burial plot."

"Describe her," Hess said.

"Your daughter?" Kovarek rubbed his jaw.

"She is not my daughter."

"An attractive woman with blonde hair, five feet eight, thirty years old. She had the key and the rental agreement."

Kovarek had just described Colette Rizik. "Was she alone?"

"No, sir, there was a dark-haired gentleman with her, six feet tall, fortyish."

Harry Levin's face flashed in his mind. Levin and the journalist. They had found the key to his hotel room, the keys to his briefcase and safe deposit box. They had obviously gone to his room before the police. "So you are telling me the box is empty?"

"Yes sir, Mr Klaus, and the contract has been terminated."

"Let me see the death certificate."

"I don't have the original. All I have is a copy of a certified copy."

Kovarek stood and went to a bank of file cabinets against the wall, opened a drawer and took out a green folder. He came back to the desk and handed Hess a piece of paper. At the top in a heavy font it said: *Certified Copy of Record of Death*, and in smaller type under that: *County of Broward, State of Florida*.

The deceased's name was Gerd Richter Klaus. Cause of death: heart failure. Birthplace: Stuttgart, Germany. Born: April 1, 1920. Mother's and father's names not available. The document was signed by A. Robert Stevenson, Clerk of Palm Beach County Commission, West Palm Beach, Florida, dated October 17, 1971.

"As you can see, Mr Klaus, it follows the legal guidelines set forth by the State of Florida. Is there anything else I can do for you? Would you like to lease another safe deposit box, sir?"

Hess wanted to pull the .38 and shoot the little four-eyed weasel. Instead he smiled and said, "Perhaps another time."

Kovarek handed him a business card. "If you have questions about any of our banking services, don't hesitate to call."

Hess could feel the grip of the revolver in his pocket. It took all the willpower he had not to shoot the idiot.

The safe deposit box had contained his real passport, $10,000 in cash and a locker key. Harry Levin and the journalist would have no idea where the locker was, or how to find it. Hess was thinking about this as he drove back to Seabreeze, approaching Lynn Risdon's house, when he saw police cars parked in front on the street, and a crowd standing behind yellow crime-scene tape strung across the outside perimeter of the property. Someone had discovered the body.

Hess drove past the house and turned right on South Ocean Boulevard. It occurred to him the police would be looking for Lynn Risdon's car. He cut over to Worth Avenue and parked the Mustang, got out, walked to a men's store and bought new clothes, Palm Beach attire: light blue trousers, white belt and matching shoes, orange golf shirt, blue blazer, aviator sunglasses and golf cap. He paid cash and wore the new clothes out of the store. The old clothes were in a bag he dropped into a decorative Palm Beach trash bin on the street.

He had to get off the island, but first he had to take care of some unfinished business. Hess went to a cafe across the street from Sunset Realty, sat at a table next to the window, sipped iced tea and glanced at the *Palm Beach Post*. He saw Joyce Cantor walk out of the office at 5.30 p.m., left a $5 bill on the table and followed her.

# Nine

They had checked out of the motel and gone back to Harry's place. First he made Colette wait in the car while he walked around the house with the .357, checking every room. Zeller's clothes were gone, but nothing else was missing except his antique rug the rednecks wrapped Colette in and he knew where that was.

Now they were in the kitchen having breakfast, scrambled eggs, English muffins and coffee. "Who do you think hired Zeller?" Harry said to Colette.

"Any number of people. Hess' wife. His mistress."

"I didn't know he had one."

"Her name is Anke Kruger, a former model." Colette poured herself a cup of coffee and stirred in some cream. "Would you like more?"

Harry shook his head.

"Or maybe the Christian Social Union hired him. Hess was well connected, politically important."

"Why would they want to find him? He's an embarrassment to the Christian Social Union, to the whole country. This is the last thing the German government needs, a lunatic former Nazi going around murdering people, with the Olympics coming to Munich next year." Harry took Hess' locker key out of his pocket and handed it to Colette. "Remember this? Whatever

74

is in the locker, I think Hess was going to bring it with him but changed his mind."

She held the key between her thumb and index finger, looking for a mark, something that would indicate where it came from.

"Where is the locker, Harry?"

"Who knows? How did Hess get to Detroit? There isn't a direct flight from anywhere in Germany, I know that. So he had to make a connection. Find out what airline he flew and where he flew out of, and go to the airport. Find the locker and see if the key fits. I know someone who might be able to help us." He'd call Bob Stark, his pit-bull attorney, put him on the case.

"Soon as we're finished I'm going back out to the farmhouse, get my rug and look around."

"What if they're still there?"

*

Harry pulled up in front thirty minutes later, sat for a while, watching the place. No cars or trucks in the driveway. No one around. He'd taken Colette to his niece Franny's apartment. He pulled in the driveway and parked next to the house. Drew the .357 Mag from a coat pocket, turned the cylinder and put the hammer on a live round.

He got out of the Mercedes, walked to the barn, opened the door and looked in at a tractor and a huge combine harvester. No sign of a green Ford pickup or Zeller's Chevy Camaro or a white GMC van that said *Acme Carpet Cleaning* on the side.

He walked to the house. The side door was unlocked. Went in the kitchen. There were beer cans on the counter, dirty dishes in the sink, the stale lingering smell of cigarette smoke in the air. He walked through the dining room into the semi-dark living room, shades pulled down over the windows, and saw his antique rug spread out on the hardwood floor. He bent to roll it up and noticed a plastic six-pack tightener and a pack of matches on the floor half under the ratty-looking couch.

Harry went over, picked up the match book, looking at the white cover with black type that said *Rodeo Bar*, illustrated to look like a cattle brand. The address was in Pontiac. Harry went upstairs and checked the bedrooms, went downstairs and checked the basement, but didn't find any more clues or anything that would help him find Zeller.

*

Harry drove past the Rodeo Bar, big gravel parking lot about a quarter full at 11.50 on Saturday morning. The building looked like it had once been a Knights of Columbus hall, low-slung cinderblock painted gray, peaked roof in front with a sign that said *Rodeo* and a neon cowboy riding a bull. Harry waited across the street in a strip mall, watching the lot fill up, pickups outnumbering cars four to one. Harry scanned the stores behind him. The strip mall had a Kresge's and a hardware store, cleaners, a Pancake House and a drug store. Earlier Harry had phoned Bob Stark to see if Stark could find which city Hess, alias Gerd Klaus, had flown out of, which airline he'd flown, and where he'd made his connecting flight or flights to Detroit. Harry was thinking what he'd said to Colette. "Find the city and maybe you'll find the locker."

*

He sat for a while, got out, went to the drug store and bought a *Free Press*. Got back in the Mercedes, glanced at the sports section. The Lions were playing Minnesota, the Purple People Eaters, on Sunday, a team Detroit had lost to the last six times they'd played.

A little after noon a green Ford pickup truck pulled into the parking lot across the street. A heavyset guy wearing overalls and a cap got out, walked to the door and went in the bar. Harry was pretty sure he was one of the rednecks from the farmhouse who'd kidnapped Colette, and it sure looked like the same truck.

Harry got out of the car, locked the door, crossed the road, moved through the Rodeo Bar parking lot to the green pickup. It was the truck all right, unless there was another green Ford with a rebel flag on the tailgate. He opened the passenger door, sat on the bench seat and looked around. The ashtray was overflowing with tan cigarette butts and there were half a dozen empty Pabst Blue Ribbon cans on the floor. He remembered seeing the same cans on the kitchen counter at the farmhouse. Looking through the driver's-side window he could see the front door of the bar about thirty yards away.

Harry opened the glove box, found the registration. The truck was a 1966 Ford F-100. The owner was Gary Boone, address on Clark Street in Pontiac. Harry considered his options. He could wait till Gary came out and follow him home, or talk to him right here.

Harry sat in the truck and watched the parking lot fill up. At 2.15 the front door opened, Gary Boone came out squinting, made a visor with his hand to block the afternoon sun, looking across the lot trying to spot his truck. Harry tracked him all the way, and when the redneck got close Harry drew the Colt and rested it in his lap. Gary Boone stopped at the side of his truck, spit and took a long piss, lit a cigarette, opened the door and got in. He was reaching to put the key in the ignition when he noticed Harry and said, "Jesus. What the fuck! Who the hell're you?"

Harry aimed the big revolver at him. "The guy that's going to blow your head off you don't tell me what I want to know."

Gary Boone sat back against the seat. "Who you kidding? You're not going to shoot me here. I know that."

Harry pulled the hammer back with his thumb. "You sure about that?"

"Get the fuck out."

Harry lowered the Colt, squeezed the trigger and put a round between Gary Boone's feet that sounded like an explosion bouncing around the small confines of the interior, ears ringing from the noise.

"Jesus sucks Jew cock," Gary Boone said. "What're you, fucking crazy? You put a hole in my truck."

"Next one's going to find you," Harry said. "Where's Zeller?"

"Honest to God, I don't know."

Harry pulled the hammer back again.

"I can give you the number where he's at, but that's it. It's in my wallet."

Gary reached behind his back, pulled it out, opened it and handed Harry a scrap of paper that had a phone number on it.

"Start the truck and pull out. We're going to take a drive."

"Where we going?"

"I'll tell you when we get there."

Harry directed the redneck north to a secluded area, an empty desolate stretch of road covered with red and orange leaves somewhere just outside Walled Lake. "Pull over."

"Pull over? We're in the middle of Bumfuck, Egypt," Gary said, glancing at the gun and slowing the truck, pulling over on the shoulder, putting the shifter in neutral. "Now what?"

"Get out."

"Where am I supposed to go?"

"That's up to you."

"Listen, I didn't lay a hand on your lady. Was Squirrel done it. Man's got the couth of an opossum."

Harry pointed the Colt at his right foot. "Want to try this again?"

"Hey, what about my truck?"

"It's mine now," Harry said.

"What're you doing? You can't take a man's truck."

Gary Boone got out and started walking north. Harry slid over behind the wheel and drove back to the strip mall where his car was parked. Made a phone call from the drug store, tried the number Gary had given him. It rang several times before a woman's voice said, "Your party is not available. Please press one to leave a message or press zero to speak to an operator." It was a recording. Harry pressed 0 and a live woman's voice said, "How may I direct your call?"

Harry said, "I'm trying to reach a friend, Albin Zeller."

"Is he a guest at the hotel?"

"Yeah," Harry said. "Where am I calling?"

"The Kingsley Inn, sir."

Harry hung up and ran to his car. Drove to the hotel at

79

Woodward Avenue and Long Lake. He parked, walked in, stopped at the front desk and asked for Zeller.

"I am sorry, sir," the clerk said, "Mr Zeller checked out."

"When?"

"A few hours ago."

"Did he say where he was going?"

"No sir, but maybe one of the bellmen knows something." The clerk called the concierge and three young guys in green uniforms appeared in the lobby. "Any of you help Mr Zeller with his luggage?"

"I did," said a longhaired guy named Scott.

"He say where he was going?"

"Asked how long it would take to get to the airport."

"Anything else?"

"He had a plane ticket in his shirt pocket but I couldn't see where he was going."

"You know what airline?"

# Ten

Cuffee Johnson phoned the Palm Beach detective, Conlin, giving him the bad news. The man definitely had an attitude. Like it was beneath him to deal with Bahamian law enforcement. Cuffee told him the suspect had escaped, and had also murdered a nurse named Paulette, wife of a friend and mother of two little ones.

"I thought you were gonna have somebody there watching him around the clock," Conlin said. "Did I tell you to put him in leg irons? That's what we do with suspects we think are dangerous here in Palm Beach County, make sure they don't kill people and get away."

Hearing the man's critical tone made his blood pressure rise. "A couple days ago this dangerous suspect, his nurse tells me, was too weak to stand on his own feet," Cuffee said, giving it back to him. "Man can't walk, didn't seem to be a flight risk."

"Well either he was playing you, or he made a miraculous recovery."

"One or the other," Cuffee said, "but listen, why are we wasting time talking about it? The question now, how we going to catch him?"

"You mean how am I going to catch him?"

This American detective was really full of himself. "What I

want to know," Cuffee said, "how'd this killer get away from you the first time, come to Freeport?"

That shut him up for a few seconds.

"Okay," Conlin said. "Tell me what you know."

"I know after sneaking out of the hospital the man broke into a store down the street, stole clothes and money. I know the next morning he took a cab to Lucaya, had breakfast at a restaurant at the marina. And I know he made friends with an American couple, hijacked their yacht and left them stranded on a little deserted island, lucky a fisherman come by when he did. They were thirty-six hours without food or water."

"Let me guess," Conlin said. "The yacht's a fifty-one-foot Hatteras and the couple's name was Brank. Know who he is? Makes pornographic movies."

"That's what I understand," Cuffee said. "So you have the boat, uh?"

"Coast Guard towed it in last night. Nobody on it."

Now it was clear. The man was back in Florida.

Conlin cleared his throat. "What did this guy Brank say about him?"

"He was a sleeper, you know? Cool, low-key, nothing suspicious about him. Man said his name was Emile Landau, a builder from Atlanta, and Brank believed him. They started talking about boats and Brank invited him aboard. The rest of the story, I think you know."

"You met the suspect," Conlin said. "What did you think?"

"I didn't believe him. Man accused of murder but can't remember anything. A little too convenient, don't you think?"

"I felt the same way," Conlin said, talking one cop to another now. "This guy Klaus was so relaxed when I questioned him, I thought he was falling asleep."

"What I don't understand," Cuffee said, "this man come from Stuttgart, had a German passport, right? Went through customs in Detroit. But he don't speak the language?"

"Said he couldn't remember," Conlin said.

Cuffee said. "Keep me posted, uh? I got a personal interest in this one."

*

Conlin had been at the crime scene since the Costa Rican maid found Lynn Risdon and called the police. The room smelled of perfume and feces, like somebody took a dump and splashed it with Chanel No. 5. That was the only perfume name he could think of.

Lynn Risdon was on her back fully clothed, lying in her own waste. Face frozen. Eyes open. There was rope binding her wrists and ankles. According to the medical examiner the probable cause of death was asphyxiation. The phone line had been pulled out of the wall, but there was no sign of a struggle.

They found grey stubble on a razor in the bathroom, and grey hair webbed on a brush and on the bottom of the tub. Looked like whoever killed her had showered and shaved. May have had a snack too. There was an empty milk glass and two plates in the sink. Forensics had been able to lift a couple prints and were checking to see if they matched the prints Conlin had taken of Klaus in the Bahamian hospital.

The deceased was wearing a two-carat diamond ring and a Rolex. Her cash and credit cards were still in her wallet. So apparently robbery wasn't a motive. Conlin dumped the contents of her purse on the kitchen table: brush, comb, makeup, condoms, lipstick and wallet. He opened the wallet, took out the driver's license. Lynn Risdon was forty-one, five six, 130 pounds, dark hair parted down the middle. There was a registration for a 1969 Ford Mustang, but the car wasn't on the property or out front on the street. Maybe she met the killer somewhere and he brought her here in his car. As he was putting her things back in the purse he noticed a receipt from a bar/restaurant on Gulfstream Road.

According to a neighbor Lynn Risdon was divorced and collecting $3,200 a month in alimony. Her relationship with her ex was acrimonious. He didn't know the exact definition of the word, but he knew it wasn't good. Looking for a motive, Conlin thought? There it was.

*

The bartender was a big guy with a gut, looked like a former athlete. He was busy behind the bar, getting ready for the happy-hour rush. Conlin walked in, got his attention and held up his shield.

The bartender grinned and said, "I'm innocent." Thinking he was funny.

Conlin let it go and said, "I need to ask you some questions."

"I'm kinda busy. The boozehounds are on their way, be here any time."

"You can work while we talk."

The bar was empty except for a couple of old dudes in golf shirts down to his right, drinking martinis. He could hear 'Joy to the World' by Three Dog Night coming from speakers somewhere in the room. Conlin held up a snapshot of Lynn Risdon he'd found in a desk drawer at her house. "You know her?"

The bartender looked up and nodded. "She's a regular. Comes in has a few and leaves. Saw her last night." He was slicing lemons and limes on a plastic cutting board.

"Was she with someone?" Conlin sat on a barstool, elbows on the bar top like a customer, thinking how good a beer would taste.

"Guy next to her, ordered a single malt, they started talking."

"What'd he look like?"

"Salt 'n' pepper hair, late forties, fifty, little shorter than you, little heavier. What happened?"

He slid the cut slices off the cutting board into a white plastic bucket.

"This guy she was talking to, they know each other?"

"I don't think so."

"How do you know?"

"I'm a bartender," he said, like being a bartender was an elite profession—right up there with neurosurgeons.

"What were they talking about?"

He looked up from the cutting board and shrugged.

"I thought you were a bartender."

"He was telling her he was a producer, made porno flicks. I don't know if he was making it up or not, but she was into it."

"They leave together?"

"She had four martinis, could barely walk. He helped her out, practically carried her."

"He drive her home?"

85

"How do I know? Ask Joey, the valet."

"This look like him?" Conlin said, showing him the artist sketch of Gerd Klaus.

"Yeah."

*

Joey looked like a valet, skinny dark-haired kid with a goatee, wearing skintight black Levis, black tee shirt and a red vest. Joey, Conlin noticed, had a ring on every finger. He was setting up his booth near the door when Conlin walked out of the restaurant at 5.12 p.m. After introductions, Conlin said, "What's with the rings?"

"Each one represents a special memory."

"A special memory, huh?" Conlin said, thinking this guy had to be a fruit. He showed him the picture of Lynn Risdon. "Know her?"

"She's here a lot. Drives a white '69 Mustang."

"See her last night?"

"Uh-huh. Pulled in at six thirty. Left at around quarter to ten. She was wasted, couldn't walk, some guy was helping her to her car."

Joey had a heavy Boston accent. Conlin had to really listen to understand him. "He drive her home?"

"I don't know, but he drove her somewhere."

"What about his car?"

"Don't think he had one. I saw him walk in from Gulfstream Road at about seven fifteen." He paused. "I was here till closing, never saw him again."

"Ever seen him before?"

86

"I don't think so."

Conlin showed him the artist sketch. "This look like him?"

"Definitely."

*

Conlin got to Sunset Realty at 5.33, parked on Worth, went in, flashed his shield and told the bleached blonde receptionist with silver hairpins holding up the front of her hair he was looking for Joyce Cantor.

"You just missed her. Went out the door a couple of minutes ago. She's walking home. Lives at the Winthrop House. Know where that's at, don't you?"

Conlin nodded, thanked her and walked outside, looked east, trying to spot Joyce on the congested sidewalk. Didn't see her. He got in his car. Worth Avenue was one-way so he drove to Cocoanut Row, went right and right again on Peruvian and took it all the way to the beach road, ocean straight ahead, took another right and pulled over in a no-parking zone in front of the Winthrop House. On the way he got a call from headquarters saying a patrolman had found Lynn Risdon's car parked on Worth Avenue, first block.

Conlin had taken Joyce Cantor's statement two weeks earlier in connection with the homicide of a security guard killed on the estate where Joyce was staying. Said she hadn't heard a gunshot and had never met a German manufacturer's rep named Gerd Klaus whose rental vehicle was discovered near the scene of the crime. Joyce's story was corroborated by Harry Levin, and by a colored guy named Cordell Sims, who were also staying at the estate owned by some rich guy named Frankel from New York. Talk about a clusterfuck.

Conlin knew they were bullshitting him, but he couldn't prove anything and had to let them go, all except for Sims who had an outstanding warrant against him—felony firearm—and ended up spending a day in county lockup until his legal problems were miraculously resolved. Now the German was back and he had a feeling Joyce would be interested to know about it.

*

Hess walked out of the restaurant and followed Joyce from the opposite side of the street, strolling along Worth Avenue in his new Palm Beach disguise, golf cap low over his eyes almost touching the frames of the aviator sunglasses. As far as Joyce was concerned he was dead. No one could have survived being shot and thrown in the ocean. That's why he believed God had intervened.

He was thinking of the last time he'd seen her—she'd been right there on the bed a few feet away—regretting he hadn't pulled the trigger when he had the chance. But there had been extenuating circumstances—like a crazy Jew with a gun, shooting at him.

He passed a police car double-parked next to Lynn Risdon's Mustang. The policeman was on the passenger side, looking in the window. Hess continued on, a Palm Beach retiree, glancing at his reflection in store windows. Just past South County Road he crossed over on Joyce's side of the street, thirty paces behind her, slowing down to maintain the distance between them.

A Rolls-Royce Silver Cloud was approaching, two-tone, silver and black, Hess admiring the classic motorcar with its long hood. When he looked down the sidewalk Joyce was gone. He quickened his pace, glanced left into a boutique, a big open shop, but didn't see her. Passed two more stores and finally spotted her in a flower shop.

There was no place to stop and wait without being seen, so Hess walked to the end of Worth Avenue, crossed South Ocean Boulevard and leaned his hip against the seawall, gazing out at the Atlantic. He watched a seagull dive in the water and rise up with a fish twisting in its beak. He looked over his shoulder and saw Joyce on the sidewalk, coming toward him, carrying a bouquet of flowers wrapped in paper. He watched her stop, cross Worth Avenue and go into the Winthrop House through a side entrance. Hess crossed too and followed her into the building. The lobby was crowded with people talking, watching television, playing cards and backgammon. Joyce, he noticed, was at the reception desk in conversation with Conlin, the detective who had visited him at the hospital in Freeport.

*

Conlin flashed a grin. "For me?" he said, glancing at the flowers she was holding. "You shouldn't have."

"What can I do for you, Detective?" Joyce said, surprised to see him in the lobby. Assuming he was back to question her.

"Remember the perp you didn't see, shot the security guard? Missing person whose car we found outside the Frankel estate." Conlin unfolded a piece of paper showing her a police artist's sketch of a square face with a wide nose and salt-and-pepper hair. "Look familiar?"

Joyce shook her head, looking past Conlin now, across the crowded lobby and saw a well-dressed man in a blue blazer, face partially hidden under a blue-and-white cap, something familiar about him, his sturdy build and the way he moved, and thought it was Hess. But how could it be possible? Hess was dead. She'd seen him with a bullet hole in his chest, lying in a pool of blood. And yet she'd swear it was him.

"You all right?" Conlin said, staring at her.

Joyce was light-headed all of a sudden, face cold, clammy. "Maybe it's low blood sugar. I haven't eaten all day." She rubbed her hands together and took a breath. Glanced back and he was gone. Scanned the lobby but didn't see him.

"You better sit down," Conlin said.

"Maybe I better."

"You might be more comfortable in your apartment."

"This is fine." Joyce didn't want to be alone with Conlin right now. She might break down and tell him everything. It was a difficult position to be in. Hess was alive and back in Palm Beach but she couldn't tell the police. They sat in two chairs against the wall, Conlin's body angled, facing her.

"You going to tell me what really happened that night?"

"I did."

"You saw him, didn't you?"

"Who you talking about?"

"This guy Klaus, or whatever his name is, killed your friend Lenore. But he was looking for you, wasn't he?"

"Why would he be looking for me?"

"That's the hundred-thousand-dollar question, isn't it?"

Conlin paused, staring at Joyce. "I talked to Mrs Frankel, she said you were staying at her estate while your apartment was being painted. You told me you were staying at Frankel's so you could put up Harry Levin from Detroit and his buddy, Cordell Sims. Which one is it?"

"Both."

"Both, huh? How do you know Harry?"

"We're old friends, went to school together. We've kept in touch."

"Yeah, where was that at?"

"The Jewish day school."

"And out of the blue he decided to come and visit?"

"What's wrong with that?"

"Which one of you shot the German? Or was it the colored guy, Sims?"

"I don't know what you're talking about."

"Sure you do. My guess would be Harry Levin?"

"Then why're you asking me?"

"According to Detroit police he's got a permit to carry a firearm. Big one, too, .357 Mag." Conlin took a pack of cigarettes out of his shirt pocket, tapped one out and lit it with a silver Zippo. "I was in Freeport a few days ago visiting a guy looks a lot like this." He held up the artist sketch again. "Shot with a high-caliber round—through and through, and dumped in the ocean. Sound familiar? That's usually enough to get the job done. But this German is either tough or lucky or both. But you don't know him, uh?"

Joyce met his gaze but didn't say anything. Conlin's hunch was right on the money but there was no way he could prove it.

"You might be interested to know Klaus escaped from the

hospital in Freeport, hijacked a boat and took it to Palm Beach. Went to a lot of effort to get back here. Like he had some un- finished business to take care of. But you don't know anything, is that right?" Conlin paused for effect. "You probably have nothing to worry about then."

He got on his feet. "There is one more thing I should tell you. You read about that woman was strangled last night a few blocks from here? Klaus is our main suspect. Murdered her, took a shower, fixed himself a snack. We've got a real wacko on our hands. Fingerprints match the prints on the security guard's handgun and flashlight. They also match the prints in Lenore Deutsch's house. But from what you tell me he's not after you, so you've got nothing to worry about. Listen, you have a nice evening, Ms Cantor."

*

The phone was ringing when Harry walked in the kitchen. He threw his keys on the counter and picked up the receiver. "Hello?"

"Harry, I think I just saw him."

It was Joyce.

"Who're you talking about?"

"Hess. He's alive."

"Not unless he's back from the dead," Harry said. "No way he could've survived. It's impossible." Although there had been a shred of doubt in the back of his mind when he dumped Hess' body in the ocean and watched the current take him out to sea.

Joyce told him about seeing Hess in the lobby and everything Detective Conlin had said.

"Harry, I'm scared. I don't know what to do."

"Call Cordell. He'll take care of you till I can get down there."

# Eleven

It was almost dark when Hess checked into the Vista del Mar, a motel on the ocean in a little town called Pompano Beach, thirty minutes south of Palm Beach by taxi. There were two couples sitting in lounge chairs by the pool, drinking beer, talking loud and laughing as Hess walked past them, went to the office and checked in.

His room was on the first floor facing the pool. He looked around. It was small and clean—nothing special. He walked out, closed the door and put the key in his trouser pocket, passed by the couples sitting there and one of the women said, "Ever stay here before?"

It was dark, he couldn't see her face. "No," he said.

"Well, you're going to love it."

"I'm sure I will," Hess said. He walked down the street to the Oceanside Shopping Center, bustling with activity, cars driving in and out, people everywhere. He went to Pompano Drugs and bought a toothbrush, toothpaste, comb, shaving cream, razor and a shampoo called Head & Shoulders. He walked down the sidewalk to a men's store and bought khaki trousers, a dark blue golf shirt, underwear, socks and a pair of brown Docksiders.

Back outside he noticed a post office, closed now. He would see about renting a post-office box in the morning. Hess carried his purchases to a phone booth, set the bags on the floor, picked up the receiver and fed a nickel into the coin slot, pressed o for the operator and made an overseas phone call to Munich.

After half a dozen rings, Ingrid said, "Hello," in a tired voice. It was almost 1 a.m. Munich time. She had probably been asleep.

"It's Ernst."

"My God, are you all right? I have been so worried. The police came to the office. They're going to arrest you for war crimes and crimes against humanity. Your bank accounts have been frozen. If you return to Germany you will be arrested."

"I need your help with something."

"Yes, of course, Ernst, anything." Ingrid took a breath. "Can you at least tell me where you are?"

He could hear voices and the clatter of shopping carts outside the phone booth. "There is fifty thousand dollars in the safe in my apartment." She had a key. He gave her the combination. "I'll phone you tomorrow and let you know where to send the money."

Hess walked back to the motel thinking about Ingrid. He knew he could count on her. They'd had a brief affair years earlier. She had been twenty-five at the time, slightly overweight and insecure, and Hess had taken advantage of her.

The way Ingrid still looked at him, he didn't think she had ever gotten over him.

He entered the courtyard and noticed the two beer-drinking couples were gone. The pool lights were on, making the water look green and murky. Hess went to his room, took off the elegant Palm Beach outfit and dressed in the clothes he had just purchased. The light blue trousers replaced by khakis that were too long, the orange short-sleeved shirt replaced by a blue golf shirt with a penguin on the upper right side, the white leather loafers with gold bars replaced by stiff brown Docksiders with rawhide laces. The finishing touch was a dark blue cap that said *Pompano Beach*, the words stacked on the front. Hess glanced at himself, posing in the mirror, and saw a tradesman on holiday.

It was 7.30. He stuffed the Palm Beach clothes, including the blue blazer, into the shopping bag, and dropped it into a trash bin on his way to a Chinese restaurant he'd seen earlier. It was across the beach road from the shopping center. Hess went in, moved past the hostess through the loud dining room to the crowded bar, found a seat between a frail, heavily made-up woman in her seventies and a grey-haired guy about his age, took off his cap and ordered a Macallan's neat.

The bartender, in a Hawaiian shirt, said, "You two guys brothers?"

Hess glanced to his right and met the gaze of the man next to him. He looked older from this angle, but there was a definite resemblance. He could have been related, Ernst's cousin or older brother.

"Max Hoffman," the guy said, hint of a German accent, offered his hand.

Hess said, "Harry Levin." They shook, manly grips from both of them.

Hess said, "You're German. I can hear the accent."

"Born in Berlin. Five generations. What about you?"

"Bavaria," Hess said. "Schleissheim, just north of Munich."

"Maybe we're related after all."

Max Hoffman set his drink down and placed his left hand flat on the bar top, and now Hess could see the faded vertical sequence of numbers tattooed across the top of his forearm. "You were at Auschwitz," Hess said, knowing it was the only camp where the Nazis tattooed prisoners. More than four hundred thousand inmates had been assigned serial numbers.

Max nodded. "We were rounded up and packed into a cattle car. Rode three days without food, water or bathroom facilities. Arrived May 12th, 1942." He sipped his drink. "The door opened and I saw the electric fence and the towers and a line of SS guards with machine guns, standing next to the train. I stepped over the bodies of those who had died during the travel, climbed out of the car and stood in a long line, walking toward a man in a white physician's coat, standing on a platform, a German shepherd sitting next to him. The man studied each of us with detached indifference, directing the fittest among us to the right and those who were going to die in the gas chamber to the left. I found out later he was Dr Mengele. With his arms outstretched, wearing the white medical coat he looked like a white angel. The Jews in the camp called him the Angel of Death." Max Hoffman paused. "There was a putrid stench in the air. I said to Wineman, a friend who was in front of me, 'What is that awful smell?' A guard standing nearby heard me and said, 'Your parents.' I was strong in those days. I had been an athlete. I wanted to grab the guard and break his neck." Max Hoffman picked up his drink. "I was there till the 26th of January, 1945, the day Russian troops liberated us."

"How old were you?"

"Twenty-eight when I got out."

"I was at Dachau," Hess said. "November 1942 till I escaped in May of '43."

Max said. "How'd you do it?"

"The Nazis said we were being transferred to a sub-camp to work in a munitions factory. It was believable, prisoners were transferred all the time. And I wanted to believe it. Any place had to be better than where I was." Hess sipped his whisky. "Fifty of us were packed into the back of a truck and driven a few kilometers from the camp. When the truck turned into the woods I knew the real purpose of our journey. SS guards in kübelwagens were following us, but there was a stretch where we lost sight of them and I jumped off the back of the truck."

"That took guts. How old were you?"

"Sixteen." Hess took a swallow of whisky. "I followed the truck to a clearing, stood behind a tree and watched the SS guards direct prisoners to a pit that had been dug. Twelve at a time were brought to the edge and shot in the back of the head, the velocity of the rounds blowing the bodies into the hole. More trucks came and more prisoners were executed. At some point the SS murderers started drinking schnapps to calm their nerves. Late in the afternoon when it was over many of the guards were drunk. But someone saw me. I was brought to the edge of the pit, hit on the side of the head with the butt of a carbine and thrown on top of bodies, some still alive, and burrowed down under the dead while the guards were shooting at me." That was Hess' recollection of what happened to the real Harry Levin. He could see Max hanging on every word. Hess finished the whisky and signaled the bartender. "A refill?"

"I better," Max said, "if I am going to hear any more of this."

"Another round," Hess said to the bartender, then glanced

at the Jew. "I awoke hours later, feeling the weight of the bodies on top of me. I couldn't see or breathe. The pit had been filled in with dirt. I clawed my way out. It was dark. I ran to a farmhouse and hid in the barn."

"Where was your family?"

"Killed by the Nazis."

Max Hoffman shook his head.

The bartender put fresh drinks in front of them.

Hess picked up his whisky, waited for Max to pick up his and clinked his glass. "To us, the survivors."

"I don't think that's appropriate," Max said. "How can we celebrate our lives when so many others have died? It's arrogant. Any way you look at it, we were lucky."

"You're right." Hess hadn't considered it from a Holocaust survivor's point of view. But then, how could he? "To the six million who were murdered."

The Jew gave him a sympathetic nod.

"What about you, Max? What else happened?"

The Jew drank some of his drink that looked like a Manhattan, staring into the glass as if the answer were floating next to the cherry.

"I was in the *Sonderkommando*."

"What was it like to be so close to death every day?"

"Worse than you can imagine."

"But at least you were well fed."

"Well fed? You have no idea what you're talking about."

"Better than the others, and you had your own quarters." Hess was enjoying himself, but had to be careful not to go too far.

"What are you saying?" Max's face was flush with anger. "You think it was special treatment? Let me tell you how special it was." He paused, glancing down at the bar. "We were outcasts, isolated from everyone, hated, despised. I remember looking across the yard at the Jewish girls, wishing I could talk to them. The Nazis were very clever to put us in charge of the gas chambers and the ovens, making us their accomplices."

The Jew drank his drink. "We planned the division of labor based on the size of incoming transports. The Jews would arrive confused, agitated, exhausted after spending days packed in a cattle car. We would take them to the undressing hall, try to keep them calm as we searched for valuables. Deceiving our own people, telling them they were going for a shower as we led them to the gas chamber."

Hess said, "How did you know when they were dead?"

"When the screaming stopped." Max took a breath. "There were fingernail scratches on the walls and ceiling."

"What choice did you have?"

The Jew met his gaze but didn't answer, paused for a few seconds and said, "We had to carry the bodies out and pull the gold teeth from their mouths with pliers. Then we sheared off the women's hair. Later it was washed and stuffed in sacks and used to make clothing." The Jew paused again. "You still think it was special?"

"Forgive me, Max." It was getting good. Hess had struck a nerve.

"And we were the stokers," Max said. "Operating the furnaces, sliding bodies into the ovens. We would be covered with ashes. I couldn't get the smell of death out of my nostrils." Max cleared his throat, pinched the bridge of his nose and inhaled.

"One day I picked up an emaciated body, a woman that looked familiar. It was my wife, Faga."

"What did you think?" Hess said.

"I was numb, paralyzed. Or maybe hypnotized. The world I knew had been turned upside down."

"I am sorry for you," Hess said, with as much sincerity as he could muster. "How many Jews were cremated at Auschwitz?"

"I don't know, a million, maybe more. I didn't count them."

"What did you do with all the ash? You must have had mountains of it."

"We dumped it around the camp. We loaded it on trucks and dumped it in the Vistula River and also the Sola."

Hess could see it, the dust of one million Jews, polluting the water table of southwestern Poland. "Did you feel guilty?" he said, rubbing Max's face in it now.

"Of course I did. It was a moral dilemma. But I wanted to live. I was obsessed with living. For an hour, a day, a week."

"I understand," Hess said. "It was all that mattered."

Max said, "What did you miss the most?"

"My family. And food. My mother was a wonderful cook. And also the Symphony, the Philharmonic," Hess said, trying to sound like a survivor.

They finished their drinks and Hess invited Max to have dinner with him. He wanted to learn more about this man who bore a striking resemblance to him. In the dining room over plates of sweet and sour chicken, beef chow mein and egg rolls, Max told him he had been a school teacher in Cleveland, Ohio, taught history and accounting for twenty-five years and had retired after his wife died of cancer a year earlier. He had purchased a house in Pompano on the Intracoastal. "I sit outside next to the pool and watch the boats."

Max had no children. No relatives. No pets. Hess told his new friend he was a scrap-metal dealer from Detroit, down for a week to relax, staying at a motel on North Ocean Boulevard. He was married and divorced and had a seventeen-year-old daughter. When they finished dinner Hess paid the bill and they walked outside and stood in front of the restaurant sign that said *Mon Jin Lau* in red neon. It was cool and dark, the sky lit up with stars. Not only did he and Max look alike, Hess noticed, they were about the same height and weight.

"Harry, thanks for everything. Why don't you come by tomorrow afternoon. We'll have a swim and a drink." Max wrote his address on a piece of paper and handed it to him. "It's that way," he said, pointing west. "Over the bridge and down five streets north, last house, on the Intracoastal, vacant lot next door."

"I'll do that," Hess said, marvelling at the situation. Max Hoffman, *Sonderkommando*, had cheated death once, and now fate had brought Hess back to reclaim him.

# Twelve

Cordell had met the Colombians through a black dude name High-Step, on account of one leg was shorter than the other and he had to wear a special shoe. High was tall, six four on one side and skinny. He had receding hair that reminded Cordell of Cazzie Russell.

They met at a bar in Hialeah, High making the introductions. The Colombians were Alejo, short, maybe five eight, with dark oily hair, and either he needed a shave or was growing a beard. Alejo wore a wrinkled white suit and did the talking for the Colombians. His partner was Jhonny, who Alejo called El Pibe, a name High said later meant kid in Spanish. It made sense 'cause Jhonny had nice olive skin and like six hairs on his face and looked about sixteen. The Colombians sold this sappy, fuck-you-up weed Alejo called woo woo for $100 a pound, the wholesale price. Cordell had heard it called a lot of things, bammy and boom and woolah, but never woo woo.

"How much you want to buy?" Alejo said when the four of them were sitting at a table in the dark bar, the Colombians drinking Cuba Libres, Cordell and High-Step Courvoisier and Coke.

"Let's start with twenty, see how it goes," Cordell said, thinking, okay, invest two grand, bring home six, calculating its street value. Maybe make a little more depending how he cut it up. High'd get ten per cent, $200, for introducing them.

"My man buy twenty, going to give him a quantity discount?" High-Step said to Alejo, sounding like a professional marijuana broker.

"I'm sure we can work something out." Alejo glanced at Cordell and grinned. "Man, you got a lot of ambition, uh?"

"My man get to check it out first," High said. "Make sure it quality shit."

"Of course," Alejo said. "Satisfaction guaranteed or you money back."

They met at a farm off Military Trail the next day. There was a white two-storey house and a crooked barn looked like it was about to fall over. There were fields but it didn't look like nothing was growing on them, and there was no one around. Just their two cars parked on the dusty yard in front of the barn. Alejo popped the trunk on his black Road Runner that had a layer of dust on it and handed High-Step a black plastic garbage bag knotted at one end.

"Twenty pounds of Colombia's finest woo woo," Alejo said.

High-Step, earning his commission, handed the bag to Cordell. It was heavy, felt like twenty pounds. Cordell untied the knot in the trunk of his Z28, pulled the plastic back, looked in and picked up a handful of sappy weed, smelled like it could send you to a far-off galaxy.

"What you think?" Alejo said. "You like?"

Yeah, he liked. Took twenty $100 bills out of his back pocket and handed the wad to Alejo. Alejo speed-counted it and gave Cordell back $200.

"You discount, man."

That's how Cordell's new enterprise had started. He took the weed back to his apartment in West Palm, filled plastic bags and weighed them on his new scale, got twenty lids per pound, four hundred total. At $15 each that was $6,000. It went fast too, Cordell making the rounds in Fort Lauderdale, the Elbow Room, the Student Prince and Penrods, selling to longhaired, pea-eyed hippies who looked like they were already in orbit, and vacationing students who wanted to get there. Everybody interested in a lid of Grade A, no-bullshit Colombian, smoke it, you'd be under the influence of a higher power.

A second market that looked promising was the crowd at the Windjammer, tap into the young rich professionals. Cordell sat at the bar next to a dude in a starched white dress shirt, unbuttoned to his navel, drinking a Salty Dog. Cordell said, "How you doing? Like to get high?"

"You taking a poll, or selling?" dude wearing a gold Rolex said.

"It's Colombian," Cordell said. "Sends you up like NASA."

"When I smoke grass it's Acapulco Gold," the dude said, getting all haughty.

"I'm impressed," Cordell said. "Shit I got makes Acapulco Gold smoke like oregano, man."

"How much?"

"Thirty dollars an ounce, limit four ounces per customer," Cordell said and grinned.

"Why is there a limit?"

"Shit's so good I can't be responsible what happens to you."

"Got it with you?"

Cordell sold the whole batch, four hundred lids in a couple days, and was on the phone to Alejo. "I'm out, man. Got more? I'll take fifty pounds this time."

"That's a lot of woo woo," Alejo said.

"Got a lot of people want to get high."

They agreed to meet at the farm again. No High-Step this time, just Cordell and the nickel-plate semiautomatic under the seat, in case he needed back-up. He looked in the rearview, tires on the dirt road kicking up a trail of dust, getting the blue Z28 with white stripes all dirty, just had it washed.

Alejo and Jhonny were waiting in Alejo's black Road Runner when he pulled up next to the barn. The Colombians got out, Jhonny popped the trunk, reached in and pulled out two garbage bags, brought them over to Cordell. He opened them and checked the shit, smelled just like the last batch. Cordell gave Alejo fifty $100 bills, and that was that.

Drove back to his apartment in West Palm and went to work. He'd filled and weighed twenty-five bags when the phone rang. Cordell picked it up said, "Yo?"

"It's Joyce." Kinda quiet voice like she didn't want no one to hear what she was sayin'. Cordell thinking, Joyce. Joyce who?

"I need your help. The Nazi's back," he thought she said, sounding upset, talking fast.

Okay, now he got it. "Yo, Joyce, slow down, tell me what's going on."

She was afraid, asked Cordell to come pick her up and she would explain everything. Man, this was bad timing, but then he thought, hold on, be cool. He could put her in the guest room, free room and board, she could help with the operation. Bagging and weighing weed you could teach a monkey to do, and Joyce, from what he remembered, was fairly intelligent. Not that he knew her all that well. But they had this connection.

Cordell left everything where it was, drove to Palm Beach

and picked her up. She was waiting in the lobby. He walked her out, Joyce all nervous, looking around while Cordell put her suitcase in the trunk. On the way back to the apartment Joyce told him what had happened, and Cordell thought it was hard to believe. He'd seen the Nazi on the kitchen floor with a bullet hole in his chest, and if the motherfucker wasn't dead, man was a vampire. But he didn't say nothin'. Joyce helped him one time so he was going to help her back.

Cordell opened the apartment door and knew something was wrong. The green plaid drape on one side of the window had been pushed through the broken glass and was blowing in the wind. Joyce was looking at it too, and then at him, could read his expression, see something wasn't right.

"What happened?"

"Look like somebody broke in."

He stepped in the apartment behind Joyce, put her suitcase on the floor and closed the door.

"You don't think they're still here?"

Cordell didn't answer, he was moving into the room, seeing the twenty-five lids he'd left on the table, gone, plastic garbage bags on the floor, gone too. All he could think of was the Colombians. Who else? Followed him from the farm. They had his money and now they had the woo woo. Sell it again to some other dumbass, steal it back. But it didn't make sense. Okay, they took five grand off him. But could've made ten times that or more dealing with him straight up. They had the weed and he had the clientele. Cordell went into the kitchen, got on his knees on the yellow-and-white linoleum, pulled out the strip of wood under the cabinets, grabbed the money, twenty-five grand, and the nickel-plate semiautomatic, thinking, call High-

Step, find out where the Colombians was at, settle up. But what about Joyce?

She came in, stood over him and said, "Will you please tell me what's going on?"

"Colombians stole my weed."

With that Joyce started crying. "Tell me this isn't happening."

Cordell got up, put his arms around her and said, "There, there now. Everything gonna be okay."

*

Stark phoned early evening, gave Harry the flights Hess, alias Gerd Klaus, had taken.

"Flew Stuttgart–London on Lufthansa, September twenty-eighth. Had a two-hour layover. Flew London–Detroit on Pan Am, arriving on the twenty-ninth, checked into the Statler Hotel downtown."

"Amazing," Harry said, writing the information down on a lined yellow pad. "How do you do it?"

"I have friends in high places," Stark said. Harry could hear him drawing on a cigarette and blowing out the smoke. "Tell me what's going on. I thought this guy was dead."

"Well, evidently there's been an eyewitness account of his resurrection."

"What do you think?"

"I don't see how it's possible. I told you what happened." Harry assumed Joyce was just being paranoid.

"I remember," Stark said. "Who could survive that?" He paused. "What's it have to do with this information I just got for you?"

"Nothing," Harry said. "That's something else."

"But, I suspect, related."

"Could be."

Harry hung up, ripped the paper off the pad and handed it to Colette. "Find the locker and you might have your next story."

"What do you think is in it?"

*

Joyce called again while they were having dinner.

"Harry, I'm sorry to bother you, but we've got a problem." She told him about the Colombians. "I can't stay here, Harry."

"Go to a friend's," Harry said. "Go to a hotel till I can get down there." He paused. "Put Cordell on, will you?"

"He wants to talk to you," Joyce's voice sounding faint.

"Yo, Harry, my man. How's everything in the Motor City?"

"You're back at it, huh?"

"It's the only trade I know."

"I don't want Joyce involved in this."

"She ain't involved. You involved?" Cordell said to Joyce. "No she ain't involved."

"Get her out of there, will you?"

"Harry, tell me you don't believe the Nazi's back. No offense," he said to Joyce.

"I saw him," Joyce said.

"Keep an eye on her," Harry said to Cordell. "I'll be down as soon as I can."

# Thirteen

Colette kissed Harry and put her arms around him, holding on tight. "Harry, I am going to miss you so much."

They had talked about when they were going to see each other again. Harry had been kicked out of Germany for carrying a concealed weapon. If he returned he would be arrested, prosecuted and sent to prison.

Harry had said, "Let's see how it goes. You might be happy to get away from me for a while. You might get home and not think about me."

And Colette had said, "You might get lonely and call Galina."

"Don't worry. She's mad, not talking to me." Harry kissed her. "When are you coming back?"

"Oh, now you want me."

"You don't have to worry about that," Harry said. "I don't know what I'm going to do without you."

She saw the last of the passengers moving through the gate into the jet way. She heard last call for her Pan Am flight to London on the intercom.

"Harry, I have to go." She kissed him one more time, showed her ticket to the gate agent and walked toward the plane.

*

Colette was in London seven hours later. Going through customs took forever. She didn't have a lot of time. Her flight to Stuttgart was scheduled to take off in thirty minutes. Colette went down to baggage claim where the lockers were, tried to insert Hess' key in locker number 48 but it didn't fit. Now she had to get to the Lufthansa gate that was on the other side of the terminal. She ran most of the way and made it with only a couple minutes to spare.

In Stuttgart Colette went to baggage claim, retrieved her suitcase and went through customs. She found the lockers, but again the key didn't fit. So now she was concerned. How did Hess travel from Munich to Stuttgart? He could have gone by train, but she doubted he would take that chance. Hess was well known and recognizable in Bavaria. And if he had booked a flight, Hess' name or his alias, Gerd Klaus, would have been on an airline manifest. Based on that supposition, Colette believed Hess had driven to Stuttgart. And since he was flying to London the locker had to be in this terminal. Colette talked to a Lufthansa ticket agent and learned that the Lufthansa lounge on the third floor had lockers.

She checked it out, found locker 48, and tried the key. It didn't fit. So, if not Stuttgart, where? Munich was the final possibility and she was going there anyway. First the airport and then the train station.

*

Franz Stigler was returning from the men's toilet when he saw the blonde enter the locker area. Eyes glued to her perfect butt in tight jeans, the denim fabric straining to hold it in, as he walked back to the bench where he had been sitting, grabbed

III

the folded sections of a newspaper, opened one, using it as a prop, glancing over the fold, studying the blonde. He was sure he had seen her before but who was she?

Franz had been waiting in the train station for the better part of three days. Ever since Ernst Hess had phoned and said he needed Franz's assistance with an extremely delicate but important mission. Franz was stunned to hear his voice and afraid to get involved. Ernst Hess was a fugitive. Anyone who helped him in any way would be prosecuted. But Ernst Hess had also been instrumental, both financially and philosophically, in the rise of the neo-Nazis. He replayed the conversation in his head.

"Franz."

"Yes, who is this please?"

"Ernst Hess."

He had paused, not sure what to say, at first thinking one of his friends was playing a joke. "Herr Hess, is this really you?" A dumb thing to say, but it slipped out.

"No, it is the Führer. I've come back from the dead. Of course it is me, you idiot." The belligerent tone confirming it. "I need your help."

"Of course, anything."

"I want you to go to the train station first thing in the morning."

Franz was an electrician. He had jobs lined up the next day and all week. "For how long?"

"As long as it takes," Hess said, voice firm. "It could be several days."

"Several days? Herr Hess, I have responsibilities."

"You have responsibilities to me," Hess said, raising his voice.

Hess explained what he wanted Franz to do, but made no offer to pay him for the work he was going to lose. Franz was married with two teenage children. How was he going to explain this to his wife? Franz had been the master of ceremonies at a few Blackshirt rallies. He enjoyed the notoriety. But going out for an evening was one thing. Devoting work hours to the Cause was something else. But there was no way he could refuse Ernst Hess. Refuse, and Hess might have him killed.

The blonde was opening locker 48, removing a parcel wrapped in brown paper. She turned, their eyes met. She looked away, walked out of the room. He got up and followed her and then it hit him. This was Colette Rizik, the journalist.

He followed her out to the taxi queue, stood behind her in line, and had his taxi follow hers to Schwabing. Colette got out at Wagnerstrasse 12. The driver opened the trunk, handed her the parcel that was in the locker, put her suitcase on the sidewalk and drove off. Franz watched Colette enter the apartment building.

*

Colette opened her apartment door, stepped in with the suitcase, put it on the floor and locked the door. She moved through the salon to the window, glanced through a crack in the drapes, scanned the sidewalk and street, looking for the man at the train station. She saw him follow her from the lockers out to the taxi queue, then saw him behind her in line.

Could it all have been coincidence? Possibly. After all that had happened Colette was understandably jittery. A young couple walked by her building and she saw a car pass, but she didn't see a thin dark-haired man wearing glasses with round metal frames.

Colette went in the kitchen, turned on the light over the table, and placed the package under it. She went into her darkroom and came back to the table with a razor blade and made an incision across one of the hard narrow sides of the package and pulled the paper off. It was a painting, bright colors, a man standing between two trees. It was signed 'Vincent'. She phoned Gunter, her editor at *Der Spiegel*, and described the painting.

"It sounds like *The Painter on the Road to Tarascon* by Van Gogh. It was supposedly lost in a museum that was bombed by the Allies during the war. Where did you get it?"

"Ernst Hess left it in a locker at the train station in Munich."

# Fourteen

Hess walked to the shopping center, rented a box at the post office and phoned Ingrid at her apartment in Munich. She had picked up the money. No one, to her knowledge, had seen or followed her. Hess gave Ingrid the Pompano Beach box number and address. "Send it to Max Hoffman."

She said he would receive the package on the 27th. Was that all right? No, but what choice did he have? Hess said he would contact her when it arrived.

He bought a *Palm Beach Post* and read it, sipping coffee at a restaurant on South Atlantic Boulevard. On page 3 a headline caught his eye: *Murder Stuns Palm Beach Residents*. There was an artist sketch of the suspect. Hess studied it, a face under a cap with a wide nose and three days of whiskers, and decided it looked nothing like him. The article went on to say that a forty-one-year-old Palm Beach woman had been strangled in her home on Seabreeze Avenue. Palm Beach police were investigating. Nothing further on the abandoned Hatteras.

Hess had an idea and went back to the shopping center and bought a bottle of Macallan's for himself and a bottle of Canadian Club for Max. Then he went next door to the supermarket and picked up two porterhouse steaks. He would arrive bearing gifts.

At 12.15, Hess crossed the bridge, went north on NE 26th

Avenue to 5th Street and went right through a residential neighborhood of single-storey houses painted soft pastel colors and built on small treeless lots.

Max's house was at the end of the street on the Intracoastal. To the north was a vacant lot with a *For Sale* sign on it. To the south was a house, Max's nearest neighbor. It was a hot day and Hess was perspiring when he arrived at Max's front door, holding a bag of groceries against his chest, and rang the bell.

*

Hess watched former *Sonderkommando* Max Hoffman floating on an orange vinyl pool raft. Max was in good shape for a man fifty-four years old, barrel chest and flat stomach covered with grey hair that looked like a dove-colored sweater. He would drift around, eyes closed, occasionally pushing himself away from the side of the pool. Or he would slide off the raft into the cool blue depths, and come back up wiping water out of his eyes, saying, "Harry, come on. You don't know what you're missing, get in here."

"I'm fine," Hess would say from his chair on the pink patio, watching the endless parade of boats move past on the waterway. "Perfectly content right here."

There was an apartment building with a swimming pool directly across the Intracoastal, thirty meters away, retirees lounging under wide-brimmed hats and umbrellas, two couples at a table, playing cards. Hess, expecting quiet and seclusion, was surprised by all of the activity. Max, in the shallow end, climbed out of the pool, grabbed a striped beach towel off a chair, dried himself and took a seat next to Hess.

"What I tell you? Not bad, uh?" Max said, swinging his arm open like an impresario, indicating the pool, the house, the property.

Hess nodded, the nod answering both questions in the affirmative.

"I wish Ellen, God bless her, had lived long enough to enjoy it with me. If my fellow teachers at Rocky River high could see me now."

Hess didn't think the modest house built on a treeless lot on the busy polluted Intracoastal warranted such praise.

"I taught history, I think I told you, and also accounting. I used to say to the kids: 'Assets equal liabilities plus proprietorship. What? Assets equal liabilities plus proprietorship. What are you going to say to me on the street in thirty years?'" Max was beaming. "I have to tell you, I miss it." He paused to reminisce. "How about a dividend?" Pointing at Hess' empty cocktail glass.

"Only if you're having one."

"Twist my arm," Max said, getting up and grabbing Hess' glass off the round plastic table that had an umbrella through the middle, and disappeared in the house.

Max was a lot more personable and outgoing on familiar turf. That, or he was getting more comfortable with Hess. Ernst was standing at the edge of the waterway, admiring a seventy-foot pleasure yacht, two shapely blondes in bikinis sunbathing on the aft deck, when Max returned with the drinks. Three fingers of Macallan's for Hess and a dark lowball cocktail for himself.

"I remember this feeling of freedom when we were liberated. I remember being in Krakow, walking through the town square shouting, 'I'm a Jew. I'm a Jew.' Finally able to say it and proud that I was."

"I know what you mean," Hess said. "The stigma was finally gone."

Hess saw a woman in a bathing suit standing by the pool next door. She glanced at them and waved. Max saw her and waved back.

"Who's that?"

"My neighbor, Lois Grant. Lost her husband eight months ago. We've gone out a couple times. Nothing serious."

"How old?"

"Forty-eight."

Hess said, "You like the young ones, huh?"

Max grinned. "I'll introduce you if you want. Nice lady." He sipped his drink and got up. "Harry, relax, I'm going to take a shower, wash off the chlorine. I'll light the grill when I come back. You hungry?"

"I'm always hungry."

The afternoon sun had dipped over the house. Hess, sitting in shadow, felt a slight chill. The retirees across the way, he noticed, had disappeared, gone back to their apartments. Hess knew he had to seize the opportunity. He went inside, locked the patio door and closed all the windows.

Hess walked down the hall to Max's bedroom, went in and stood listening at the bathroom door. He could hear the shower, and heard the doorbell ring. He moved to the front of the house, looked out and saw a maroon Ford parked in the driveway and a tall man with dark shoulder-length hair at the front door. Hess watched him press the doorbell again and heard it echo across the foyer to the patio doors. When no one responded, the man knocked impatiently. Hess waited him out, saw him go to the car, glance back one more time, get in and drive away.

Hess returned to the bathroom door, heard the shower turn off and the rattle of the shower curtain being pulled open. He drew the revolver and knocked on the door, heard Max say, "Just a minute."

The door opened, steam floating through the crack, Max visible now with a towel wrapped around his waist, wet hair dripping water on his chest.

"Someone is at the door," Hess said, holding the gun down his leg, pillow on the floor against the wall.

Max opened the door halfway. "Who is it?"

"Some guy wants to talk to you."

"Tell him to hang on."

Hess raised the revolver and shot Max point blank in the chest. Max glanced down at the little spot of blood just above his right nipple, and charged through the doorway. Hess stepped back and shot him again, lower this time, center chest, and still he charged, Hess retreating, firing two more times from the hallway, the .38 jumping, and now Max staggered and fell face down on the white tile, blood running out from his body in crimson streams following the level of the floor. Hess glanced at himself in the hallway mirror, spatter from the gunshots on his face, shirt and khaki trousers.

Hess dragged Max into the bathroom and lifted his wet naked body, first his legs, then his torso, into the tub. He found a bucket and mop in the laundry room and a bottle of ammonia and cleaned the floor, coughing at the toxic fumes. When he was finished, Hess went in the guest bathroom, wiped the blood off his face and arms with a washcloth, and changed into one of Max's Cleveland Indians tee-shirts and cap and a pair of his madras Bermuda shorts. Hess looked in the full-length mirror on the bedroom wall and barely recognized himself in the borrowed clothes.

Hess planned to stay there for a few days until his money arrived. Max had said he didn't have any friends in the area. And since they looked somewhat alike, Hess thought, as long as he maintained a low profile, he could become Max Hoffman, assume the Jew's identity. Wear his clothes, drive his car. But what was he going to do with Max's body? He could weigh him down and dump him in the Intracoastal. But what if a fisherman snagged the body and brought it up? That wasn't out of the question. Not in a fishing community such as this. No, dumping a body in water was dangerous. Hess himself was proof of that.

In a flashback, maybe triggered by the blood spatter, Hess recalled the scene in the forest outside Dachau, the pit dug, the bodies shot and thrown in, and saw the solution to his problem. He would bury Max Hoffman somewhere on his own property.

In the garage Hess found a shovel and walked around the house, trying to find an area that wasn't visible to the neighbors, which didn't leave many options. The only possibility was the north side of the house adjoining the vacant lot. There was a flowerbed that was roughly eight feet long by three feet wide.

Hess sunk the shovelhead and pulled back, lifting a shovelful of dirt and pieces of flowers that had yellow and white petals. He dug down three feet and hit the water table, but for his purposes it was deep enough. The sun was hanging on the rooftops, red highlights subdued by heavy clouds. He could see a woman down the street, walking her dog, and hear the low rumble of boats moving by on the waterway. Hess was exhausted, sweat-soaked and filthy but he had to finish the job. He found garbage bags in a drawer in the kitchen and a roll of duct tape. He cut the bags in half, taped the sections together and laid out a canvas of plastic on the bathroom floor. He grabbed Max's legs and pulled his body half over the side of the tub and then all of him, wrapping sections of plastic around him and securing the sections with silver duct tape.

It was dark and quiet when Hess dragged Max's plastic-wrapped body through the garage and out the rear door, and rolled him into the hole and filled it in with dirt. When he was finished he went in the garage, locked the door, stripped off his soiled tee-shirt and dirt-caked shorts and walked naked through the house to the guest bathroom.

He showered and dressed in a pair of Max's trousers and a blue cotton shirt, went in the kitchen and poured a much-needed glass of Macallan. He sat at the kitchen table, going through Max's wallet, which held two $20 bills, a $10, a $5 and a $1. Hess studied Max's face on his Ohio driver's license. Max had a bigger nose and grayer hair but other than that they really did look remarkably similar. He practiced forging Max's signature with its big dramatic flourishes, and finally wrote one that looked passable.

In the morning, Hess, wearing Max's white terrycloth robe that had the faint smell of aftershave, walked through the garage, out the door, and surveyed his work from the night before. There was a convex mound where he had buried Max and filled in the hole with dirt. And now, despite the missing flowers, there was nothing suspicious about the garden.

Hess carried Max Hoffman's wallet in his back pocket as he drove south down the coast in Max's light green Chrysler New Yorker that was the size of a motor yacht and only had two doors, stopping at a restaurant in Lauderdale-by-the-Sea. He ordered eggs over easy, sausage, toast and black coffee. He'd brought the *Palm Beach Post* with him and perused it while he ate. There was a small one-column article about the murder in Palm Beach and the same sketch and description he had seen in yesterday's paper.

On the next page was a photograph of Tony and Denise Brank under a headline that said *Hijacked Couple Back Safely in South Florida*. A Bahamian fisherman had rescued the shanghaied American erotic film producer and his actress wife on a remote island in the Bahamas. US Coast Guard officials said the Branks' fifty-one-foot Hatteras pleasure yacht had been returned to them.

After breakfast, Hess stopped at Publix, bought enough food for a few days and went back to Max's house.

# Fifteen

Zeller had underestimated Harry Levin, sure he was in control of the situation when Levin walked in his house. Surprised when the man pulled a gun on him. It was embarrassing. This scrap-metal dealer had made him look like an amateur. Zeller wasn't convinced Levin or the journalist knew where Hess was hiding anyway.

But that was all moot now after he had received a call from his answering service telling him Ingrid Bookmyer had the information he had been waiting for. Zeller flew back to Munich and was waiting in Ingrid's apartment the next evening, sitting in an easy chair in the darkness of the salon when he heard a key in the lock and saw the door open, casting light across the foyer. Ingrid entered the apartment, dropped her keys and purse on a table and turned on a lamp. She moved toward him but turned right into the kitchen. Zeller saw a light go on and heard the rattle of utensils. He heard the refrigerator open and close, the sound of a cork popping.

Ingrid came out of the kitchen into the dark salon and now Zeller turned on the lamp that was next to him on an end table. Ingrid, startled, dropped the wine glass. It hit and shattered on the hardwood floor.

Zeller said, "Where is Hess?"

"All I have is a post-office box in Pompano Beach, Florida."

Ingrid glanced down at the broken glass and the spilled wine moving in a stream across the floor.

"What does he want you to send him?"

"Money," Ingrid said.

"Where is it?"

"In the desk. I will show you."

Ingrid crossed the room, opened a drawer and took out a manila envelope. She came back and handed it to him. The envelope was addressed to Max Hoffman, PO Box 3456, Pompano Beach, FL 33064. "Max Hoffman, is this an alias, or an acquaintance?"

"Herr Hess did not explain."

Zeller undid the clasp, tilted the envelope and out came five bundles of $100 bills held together with rubber bands. He picked up a bundle and shuffled one of the ends to make sure there were $100 bills all the way through.

"Why would Hess have fifty thousand US dollars?"

"I don't know."

"I think you do." Zeller reached behind his back and drew the silenced Makarov, training it on her.

"He did business with American companies and traveled frequently to the United States."

Zeller could see in her eyes there was something else. "Where did Herr Hess get the money?"

"From an art broker in New York," Ingrid said. "For the Dürer."

"It was a painting?"

"No, I think an illustration. I never saw it."

"Where did Herr Hess get it?"

"All I know, it was during the war."

This was getting interesting. He knew the Nazis had stolen thousands of paintings and artwork from occupied countries throughout Europe, from private collections and museums, from churches and synagogues. Zeller was intrigued by the possibility that other stolen paintings might exist. He thought of the Van Gogh that Hess' wife had mentioned, and it occurred to him—this is what Braun was after. Hess' alleged war crimes had nothing to do with it. Hess being on the run gave Braun the opportunity.

Zeller had searched Hess' estate in Schleissheim, his place of business and his apartment. There were no paintings. Where would Hess store them? He would need a place with controlled temperature and humidity. The Nazis had hid their stolen treasures in caves and salt mines for that very reason. "Does Herr Hess own property in the country?"

"I would have no idea."

"Does he own a chalet or a summer home? Is that where the other paintings are stored?"

Ingrid fidgeted with her hands. "I don't know anything about other paintings. I only know Herr Hess had the Dürer and brought it to a broker in New York. It was authenticated and sold."

"Who is the broker?"

"A man in New York named Mauer."

Zeller had seen the name in Hess' address book. He glanced at the bundles of money in his lap and noticed there was something else in the envelope. It was a copy of *Der Spiegel*. Of course, she was sending him the article. "Does Hess know about this?"

"I told him," Ingrid said. "Herr Hess wants to read it for himself."

Zeller was trying to think if there was anything else he needed from Ingrid, and decided there wasn't and raised the Makarov.

*

"I think I misjudged you," Gerhard Braun said, "You are obviously the wrong man for the job.

"I will have Hess on the twenty-seventh of October," Zeller said. "I'll put him in a crate and mail him to you if that's what you wish."

"Well, you are confident, I'll give you that."

"It has nothing to do with confidence. It's assurance."

They were sitting on a stone bench in the English Gardens. Braun wore a long coat buttoned to the neck and leather gloves, smoking a cigar, the smoke mixing with clean cool late October air. Braun could see stands of tall trees that had lost their leaves, stretches of leaf-covered lawn and people scattered about on the walking paths. His driver sat behind the wheel of a black Mercedes sedan twenty meters away, watching them, smoking a cigarette with the window down.

"Where is Ernst?"

"Southern Florida."

"I would have guessed South America. Join the old gang in Buenos Aires."

"Too obvious."

"How did you find him?"

"It's what I do."

Zeller was still boastful and over-confident and had not ac-
complished anything. Braun puffed on the cigar and blew out
a stream of smoke.

"What do you want me to do with him?"

"Persuade Ernst to tell you where he hid the paintings."

"The paintings?"

"A few works considered degenerate art by Hitler. *Entarte
Kunst*, modern art that was deemed un-German or Jewish
Bolshevist. Many of these paintings were confiscated and des-
troyed, but some survived."

"What artists are you referring to?"

"Liebermann, Meidner and Freundlich," Braun said, down-
playing their artistic significance. Leaving out better-known
names: Picasso, Matisse, Kandinsky, Klee and Chagall.

\*

Two days later Zeller landed at Palm Beach International Airport. It was October 26, 1.30 p.m. He had been traveling for
twenty-four hours. Walking out of the aircraft he was hit by the
tropical glare and humidity. He put on sunglasses, took off his
leather jacket and folded it over his arm.

Zeller picked up his suitcase at baggage claim, rented a car
and drove to Pompano Beach. He had been thinking about his
conversation with Braun. Zeller had no doubt the paintings
Hess had looted or confiscated were worth millions, or why
would Braun be wasting his time? Find the paintings and he
would be rich.

He stopped at a Shell gas station on North Ocean Boulevard
and asked for directions to the post office. "Which one?" the

man behind the counter said. "There're two. One's on NE 16th, other's on East Atlantic."

By process of elimination, he found the post office where the package was being shipped. It was on East Atlantic Boulevard in a crowded shopping center. He had parked, gone in and checked the numbers on the boxes, a wall of them, and found Hess' number, 3456. Business hours were posted on the glass door: 8.30 a.m. to 6 p.m.

The package was scheduled to arrive the next day, so Zeller decided to postpone his surveillance operation for the time being. He wondered if there was any significance to Hess using Max Hoffman as an alias. He went to the phone booth, checked the phone book and found two Max Hoffmans. One lived on NE 5th Street in Pompano Beach. The second lived in Lauderdale-by-the-Sea, 4612 El Mar Drive.

Zeller went to a petrol station and bought a map, located NE 5th Street, drove there and found Max Hoffman's address and parked next to a vacant lot. The house, built on the Intracoastal, was pale yellow. A truck was parked down the street and a landscaping crew were busy trimming trees and cutting the lawn.

With the window down Zeller smoked a cigarette and watched boats cruise by on the waterway. He waited and watched for thirty minutes, smoked another cigarette. He started the car, shifted into drive and turned into Max Hoffman's driveway. Zeller got out, walked to the front door and rang the bell. Waited and rang again. He tried to see in the windows flanking the door, but the blinds were closed.

He walked around the side of the house, looking in windows. The interior was dark. Zeller stood on the patio, watching a speedboat, with its long hull, rumble past. Felt the sun's heat on his face and wiped sweat off his forehead. Noticed a mattress floating in the pool, and a woman at the house next door, sitting on her patio, reading a book. She glanced over at him and waved. Zeller waved back. He heard the drone of an engine and saw a biplane in the distance, trailing a banner advertising *2-for-1 Happy Hour cocktails* at Mon Jin Lau. He tried to turn the handles on the French doors. They were locked.

At 3.40 p.m., Zeller drove south on A1A to Lauderdale-by-the-Sea. The second Max Hoffman lived at Marine Terrace, a huge pink oceanfront condominium on El Mar Drive. Zeller parked in the lot, walked in the lobby and rode an elevator to the eighth floor. He found 8612 and rang the bell. The door opened, a woman with blonde hair, sixties, said, "Whatever you're selling, I'm not interested. And listen, you, there's no so-liciting here."

"I'm looking for Max," Zeller said.

"My Max?" The woman frowned. "And who're you?"

"What's going on?" a short bald man said, coming toward them.

Zeller said, "Have you talked to Herr Hess?"

"Who?"

"Ernst."

"I don't know any Ernst."

"My mistake," Zeller said. "Sorry to have disturbed you."

Zeller was back in Pompano Beach fifteen minutes later, driving on the beach road north past the pier. He saw a motel called Treasure Island, pulled in and looked around. It was built in a U-shape with a swimming pool in the center, rooms facing the ocean and a private beach.

He checked in and slept till seven, showered, walked down the beach to a seafood restaurant. He went in, sat at the bar and had two vodka tonics and later ordered grilled mahi mahi, French fries and two glasses of Chablis. After dinner he walked back to the motel, and stood on the beach at the water's edge, looking up at the stars. With any luck he would conclude his business in the next two days and be on a plane back to Germany.

# Sixteen

Squirrel said, "You going to let him get away with that?"

"I've got news for you," Dink said. "He already did." Police had located his truck in a strip mall across the street from the Rodeo Bar. Jesus lord, that had pissed him off something fierce.

"What I'm sayin' is, you going to just let it go? Man put a bullet hole in your floor board."

"What do you got in mind?"

"Something, I'll tell you that."

"Oh now that's helpful."

"You know what I mean," Squirrel said.

Dink sure did. He'd given it some serious thought too. This Kraut Zeller'd hired them and then *poof* he'd disappeared without payin' them. Nothin' they could do about that, so Dink turned his attention back to this Jew, Levin. His first instinct was to torch the man's home, show him what happens you fuck with good ole boys from east Tennessee. But what the hell good would that do?

His next idea was to clean out the man's house, empty the place, call Harry, say, "Hey, seen your furniture and such?" Sell it all back to him. Squirrel pointed out a few flaws in the plan.

"Where we gonna get a movin' van? And let's say one miraculously appears, who you gonna get to help you? 'Cause it ain't gonna be me."

Dink said, "You got a better way let's hear it. Don't keep me in suspense any longer."

"Tail the man till an opportunity presents itself," Squirrel said, tilting the beer can up to his mouth till it was empty. Then belching, filling the inside of the truck with the second-hand smell of sausage and gravy.

"Jesus," Dink said, fanning the air in front of his face with one hand and rolling down the window with the other.

Squirrel grinned, showing brown front teeth parted down the middle. "Like havin' breakfast all over again."

*

Eight hours later they were in Squirrel's El Camino, with its gunmetal junkyard hood contrasting the original white paint color, just down the street from Harry Levin's house. Squirrel had his side window cracked about an inch, hot-boxing Camels like he was going to the chair. Squirrel'd smoke one down to a nub, light a new one with it and push the nub through the opening in the window. Must've been fifteen on the street.

Dink was dizzy sitting in the cloud of smoke. It was still dark out when they got there, watching the overcast sky lighten as the sun came up, looking at the dark shapes of trees that had lost most of their leaves.

Squirrel said, "What do you know about this Nazi Zeller was tryin' to locate?"

"That's about it," Dink said. "Man was a Nazi."

"What'd Zeller want him for?"

"Didn't say."

"How's this fella Levin know where the Nazi's at?"

"No idea. But what if we find the Nazi first?"

"And then what?"

"Sell him. Somebody'll pay good money for a genuine Nazi."

"I thought you admired them."

"I do but this is commerce."

Dink saw Levin roll down the driveway and followed him along Woodward Avenue to the freeway and through Hamtramck where the Polacks lived to a scrap yard, mountain of metal rising up behind a low-slung cinderblock building on one side of the yard and a big two-storey warehouse on the other side. They had to get in there for a closer look and Dink had just the way to do it.

They drove back to Dink's rented house in Pontiac. The landlord had left an old icebox in the garage. It was white with gold fixtures and weighed enough to give you a hernia. Squirrel backed the El Camino up to the garage, lowered the tailgate, laid a tarp over the truck bed and they picked up that goddamn reefer and slid it in without too much room to spare.

"Think this is a good idea?" Squirrel said. "Man knows you."

Dink pulled the brim of the Cat Diesel cap low over his eyes. "But he's got to see me and then recognize me."

"What do you think this is, some great disguise?"

"I call it the element of surprise. He's not gonna be expectin' me. You understand?"

Squirrel, breathing through his mouth, looked at him with vacant eyes.

*

There were two trucks ahead of them in line for the scale,

colored guys sellin', by the look of it, steel and copper pipes they'd yanked out of abandoned houses. When it was their turn, the man working the scale, whose blue work shirt had a white name patch that said *Archie* on it, told them to put the refrigerator on the scale.

"Will you look at that," Archie the scale man said. "What year is it?"

He had long brown hair parted down the middle and held in place by a headband.

"1926 Gibson," Dink said.

"Where in the world you get that?"

"Garage," Dink said.

Squirrel said, "What can you give us for it?"

"I can go twenty-eight dollars, but you can probably get more at an antique store. It was made out of copper, I'd go eighty-four."

Dink said, "How 'bout it was made out of gold? What would you give us for it then?"

"I don't know."

"Oh, he don't know," Dink said to Squirrel.

The scale man folded his arms across his chest in a gesture that said he wasn't going to take any shit. "You want to sell it or not?"

"Well we're not takin' it back home, I'll tell you that."

"I need your name and address."

"Why do you want to know that for?"

"We're payin' cash for scrap, IRS wants to know who we're paying."

"Aubrey Ponder," Dink said. "Sleepy Hollow trailer park in Pontiac."

Squirrel gave him the evil eye. Dink looked at him and grinned.

The scale man wrote everything on a small piece of note-paper and handed it to Dink. Squirrel moved the El Camino, parked next to the office. They went in the cinderblock lobby that reminded Dink of his cell at the Tennessee State Penitentiary in Nashville where he done eight years for robbin' a convenience store, first and only conviction.

There was a tinted double window on the inner wall that slid back and forth. It was open a couple inches and Dink could see a desk, file cabinets and a not bad-lookin' girl with blonde cotton-candy hair, phone up to her ear. He tapped lightly on the glass with a knuckle. She slid the window open, held her hand over the part of the phone where you talk.

"Can I help you?"

"We's here for our money." Dink handed the piece of paper to her.

The blonde brought the phone back up to her face and said, "Mother, I'm going to have to call you back."

She hung it up and opened a metal lock box on the desk. Dink could see it was full of money. She grabbed a few bills, turned and handed him two tens, a five and three ones.

"Here you go," she said. "Don't spend it all in one place."

Dink grinned. "Well, I'll try not to."

They walked out of the office, got in the El Camino.

Squirrel said, "What're you doin' hittin' on that smelly, you're suppose to be playin' it incognito?"

"You're givin' her too much credit. There's nothin' about me she's gonna be able to tell anyone."

Squirrel spun the El Camino around in the yard. Dink

135

watched a crane with a grapple hook drop a load of scrap in a high-sided semi-trailer, shocks compressing, the trailer shaking.

"What you should've noticed back there was the cash box full of money."

"Believe me, I seen it," Squirrel said. "How much's in it, you suppose?"

"Enough to bother."

Squirrel gunned it past the scale man talking to a guy with a stake truck full of rusted farm machinery on the bed.

They stopped at a bar in Hamtramck, had a few cold ones and grilled kielbasa on hotdog buns with mustard and dill chips, and came up with a plan. Well, Dink came up with the plan while Squirrel guzzled four PBRs and inhaled the kielbasa.

After lunch they bought a couple six packs and drove to the trailer park where Squirrel lived. Squirrel had a chain cutter they'd use to cut the chainlink fence. Squirrel also wanted his .45. They sat around the trailer all afternoon and evening watching porno films from Squirrel's collection, starting with *Shoot the Goooo*, then *Masterbation Frenzy* and Dink's personal favorite, *Twat's Up Doc?*

They drove back to the scrap yard, arriving at 2.58 in the a.m., Hamtramck bars had been closed for an hour and the streets were deserted. Squirrel parked on a side street across Mount Elliott from the entrance, killed the lights. There was a car parked in the middle of the yard, looked like a bone stock two-door '62 Chevy Biscayne. Somebody in it, smoking cigarettes, keeping the engine running, probably listening to the radio. Dink saw the night watchman step out of the Chevy, wander over to the warehouse and take a leak, and that's when they made their move.

# Seventeen

Hess glanced at himself in the rearview mirror, blue-and-red Cleveland Indians cap pulled low, brim hiding most of his face. He had a good feeling that today was going to be the day. He eased the big Chrysler out of Max's garage, pressed the button on the remote and watched the door go down. He drove through the neighborhood, went left on Atlantic Boulevard and got stuck in traffic, waiting for the drawbridge to go down.

When it did he drove to Oceanside Shopping Center. The parking lot was crowded and he took a few minutes to find a space, parked and went straight to the post office. Hess opened the box and saw a note saying he had received a package. The box could accommodate letters and small parcels, but larger items had to be picked up at the counter.

He showed a clerk the note and Max Hoffman's driving license. The clerk went into another room, found the package, asked Hess to sign his name and handed him a square padded parcel. He carried it under his arm to the car and started back to Max's house.

*

Using a paring knife, Hess cut through the packing tape, sliced through the top of the envelope and slid three shrink-wrapped stacks of blank paper out onto the kitchen table. If Ingrid had decided to keep the money, why did she go to the trouble of sending a package at all? It made no sense . . . unless someone had gotten to her, threatened her. The package was mailed so he would be seen picking it up and followed.

Hess opened *Der Spiegel*, read the article, and now he had a better idea what was happening. The article mentioned his upbringing—father was a career soldier, mother a teacher and strict disciplinarian—and his Nazi party affiliation, suggesting his rapid rise was due to his relation to Rudolf Hess, Hitler's deputy, which was patently untrue. The article mentioned Hess and his SS murderers slaughtering six hundred Jews in the woods outside Dachau in 1943. Two survivors had escaped and identified him, although the incriminating photos of Hess posing in front of the pit filled with dead Jews would have likely been enough to convict him.

Hess walked around the house locking the doors and windows and decided, for the time being, to stay inside. The first question: who was after him? Was it Mossad? Agents from the Central Office for Nazi Crimes? The Federal Criminal Police, the Bundeskriminalamt?

Another problem: the $50,000 was money he needed to live on. Then it occurred to him that Max Hoffman had assets he could tap into. Maybe not $50,000, but something. The third bedroom, Hess remembered Max telling him, was used as an office. He went in and sat behind Max's dark heavy desk that had brass handles and looked out of place in the small room with turquoise walls and windows that let in a lot of sunlight.

He glanced at the photograph of a woman in a wooden frame next to the phone, assuming she was Max's former wife, a good-looking woman, late forties. Hess found Max's bank statements and other financial information. For a teacher he was surprisingly well off, $28,000 in cash and $105,000 in bonds, plus monthly income from an annuity and a pension from the Ohio State Teacher Retirement Fund.

With the driver's license, Hess could travel to different bank branches and withdraw money from Max's account. But depleting the cash would take time. He could also sell the house. According to the advertisements for similar waterfront homes in the newspaper, Max's house had to be worth at least $60,000. But that would have to wait. His more immediate concern was staying alive.

*

Zeller bought coffee and pastries at a bakery and arrived in the shopping-center lot at 8.15, parking with a clear view of the post-office entrance forty feet away. He sipped coffee and ate a cheese Danish, watching the shopping center come alive. At 8.30 a.m. a uniformed employee opened the post-office door. Zeller grabbed binoculars off the seat next to him, and trained them on cars pulling in, focusing on people: an elderly couple, two longhaired teenage girls standing on the sidewalk eating doughnuts, a mother pushing a stroller, shoppers pushing carts. A little after eleven, Zeller saw a stocky man in shorts and a red-and-blue cap walk along the concourse and into the post office.

Zeller trained his binoculars on the same man as he came out, carrying a package stamped with West German postal indicia. Now convinced this was Hess, Zeller watched the man return to his car, a big green Chrysler, watched him drive out of the parking lot and turn on Atlantic Boulevard. Zeller followed, saw him turn right on NE 5th Street and knew where he was going.

Zeller stopped at a hardware store on Federal Highway, bought what he needed and went back to the motel. He turned on the TV, stretched out on the bed and watched a western called *Gunsmoke*. From what Zeller could understand, it was about a lawman, Marshall Dillon, who had some kind of relationship with Miss Kitty, who ran a bordello.

Just after midnight, Zeller took his hardware-store purchases out to the car. It was dark and quiet. He could feel a cool breeze blowing in from the ocean, smelling the salty air. He drove over the bridge and through the neighborhood to Max Hoffman's house, parked on the empty street next to the vacant lot. Sat for a minute, looking around. All the houses were dark. It was so quiet he could hear himself breathe. He got out of the car, walked to the rear of the house, standing on the patio, looked through the French doors into the dark interior, saw the shapes of furniture. Behind him, a breeze ruffled the canvas awning. He saw a light coming toward him on the waterway and heard a boat go by, engine at low rpm. He took the supplies out of the paper bag and laid them on the patio stones.

The French doors had lever handles, with a simple pin-and-tumbler lock. He slid the tension wrench into the keyhole, turned it to the right, inserted the pick and started lifting the pins. Could hear them *click*, falling into place, the upper pins going into the housing, the lower pins into the plug. Zeller opened the door, went in, closed it and listened. Silence until the air conditioner kicked on. He glanced down, noticed the floor was tile, unzipped his boots, slipped out of them and moved toward the front of the house, arm outstretched, left hand gripping the Makarov.

Zeller walked past an open room to his left filled with big heavy furniture. Small room with a desk to his right, and next to it, a bedroom with an adjoining bathrooom, bed made, currently unoccupied. He saw Hess' bulky shape under a blanket in the second bedroom and tiptoed in.

"I've been expecting you," Hess said, coming up behind him. "Very carefully, drop your weapon."

Zeller heard him cock the hammer of a revolver, lowered the pistol and dropped it on the carpeting.

"On your knees."

Zeller squatted and went down like he was praying. Maybe he should. Hess kicked the gun through the doorway and Zeller heard it slide on the tile floor. Hess bound his wrists and ankles with duct tape, removed his wallet from his rear trouser pocket and sat on the side of the bed. Hess opened the wallet, looked at his driver's license.

"You are ex-Stasi, aren't you? The Makarov gives you away. It's no Walther but it is a fine weapon. Who sent you, Herr Zeller?"

He wasn't going to say a word.

"Who're you working for?"

Zeller stared at the wall. Hess got up now, moved behind him and he felt something crash into the back of his head and the lights went out.

*

Zeller's head was pounding, the pain more intense now as he

was coming awake. What had Hess hit him with, a sledgehammer? He tried to move his arms and legs, and couldn't, opened his eyes, lifted his head and saw why. He was on his back on a table or workbench, wrists and ankles tied to metal rings, head hanging over one end. There was a rack of tools on the wall to his left and a vice bolted to the end of the bench just beyond his feet. He was in a two-car garage, the big green Chrysler parked next to him. He turned his head the other way and saw the door to the house was open, and now Hess appeared, whistling a Bavarian folk tune, carrying a bucket and a hand towel.

"Ah, Herr Zeller, you're awake. I want to give you an opportunity to talk before any further unpleasantness," Hess said, like an affable uncle. Not a nuance of menace in his voice. "What did you do to poor Ingrid?"

Zeller said nothing.

"I have been trying to reach her for several days and she doesn't answer." Hess placed the bucket next to Zeller's hip. "Where is the money?"

"What money?"

"You have it or Ingrid does. I am betting on you."

Zeller's head hung off the end of the table at an uncomfortable angle. Hess covered his face with the towel, picked up the bucket and poured water into his breathing passages. Zeller closed his mouth, held his breath as long as he could, pulled at the ropes trying to free himself, turned his head from side to side but the water kept coming and he felt like he was drowning. Zeller heard a phone ringing, sounding faint and far away. Hess stopped pouring, set the bucket down and removed the towel.

"Where is my money?"

Zeller was trying to breathe, sucking air into singed nasal passages and lungs. "I have it," he said spitting water out of his mouth. "A safe deposit box in Munich."

Hess said, "Where is Ingrid?"

"I don't know," Zeller said, buying himself more time, trying to get his wind back.

"I think you do," Hess said, standing over him. "Are you thirsty, Herr Zeller? Another drink? You are making it unnecessarily difficult. You are going to tell me what I want to know. There is no reason to be a hero." Hess paused. "Where is Ingrid?"

"I don't know."

Hess put the wet towel over Zeller's face. He moved his head side to side trying to shake it off, but Hess held it in place.

"I first saw this technique at Dachau, and it was extremely effective. I was surprised to learn that it dates back to the Spanish Inquisition. You can torture your enemy without leaving a mark." Hess paused. "Water filling the breathing passages triggers the mammalian diving reflex, causing the victim to feel the sensation of drowning. But why am I telling you this, Albin? You already know what it feels like." Hess picked up the bucket, tilted the spout over Zeller's face. "Ingrid is dead, isn't she?"

Zeller nodded.

"Who sent you?" Hess' voice was calm and relaxed. "Who do you work for, the federal police, BKA?" He paused. "It was Steiger, wasn't it? God knows we've had our differences."

Zeller was familiar enough with the politics of Bavaria to know that Wolfgang Steiger and Ernst Hess had been bitter rivals in the Christian Social Union.

"And if not Steiger, then who?"

Zeller held his breath until he couldn't, water filling his nose and mouth. Neck muscles bulging, he strained to lift his head up, but Hess held him down. And just as Zeller felt himself starting to fade, Hess stopped pouring and removed the towel. He was coughing up water and trying to draw in air when the doorbell rang.

Hess turned his head, glanced at the open door leading to the house. "How many are working with you?"

The doorbell rang again.

"I am alone."

"We'll see," Hess said. He ripped a strip of duct tape off the roll and pressed it over Zeller's mouth. "Don't go anywhere."

Hess drew a revolver from his pocket and went into the house.

# Eighteen

Harry had packed a bag and was getting ready to drive to the airport, catch a flight to Florida, find out what the hell was going on with Joyce, when he got the call. It was a woman with the Detroit police, telling him there had been a homicide at the scrap yard, asking if he could come down right away.

There were two police cars, lights flashing, one in the yard near his night watchman, Columbus Fletcher's Chevy, which Harry was surprised to see, the other in the parking area by the office. Next to the police car was a black van that said medical examiner on the side—never a good sign, and next to that was an unmarked Plymouth Harry'd seen before. Phyllis' VW Bug was in its usual space.

The scene was familiar, almost a duplicate of the morning Harry'd arrived to find police investigating the murder of Jerry Dubuque. There was a cop in uniform standing next to the door.

"I'm Harry Levin," he said. "I own the place."

"Go ahead."

He walked in the lobby. Through the window he saw Detective Frank Mazza sitting at Phyllis' desk, Phyllis across from him, smears of mascara on her cheeks, Columbus Fletcher on his back, arms bent, legs apart, blood stains under him, dark against the gray low-pile industrial carpeting. A cop from forensics was dusting the lock box for prints. And someone else was photographing Columbus from different angles, flashbulbs popping.

Harry walked in the office, glanced at Phyllis first and then Mazza, noticed the metal cabinet against the wall was damaged. By the look of it someone had used a sledgehammer.

Frank Mazza said, "Mr Levin, you're keeping us busy."

"Not my intention," Harry said, annoyed by the remark.

Phyllis got up and came over. Harry hugged her and she started crying, body heaving against him. He guided her back to the chair she was sitting in.

"Perp or perps cut through the fence out there." Frank Mazza turned the swivel chair toward Harry and pointed north. "Just on the other side of the building. Broke a window, came in through the lavatory. Came in here like they knew what they were looking for. Broke into the cabinet where Ms Wampler said you keep the lock box. How much was in there?"

"Not much. Maybe five hundred dollars. I keep most of the money in the safe in my office. Leave a little for Phyllis to get started in case I'm late."

Mazza had traded his Sears wash-and-wear suit in for a tweed sport coat.

"Your night man must've heard or seen them and come in to have a look. Shot him with a .45 Colt. Cause of death was multiple gunshot wounds. Manner of death was homicide."

"How do you know it was a .45?"

Mazza took a small plastic evidence bag out of his sport-coat pocket, three shell casings in it. He pushed his heavy-looking hair up on his forehead and it fell back where it had been. "What can you tell me about Columbus Fletcher?"

"Years ago he was a fighter, middleweight."

"I wondered what happened to his face."

"Two hundred seven stitches, he told me, thirty-nine fights."

"Ever see him in the ring?"

"One time," Harry said, "exhibition bout at Cobo."

"Married?"

"Three times. Daughter works at Henry Ford Hospital."

"What was he like?"

"Quiet, likeable, easy-going. Showed up on time, never missed work."

"How would you know?"

"Everyone punches a time card."

"He use drugs?"

"I doubt it."

"He ever been arrested, convicted of a crime?"

"I don't know."

"Why don't you sit down, we'll try to figure out who had motive."

There was a swivel chair at another desk across the room. Harry wheeled it over and sat.

"Who knew you kept cash in the office?"

"Everyone we did business with. People bring scrap to us in trucks, cars, vans, trailers, you name it. We weigh it, take their name and address, send them in to see Phyllis and she pays them in cash."

"I told you," Phyllis said, giving Mazza a dirty look. She liked his hair but didn't care much for him.

"Why don't you go over all the receipts the past few days, see if anyone rings a bell."

"Say you decide to rob a scrap yard. You come in for a look, sell a load, see the money. You think they're going to give us a real name and address?"

"People are dumb," Frank Mazza said. "You wouldn't believe it."

Phyllis got up, moved to the other side of the desk, knelt next to Mazza, opened a drawer and took out a manila envelope. She folded back the metal clasps and handed it to Harry. Harry dumped the receipts on the desktop. Frank Mazza got up, tapped a Lucky out of the pack and said he was going outside to smoke. Harry sat where Mazza had been, shuffling through the receipts, looking at names and dollar amounts: Clarence Cherry, an address on West Grand Boulevard in Detroit, $68.75, Donnell Lewis on 2nd Avenue, $159.33. He looked at forty more, all from the inner city, and then he came to Aubrey Ponder, a trailer park in Pontiac, $28. Right away that one struck him as odd. Harry didn't get many customers from the suburbs. And it was a long way to come for hardly any money. Harry handed the receipt to Phyllis. "Remember who gave you this one?"

She studied it and looked at him. "There were two of them, sleazy-looking, like they hadn't used soap and water in a while. They were wearing caps. One said Red Man, the other Cat Diesel. Guy that did the talking had a southern accent."

Based on that description they sounded like the two who kidnapped Colette. "How do you remember so much?"

"I handed the guy twenty-eight dollars and said, 'Don't spend it all in one place.'"

"Were they driving a green Ford pickup by chance?"

"I don't know."

Harry went outside and talked to his scale man, Archie

148

Damman, saw Mazza smoking, talking to the cop he'd met on the way in. "Remember two guys came in yesterday, wearing caps, one had a southern accent?"

"Both did. Drove up in a white El Camino with a primer gray hood. They brought in an old icebox from the twenties, weighed a ton. Couple of confederates."

"What do you mean?"

"There was a rebel flag on the tailgate," Archie said. "They have something to do with what's going on here?"

"Looks that way."

*

"Here you go," Harry said, handing Mazza a piece of notepaper. "The two that killed Columbus. Gary Boone lives on Clark Street in Pontiac, drives a green Ford F-100, and Aubrey Ponder lives in a trailer park at that address."

"You know them?"

"I can't say that," Harry said.

"What's going on, they have something against you?"

"You'll have to ask *them*." Harry paused. "If there's nothing else . . ." He would've preferred to go after the rednecks himself, but Columbus Fletcher was dead, and Joyce was still alive.

# Nineteen

Someone was knocking on the door. Hess crossed into the salon, glanced out the window and saw Lois Grant standing at the front door, holding a silver tray covered with tin foil. That's right, Max had said she would bring him food, baked goods.

Lois rested the tray on brick steps, moved toward the living-room window, placed an outstretched palm over her eyes, trying to cut the daylight glare and see inside. Hess stepped away from the window, out of sight, his back against the living-room wall. He could see Lois' face close to the glass.

Then he saw her through a side window, carrying the tray, walking back to her house. Hess didn't like it. He couldn't be sure what this woman was going to do next. Hess went back in the salon, stood at the window, scanned the street. Zeller's Ford sedan was parked in front of the vacant lot, Hess wondering when the reinforcements were coming. He believed Zeller was federal police, BKA, and knew they would have sent more than one agent. They would need at least four to set up surveillance, to find and apprehend him, or take him out.

Hess filled the bucket at the kitchen sink, listening to a message on Max Hoffman's answering machine. It was Lois Grant saying, "Max, where are you? I've left three messages. That car parked next to the vacant lot, nobody in the neighborhood knows who it belongs to, so I called the police."

He carried the bucket to the garage, surprised by how much water had pooled under the worktable on the seal-coated concrete floor, streams running all the way to the garage door. Zeller's white shirt was so wet Hess could see right through it—his skin and the hair on his chest. Hess could hear Zeller forcing air through his damaged nasal passages, the exhale sounding like a snort, face wet, watery bloodshot eyes watching him.

Hess ripped the duct tape off Zeller's mouth leaving red marks where the adhesive had stuck to his skin. Zeller's arms flexed, pulling at the restraints.

"You are with Bundeskriminalamt."

"No."

"Where are the other agents?"

"I'm alone."

"Sure you are." Hess wrapped the wet towel around his face, picked up the bucket and started to pour.

*

Zeller knew that as soon as he gave up Gerhard Braun's name it would be all over. Hess would finish him. He tried to hold his breath but the water came and kept coming and now he was gagging, pulling on the ropes, muscles flexing, chest heaving, lungs burning. Then he was drowning, under water, and his air was gone and he started to lose consciousness, started to fade and the water stopped. Hess removed the towel, Zeller spat water out of his mouth and blew it out his nose, tried to focus on Hess through bleary eyes.

"Who sent you?"

"Give me a minute."

Hess draped the towel over his face again before he could take a breath, and then water filled his nose and mouth and he was gagging, out of air, experiencing fresh trauma, the pain severe and then, like before, he was starting to go under.

*

Zeller opened his eyes looking up at the rafters. There was a strip of tape over his mouth and his nose was plugged. He snorted out water and felt the passages clear, inhaling as much air as he could. He heard the faucet on in the kitchen, Hess filling the bucket again. Zeller didn't know how much more he could take.

He heard a car drive in and park next to the house, and a car door open and close. Heard the doorbell ring. The faucet in the kitchen was turned off. He heard someone banging on the front door. Heard voices and then footsteps on the concrete outside the garage. And then someone banging on the garage door, the echo reverberating around him.

A voice said, "Pompano Beach Police. Is anyone home?"

Zeller grunted under the tape, tried to lift his head, neck muscles bulging but he didn't have the strength to do it. He heard footsteps going back to the car. He heard the door close, the engine start, and the car drive off.

*

Standing at the kitchen sink, Hess heard the phone ring, and the answering machine click on. A woman's voice said, "Mr

Hoffman, this is the Pompano Beach Police. An officer will be arriving at your home any minute. Please answer your door."

A Palm Beach cruiser rolled up the driveway and parked next to the house. A policeman in a tan uniform got out, looking around. He seemed to be focusing on water that had streamed out from under the garage door and pooled on the concrete driveway.

Hess heard the doorbell ring. He moved through the house to the living room, saw the policeman at the front door. On the street a tow truck was backing up next to Zeller's Ford sedan. Out of the corner of his eye he saw Lois Grant approaching. She and the policeman talked for several minutes, Lois pointing at the tow truck.

Lois walked around the house, looking in windows. He heard the French doors rattle, Lois shaking the handles, face distorted, pressed against a glass pane. After a while she gave up and went back to her house, and Hess went back to the living room. He watched the police car back down the driveway. On the street the tow truck was lifting the front end of Zeller's sedan.

Hess finished filling the bucket and carried it into the garage. Zeller had had a nice long rest, and now he would have to start all over. Zeller's eyes were closed. Hess stood over him, ripped the tape off his mouth and Zeller's eyes popped open. "You can stop the pain. You can save yourself from any further discomfort. Tell me who sent you."

"Gerhard Braun," Zeller said.

Good old Gerhard, Hess was thinking. You can't trust anyone.

"Mr Hoffman, don't you get nervous carrying around that much cash?" the homely, big-breasted teller said. "I know I would be."

"That's just it," Hess said. "Nobody would suspect someone of carrying that much. It is totally unexpected."

"You have a wonderful day," the fat teller said.

Hess walked out of the National Bank of Florida with $6,500 of Max Hoffman's savings. Earlier he had stopped and withdrawn like amounts from two other NBF branches, and now had a total of $19,500. That was enough for today. Hess was concerned about attracting too much attention.

He had had a relaxing afternoon on the beach across from the Winthrop House, resting and looking at women in bikinis. From the cabana Hess could train his binoculars on select females, studying them, wondering how they would perform in bed. It had been over a month since he had been with a woman and he was feeling the urge. Thinking about finding a prostitute, but he wanted a woman with class, not a street hooker.

By five most of the sunbathers had packed up their belongings and departed. The sun was fading. Hess felt a cool breeze blow in from the ocean. He focused the binoculars on Joyce Cantor's empty balcony, hoping to see her standing there but didn't.

Hess drove back to Pompano, cruised past Lois Grant's house, turned into Max's driveway, pushed the remote and backed into the garage. He closed the door and opened the trunk. Zeller was right where Hess had left him, head over the edge of the worktable, duct tape over his mouth, panic in his eyes, pants wet where he had urinated.

"I have good news. You are going to be released soon."

Zeller was making sounds under the tape. He obviously didn't believe it. He wanted to talk. Of course he wanted to talk. Hess pulled the tape off his mouth. "You were saying, comrade."

"Bring me the phone. I'll tell Herr Braun you're dead."

Hess smiled, he couldn't help himself. He thought Zeller would say something like that. A person in this situation would say anything to stay alive.

"That won't be necessary."

He ripped a fresh strip of tape off the roll and fit it over Zeller's mouth.

*

At 3.00 a.m. Hess went out to the garage. Zeller was asleep. He could hear him breathing through his nose, a nice easy rhythm. Zeller awoke while Hess was taping his ankles together. The man struggled as Hess turned him over and taped his wrists together. Hess moved the car closer to the worktable, slid Zeller off of it into the trunk and closed the lid.

He took Interstate 95 north to PGA Boulevard and east toward Singer Island. Past A1A Hess could see glimpses of Lake Worth. The causeway between North Palm Beach and Singer Island was dark. He had driven this stretch of road earlier and decided it was the perfect place to dump a body. With Lois Grant snooping around he couldn't take a chance burying Zeller on Max's property.

When he could see water on both sides of the road Hess slowed down and pulled over. He got out, looked up at a half moon, felt a breeze come at him from the lake. He opened the trunk, reached in, took hold of Zeller, pulled him out and dropped him on the hard-packed dirt roadside. Hess, breathing hard from the effort, bent over, hands on his knees. When he got his wind back he squatted, lifted Zeller's ankles and started to drag him toward the water. Zeller bent his legs, kicked and sent Hess to the ground holding one of Zeller's shoes that had come off. Hess scrambled to his feet, moved to Zeller, kicked him in the face, took the fight out of him. Zeller was conscious but woozy as Hess dragged him to the water's edge. Hess heard something, looked and saw headlights approaching from the island. He pushed Zeller in the lake and watched him thrash, trying to stay afloat, and then disappear in the dark water, bubbles rising to the surface.

The car was approaching, slowing down. It crossed the center line and stopped on the side of the road in front of Max Hoffman's Chrysler. It was a police cruiser. The policeman got out with a flashlight and came toward him, aiming the high beam in his face. Hess blinked and squinted, brought his hand up to shield his eyes.

"What're you doing out here middle of the night?" the policeman said, southern accent. He moved to the Chrysler and aimed the flashlight beam in the trunk. Hess put his hand behind his back, felt the handle of the .38 under his shirttail.

"What'd you dump?"

Hess said, "I couldn't sleep so I decided to take a drive."

The policeman moved toward the water, shined the light where Zeller had gone under. "Got some ID?"

"In the car," Hess said.

"Get it."

Hess could feel the man behind him as he walked to the Chrysler and opened the passenger door. The dome light came on. He reached in, picked up Max's billfold, opened it and handed the driver's license to him. The policeman looked at the license and back at Hess.

"You're a long way from Pompano. I'm going to ask you one more time. You don't have an answer I like, I'm gonna take you in."

The policeman was big, the tan uniform tight across his chest and shoulders, revolver in a black holster on his hip.

"You dumped something in the lake is what I think. Now you better start talking."

"My dog died," Hess said in a burst of inspiration.

"What kinda dog?"

"A dachshund."

"A what?"

"Little dog with a long body and short legs."

"Looks like a sausage."

"Exactly."

"What'd it die of?"

"I don't know but Fonzie was almost fifteen."

"Well there you go. That's a long goddamn life for a dog. My doberman, Pepper, passed at thirteen." The policeman shook his head. "Why'd you throw it in the lake?"

"I was upset, I wasn't thinking clearly."

"I'm sorry for you, buddy. It's a sad day man loses his best bud. You take her easy and keep it between the ditches. Next time bury it like a normal person, okay?"

Hess closed the trunk and got in behind the wheel. The policeman, still standing next to the Chrysler, waved. Hess turned the key, heard the engine rev, backed away from the police car and made a U-turn. He was calm, steady, thinking you never knew what was going to happen in a situation. He had been ready to pull the .38 a couple of times, sure his only way out was to shoot the man.

# Twenty

Joyce could see cars zipping along on the turnpike in the distance. She and Cordell had adjoining rooms at a Howard Johnson's Motor Lodge, which Cordell had said was safe.

Joyce had said, "Compared to what, your apartment?"

"Colombians got what they wanted. They're not gonna be comin' back."

"I'm not worried about Colombians, I'm worried about Ernst Hess."

"You seen him on the floor with a hole in his chest and blood everywhere," Cordell said. "Man's still alive he a vampire."

"A Palm Beach detective told me he was picked up by a fisherman in the Bahamas."

"Bahamas is like seventy miles away. How you think he got there, the backstroke?"

Joyce said, "The same man escaped from a hospital in Freeport, hijacked a boat in Port Lucaya, left the owner and his wife stranded on a remote island, and headed for the Florida coast. That night he strangled a woman in her house in Palm Beach. The police say the prints they found in the dead woman's house match the prints they found on the security guard's car, gun and flashlight, and the prints found at my friend Lenore Deutsch's house. I know you don't believe me but I'm telling you I saw Hess in the lobby of my building earlier tonight."

Cordell said, "Why don't you think I believe you?"

"Maybe it's that look on your face, that grin you can't hide." Joyce walked over, put the chain on the door, and wedged a chair under the door handle, a security precaution she had seen in a movie.

"Anyone try to get in, I be on the motherfucker," Cordell said, pulling the gun he referred to as his nickel-plate.

They kept the doors between the rooms open, and Joyce had to admit, knowing Cordell was right there put her at ease.

*

Early the next morning he popped his head in her room, said he had to take care of some business. "You be okay? I'll check on you in a while."

Joyce, still in bed, yawned and said, "See you later." Thinking he'd be back reasonably soon. She heard his door close and saw him walk by the window. Joyce locked the door between their rooms and called her office. Told Amy, the office manager, her aunt died. She was going to Baltimore to sit shiva.

Joyce showered, dressed and had breakfast in the motel restaurant, first looking out the window from the second floor, scanning cars in the parking lot, looking for Hess. Over cereal and fruit and coffee she paged through the *Palm Beach Post*. There was another article about the woman murdered in Palm Beach a few days before. This time there was an accompanying passport photograph of the suspected murderer. The article referred to him as Gerd Klaus. But it was Hess. The article went on to say he was considered armed and dangerous. Anyone with information about this man should contact the Palm Beach police immediately.

*

High-Step was barefoot and Cordell could see the left one was smaller than the right, it didn't even look like a foot—all mangled and deformed as it was. Cordell didn't want to look but it was so strange he had to, like looking at the alligator-skin girl at the state fair.

"Hey motherfucker," High-Step said, "why you lookin' at my feets?"

"I wasn't," Cordell said.

"What you mean, you wasn't? I seen you."

Cordell said, "Why don't you put your special shoe on, you're so sensitive 'bout your foot."

"Why don't you go fuck yourself."

High was pissed about something, that was for sure. "We gonna talk about the Colombians?"

"Why didn't you kick me in on the second deal? I was involved they never woulda pulled that shit."

Now they were getting to it. "You made the intro. I took care of you, didn't I?"

"Then what you doin' here? You's here 'cause you need High's help. Well this time I don't want no two hundred dollars, I want half."

"Half. What you been smokin'?"

"It's called wise-the-fuck-up weed, motherfucker."

Cordell looked at him and said, "You're fuckin' with me, aren't you?"

"How much you got right now? Nothin'. I'm gonna get the weed back and the money, and for that I want half."

"How you gonna do that?"

*

High-Step was from Detroit, had lived on the same street as Cordell and his momma. High made his money selling firearms, assorted pistols and revolvers. One of his homeboys worked in shipping and receiving at the Anniston Army Depot in northeast Alabama, supplied brand new just-out-of-the-crate M16s.

High's real name was Carlos Bass, seven years older than Cordell, and successful. Never got busted in the Motor City, moved to Miami after the riot in '67, police coming down hard on black entrepreneurs involved in illegal activities. High had a house in Coconut Grove with a swimming pool in back, and even with his fucked-up foot always had fine-lookin' poon hangin' around.

They listened to Motown tracks on the way to Greaser Town, and when they got there, sat in the car, lookin' up at an apartment building High said was where Alejo and Jhonny stayed.

"What're we waiting for, man?" Cordell already impatient. "Let's go talk at him."

"How you know he in there? And he is, who in there with him? What I'm sayin', we don't rush, we take our time, do it right. Now you met Alejo and Jhonny the kid, but they got two others, can't think of their names. And they all armed. How do

I know this, right? Is that what you're thinkin'?" High lit a cigarette. "I sold them the guns that's how I know."

"What'd you sell 'em?"

"Two Colt .45 Commanders, stainless with black grips, one 870 Wingmaster twelve-gauge, and one Smith & Wesson .38 revolver," High said like he was reading a sales order. "That's why I want to know who in the apartment before we go up."

It was almost one in the afternoon, car runnin', engine workin' hard with the air on, Cordell watching the Latin babes go by on the street, young ones in tank tops and short shorts, hard tight bodies, dark hair, long brown legs, and the older bitches with heavy legs and tits down to their waist. Cordell thinkin' about age, wondering how many years before he got old and fat? His momma was already there but she'd had a hard life, smokin' rock. Her only exercise, walkin' to a dope house. Cordell only had fuzzy memories of his father, like photographs out of focus.

After a while, Alejo, Jhonny and two other greasers came down the stairs, all wearing those greaser shirts hangin' over their pants, High said to hide their guns. They got in Alejo's Road Runner and drove off.

Forty-five minutes later Cordell saw Alejo's black Road Runner come down the side street and park. The four greasers got out and walked up the stairs to an apartment on the second floor.

"Okay," High-Step said. "Let's get it done."

"What're you gonna do?"

"What're we gonna do? That what you mean?"

"Whatever."

High-Step got out and opened the trunk of the '66 GTO,

came back with something wrapped in a nylon windbreaker, unwrapped it, showing Cordell a short compact sub-machine gun with a skinny black clip.

"I want my money back but I ain't gonna kill nobody for it." Cordell looked at the gun. "What you want me to do?"

"Stand outside, make sure nobody come in behind me."

There was a strap on the end High fit over his right shoulder, let the gun hang under his armpit. Put the windbreaker on, couldn't see a thing. They got out of the car, High wearin' a white sport shirt with epaulettes under the windbreaker, white captain's hat with a black brim, and sunglasses, looked like a nigger yachtsman.

They went up the stairs, moved along the balcony, woman pushin' a baby carriage on the street below, couple seagulls flew by overhead. High-Step was breathin' hard and sweatin' when they got to the apartment door. High looked back at him, nodded, knocked on the door, waited a couple seconds, knocked again. Door opened, Jhonny the kid, standing in the crack, eyes on High-Step then looking over at Cordell.

"Yo, how you doin'? My man Alejo at home?"

The kid turned looking in the room, said something in Spanish. Cordell heard a voice say something back.

Kid looked at High-Step, sounded like he said, "I doan thin so."

"I can see it's a big place—must have six hundred square feet—Alejo could be in there you don't even know it."

Cordell moved up behind High, saw two greasers on a couch looking at them.

Jhonny said, "Give us a moment, uh?"

The kid tried to close the door, but High-Step got his good

foot in the way, blocked the door and pushed it open. The kid moved backward into the room. The greasers, alert, reached behind their backs for their guns but didn't draw them. A TV was on, Cordell could hear the scratchy voice track of a Latin soap opera. And now Alejo appeared, right arm hanging down his wrinkled white pants, smiling. "Señor High-Step, man what you doing here?"

"Never guess what happened. After my man met with y'all the second time, took the woo woo home, somebody come and stole it. You believe that?"

"I can see it happen," Alejo said. "You friend got this good smoke, people hear about it, and human nature take over, huh?"

"Wasn't your human nature takin' over though, right?"

"No, not us."

Alejo looked at the greasers like he was giving them a signal.

High-Step brought out the Uzi, swung the barrel at Alejo as Alejo lost the grin and brought up a sawed-off pump gun, leveled it as High fired a burst from the silenced Uzi that sounded like a BB gun, cut Alejo down and blew out the TV, turned the gun on the greasers as they stood drawing, chewed them up along with the couch and the wall. Cordell saw Jhonny draw, but High-Step was already turning, firing.

Cordell stepped in the apartment, closed the door, saw four dead Colombians on the floor. He wasn't thinking about the money or the weed now, just getting the hell away from there. But High wasn't leavin' till they got what they came for. There were two bedrooms. Cordell found two black plastic garbage bags in the closet, the ends knotted. He lifted them and both had heft, felt like twenty pounds at least. Opened one, got a blast of high-grade woo woo.

There was a nylon gym bag on a shelf over the weed. Cordell brought it down, sat on the bed, unzipped it, looking at stacks of cash held together with rubber bands. High came in the room. Cordell showed him the money.

"Hit the jackpot," High said, flashing a grin.

He could see people looking out the apartment window next door as they passed by on the way to the stairs, and heard a siren as they were going down to the car, passing a police cruiser, lights flashing, on the way out to the freeway, and cut over to the Grove.

They had a couple drinks to calm down and split the money—$68,500, and the woo woo—fifty pounds. Cordell didn't like it, knew this wasn't the end. Somebody'd be comin' after them. But he wasn't gonna be around when they did.

*

When Cordell got back to the motel it was 7.15 in the evening. The doors between their rooms were open. Looked like Joyce had cleared out, took her suitcase and left. His first thought, the Nazi had come and grabbed her. But how'd the Nazi know where they were at? Cordell picked up the phone, called Joyce's apartment – no answer. He'd screwed up, felt bad about it. He had to find her, but where was he going to start?

# Twenty-one

Seeing the police cars and ambulance parked in front of the Winthrop House, Harry assumed the worst. Joyce had gone home and Hess had shot her. He parked the rental car in the shadow of the building on Worth Avenue and went in the side entrance. The lobby was chaotic, dozens of elderly residents trying to get the attention of two police officers in tan uniforms, trying to find out what was going on, what happened.

Harry moved around the crowd, approached the front desk manned by a sullen dark-skinned Latino in a sport jacket, losing his hair on top.

"Sir, may I help you?"

Harry walked by him, stepped into a waiting elevator and rode to the fourth floor. The door to Joyce's apartment was open. Detective Conlin was talking to a black maid in a light blue uniform in the living room. Harry walked in, looked around. Conlin saw him and stood up, said something to the maid and she got up and walked by Harry, black eyes staring straight ahead like she was in a trance.

"Another homicide, look who walks in the door," Conlin said. "Poor girl found the body. I don't suppose you saw or heard anything."

"I just got here," Harry said. "Came right from the airport. Where's Joyce?"

"I was going to ask you."

"She's not dead then?"

"Not that I know of," Conlin's hard stare held on him. "No one's seen her for a couple days."

"You try her office?"

"Manager said Joyce went to Baltimore, her aunt died. I called, talked to the dead aunt who it turns out isn't. She had no idea what was going on or where Joyce was at."

Down the hall toward the bedrooms he heard voices and flashbulbs popping.

"Who is it?"

"Night manager. Shot twice in the chest. Been dead two days or so, accounting for the odor. Ever smell a body in decomp?"

"One or two."

"Yeah? Where was that?"

"Dachau," Harry said.

"The concentration camp?"

Harry nodded.

"I didn't know," Conlin said, sounding like he was apologizing. "How old were you?"

"Thirteen."

"Jesus. How'd you get out?"

"I escaped."

A patrolman entered the apartment and said, "There's a colored guy named Sims downstairs, Detective, says he might know something."

"Send him up."

A few minutes later the same patrolman escorted Cordell into the apartment.

Conlin said, "Come out here," and led Harry and Cordell

through a sliding glass door to the balcony. It was bright and hot, sun reflecting off the white walls of the building, and the sounds of traffic coming up from the street. Cordell had his hands on the railing, looking down at the sunbathers on the beach. Conlin tapped a cigarette out of his pack, cupped his hands against the breeze and lit it with a silver Zippo. "Officer said you know something," he said to Cordell. "Tell me."

Cordell turned, glanced at the ocean.

"Hey, look at me when I'm talking to you."

Cordell turned his head back in Conlin's direction. "Joyce came to stay with me for a couple days."

"Why's that?"

"I don't know," Cordell said. "We friends."

"You two going steady?"

Cordell looked at him but didn't say anything.

"You going to raise the kids Jewish?" Conlin paused. "She left the night I was here. Something scared her, didn't it?"

"Maybe it was you. Talkin' about some motherfucker comin' to kill her."

"Back to settle things with all of you is my guess. Night manager was shot. I'm sure we'll recover bullet frags for ballistics comparison to the murder of the security guard and the real-estate lady."

Conlin tossed his cigarette over the balcony, walked back in the living room. Harry and Cordell followed him and Conlin closed the sliding door.

"Why don't you tell me about the German." Conlin looked at each of them. "And don't say what German? Don't insult my intelligence."

Harry didn't think it would take much.

Conlin went back at it. "Why'd you shoot him?"

Harry said, "Haven't we been through this?"

"That's the way you want it, huh? Well, you're on your own then. Tell me who to contact when he kills you. Direct me to your next of kin."

"Okay," Harry said. "If there's nothing else we'll be on our way."

"I may want to talk to you again. Where're you staying?"

"The Breakers."

Harry and Cordell walked out of the apartment and down the hall to the elevator. Harry pushed the button, glanced at Cordell. "Where the hell's Joyce?"

"Yo, Harry, you not gonna believe this. I left Joyce at this motel, had to take care of business. When I come back, she gone."

"Why didn't you take her with you?"

"What I had to do, it wasn't appropriate."

"I asked you to help me out," Harry said. "Come on."

"I know, I fucked up. I'm sorry." Cordell paused. "But you know we'll find her, right? Probably stayin' with a friend, someone from her office."

"I guess that's where we'll start."

"You're not buyin' this whole Hess is back from the dead bullshit, are you?"

"I don't know."

"You don't know? Harry, you the one took him out put him in the water. What're you sayin'?"

"It's possible he is alive."

"This is fuckin' crazy, Harry."

"I don't know what to tell you."

Hess was on the beach in a rented cabana when he heard the sirens. This was what he had been waiting for. A Palm Beach police cruiser arrived first, lights flashing, stopping in front of the Winthrop House, followed by an ambulance, and a few minutes later by a beige sedan. The three vehicles parked one behind the other. Hess, partially hidden by the cabana, trained the binoculars on Detective Conlin stepping out of the sedan and disappearing into the building.

All the activity across the street, including TV news crews filming the action, attracted attention. Now a crowd from the beach stood behind the seawall blocking his view. Hess aimed the binoculars at Joyce Cantor's balcony. The Negro, Cordell Sims, was leaning over the railing. Conlin, the cocky detective, was standing behind him, smoking. And to the right—this was his lucky day—he saw Harry Levin.

*

Hess had been here two nights earlier, parked down the street, got out, looking at the ocean, dark water meeting dark sky, a stiff breeze blowing in. He went in the lobby. It was quiet at 10.47, and deserted but for a gray-haired gentleman in a tie and blue blazer, seventy but clear-eyed and alert, behind the front desk. Hess had checked the directory on his previous visit, and knew that Joyce Cantor was in 412. He walked by the front desk, moving toward the elevator.

"Sir, may I help you?"

Hess glanced at the man behind the desk. "I'm here to see Joyce Cantor."

"I'm sorry sir, I saw Ms Cantor leave yesterday with a suitcase, and to my knowledge she hasn't returned."

"I left my briefcase in Joyce's condo the last time I was here and I need to get it. Do you have a key?"

"Sir, that would be against the rules. That could get me in a lot of trouble."

"What's your name?"

"Denny, sir."

"Denny, if I don't get the briefcase I'm going to be in a lot of trouble."

"I don't understand why she didn't leave it for you," Denny said. "It doesn't make sense. Ms Cantor is a very responsible lady."

"Joyce was supposed to meet me for dinner and bring the case."

"Why didn't she phone you?"

Denny, the rule follower, was starting to annoy him. "I have no idea." Hess brought out his billfold, opened it and slid two $100 bills on the desktop. "For your trouble."

Denny glanced at the money, flustered now. "Oh, I don't know."

"You could use that, I'll bet. Listen, nobody will know except you and me. I'm not going to tell anyone, are you?"

"Well, I don't see any harm as long as we're in and out quickly." Denny reached out, placed his right palm over the bills, slid the money toward him, folded the bills in half and put them in his trouser pocket. Now earning his fee, he unlocked a cabinet behind him, opened the doors, selected a key and locked it again.

They rode the elevator up to the fourth floor in silence. Denny was nervous, agitated. The doors opened. They walked down the hall to 412. Denny unlocked the door. They went in Joyce Cantor's apartment, Hess scanning the large open room, windows along one side, looking out at the ocean.

Denny said, "Sir, if you would please find that briefcase, I would really appreciate it."

"First, I want to show you something," Hess said. He directed Denny through the master bedroom into the bathroom.

"What is it you want to show me?"

"This," Hess said, drawing the revolver, and pulling open the shower curtain.

"Sir, what's this all about?"

"Get in," Hess said. "I'll tell you when it is safe to come out."

Denny was shaking. He reached into a trouser pocket and handed the $200 to Hess. "Sir, I would like you to have this back."

Hess took it. "Get in."

Denny stepped in the bathtub. Hess pulled the shower curtain closed, looking at the outline of Denny's body behind the translucent plastic. Hess wrapped a towel around the barrel of the .38, and shot him through the curtain.

Hess was thinking about the old man while he searched the apartment, regretted shooting him, surprised by the rare feeling of guilt. Hess couldn't remember the last time he had actually felt bad for someone.

He found an address book in a desk drawer in the living room, a vase of flowers on the desktop, wilting in the darkness.

Remembered Joyce carrying flowers the last time he had seen her. He sat paging through the book, a gooseneck lamp casting a bright circle on the open pages. He was looking behind the L tab and saw Harry Levin's name, address, home and business phone numbers.

Hess picked up the phone and dialed the number. It rang several times before he heard Harry Levin say, "This is Harry. Leave a message, I'll get back to you."

*

Nothing else happened for almost an hour. The TV news crews had gone. The crowd had dispersed. At 4.20 a black body bag was wheeled out of the building on a gurney. Two men lifted it into the rear of a white van that said MEDICAL EXAMINER on the side in black type. The van drove off.

Hess collected the towel, binoculars, tanning lotion, stuffed everything in Max Hoffman's beach bag, slipped into the Docksiders and moved along the sand-blown sidewalk to the Chrysler. The parking meter had expired. There was a ticket on the windshield under the wiper blades. Hess picked it up. The fine was three dollars. He ripped the ticket in half, slid the pieces in his trouser pocket.

Hess sat behind the wheel. He saw Harry Levin and the Negro come out the side entrance on Worth Avenue. They stood and talked for a few minutes. Then Sims started walking toward town and Harry got in a car that was parked on the street. Hess spun the big Chrysler around the corner, followed Harry to the Breakers, and watched him check in.

# Twenty-two

After twenty hours at the Motor Lodge near the turnpike, afraid to go out and going out of her mind, Joyce had had enough. She called a taxi and took it to her cousin Larry's in Boca. He lived on Lake Drive in an 8,500-square-foot Mission-style mansion. Larry Schiff was self-made, president of Appliance World, a business he started with $10,000, most of it bar mitzvah money he'd saved.

A dark-skinned Latin in a white guayabera shirt answered the door. "Welcome, Señora," he said, bowing with an effeminate flourish. He picked up Joyce's suitcase, carried it into the foyer whose ceiling went up to the second storey, and closed the door. She could see Larry approaching, coming down a long hallway with a marble floor. "Joycee's here. Joycee's here. Everyone stand up and cheer," his voice high and lispy. He kissed her on both cheeks like a French aunt. "Armand, meet Ms Joyce Cantor, my one and only cousin."

Armand nodded, lifted her suitcase and moved to the stairs.

"So good to see you. Want to freshen up? Armand will escort you up to the guest suite."

Joyce said, "What're you doing home? I thought you'd be working."

"We shot a commercial this morning and finished early. Guess what number."

"I don't know. Twenty."

"Try fifty," Larry beamed. "Number one appliance store chain in the country. Knock on wallboard," he said, tapping his knuckles on a foyer wall. "What brings you to Boca?"

"Oh, you know, get away for a few days, see my cousin I haven't seen in forever."

Larry smiled. "Go change, unpack. Come down we'll have a drink on the terrace."

"I may take a quick nap, close my eyes for twenty minutes. I didn't get much sleep last night."

\*

Joyce lay down on the bed, tried to sleep but her mind was racing. She got up, turned on the TV, a nineteen-inch console, while she unpacked.

*Homicide in Palm Beach*, it read over an aerial shot of the island, cutting to a blonde, blue-eyed TV reporter standing outside the Winthrop House. "Shortly after noon today, the body of Dennis Ifflander was discovered in a fourth-floor apartment bathroom by an unsuspecting maid."

Joyce was stunned, couldn't breathe. She knew Denny. He was a good guy, nice to everyone.

"This is the second homicide to shock residents of this affluent seaside community in less than a week. Detective Conlin of the Palm Beach Police Department had this to say."

"Mr Ifflander was shot twice at close range with a high-caliber revolver. There was no sign of a struggle, which indicates Mr Ifflander probably knew his assailant."

"Detective, is this case related to the murder of Mrs Lynn

Risdon less than a week ago?" She held the microphone up to Conlin's face.

"The manner of death is certainly different, but we won't know for sure until all of the evidence is examined. And, of course, we want to talk to the woman who is renting the apartment."

"Thank you, Detective."

Now Hess' face filled the screen, the grainy black-and-white photo.

"This man is a suspect in two other Palm Beach homicides. He's considered armed and dangerous. If you see him, contact police immediately."

My God. Joyce had this sudden sickening feeling Denny had been murdered in her apartment.

Now the camera went back to the blonde. "Kim Fortin reporting live from the Winthrop House in Palm Beach."

Joyce picked up the phone and called Harry's house. Got his answering machine. "Harry, it's Joyce, call me. It's an emergency." She left Larry's number. Then she called his office and left the same message. She washed her face, tried to compose herself and went downstairs.

Larry was five six in his elevator shoes, but looked smaller under the high kitchen ceiling, leaning back against one of the black marble counters, smiling in approval, watching himself on TV. Without taking his eyes off the screen he said, "You've got to see this."

In the commercial Larry was in an appliance store surrounded by washers, dryers, stoves and sinks. "Appliance World," Larry said, mugging for the camera. "Deals so good, you'll feel like dancing." Larry turned sideways, like he was walking, moving his feet faster and faster until the scene faded, and the words Appliance World appeared chiseled out of stone.

"Black dudes at the station call me the white James Brown."

Joyce had seen his commercials before. The girls in the office were talking about him one time, and Joyce finally admitted Larry was her cousin.

Amy, the office manager, had said, "What's he like?"

"Full of himself. Larry's head's so big he couldn't fit through the doorway. But he's very insecure. Say something negative about him, he looks like he's going to cry."

Amy grinned. "Why's he dance in the commercials?"

"I guess he thinks he's good."

"It's really annoying."

Joyce felt guilty for bad-mouthing him after Larry had taken her in—no questions asked, and said she could stay as long as she wanted. But he was having a party in a few hours and it was probably going to get wild and crazy.

"Ever see a pool full of drunk horny naked men committing unnatural acts?"

"Not in a couple days."

"You want to?"

"Who wouldn't?"

Larry made them white wine spritzers they took outside and sat in comfortable chairs looking out at Lake Boca that was really a widened stretch of the Intracoastal. The sun was fading and she could see lights on in the highrises across the water.

Larry said, "How's it going?"

"Okay."

"Did something happen?"

"What do you mean?"

"You've never been here before and you asked if you could stay for a while. So I figured something was wrong. Get it off your chest," Larry said. "You'll feel better."

Joyce told him most of the story, starting with the Nazi death squad in the woods outside Dachau, and when she finished Larry said, "I knew about the concentration camp, but not the rest." He sipped his spritzer. "This is an amazing story. Let me put your mind at ease. Armand was a former captain in the Cuban military. The Nazi shows up here it's all over."

Joyce could see Armand in a pillow fight maybe, but not locked in mortal combat with a crazed Nazi.

They had dinner on the terrace, paella with soft-shell crabs, watching boats cruise by on Lake Boca, Joyce looking at the glittering buildings in the distance. She let her guard down, felt relaxed for the first time in several days.

"So you're selling real estate. How're you doing?"

"Better when a Nazi murderer isn't after me."

"You're funny," Larry said. "Keeping your sense of humor even under duress."

"I better or I'm going to crack up. What time's your party start?"

"About nine. Stick around, you need to have some fun."

"I don't want to cramp your style."

"That's impossible. To say we're uninhibited is an understatement."

*

Joyce was in her room watching *All in the Family* when she heard the music come on, Tina Turner belting out 'Proud

Mary' at full volume. Joyce turned off the TV and walked out of the room, leaning over the railing, looking down at the living room empty of furniture and filled with dancing men. There were short stocky men, tall good-looking men, there were old men and young men, men dressed up and men dressed down and a few getting undressed, dancing in their undies. Joyce had never seen anything like it. She assumed they would all be tan and fit and good-looking, although Larry sure didn't fit that stereotype.

Larry was dancing with a stocky dark-haired guy wearing hospital scrubs. He looked up and waved at her to join them. She was on the stairs when 'Proud Mary' ended and 'Rainy Days and Mondays' started. Now they were slow dancing with their arms wrapped around each other. Joyce was uncomfortable seeing men dancing close, a few couples making out.

She approached Larry, who stopped dancing and introduced her. "My cousin, Joyce. Joyce, Marty Rosenberg, my significant other."

"Nice to meet you," Marty said, eyes a-glitter, chest hair sprouting out of the V-neck of his scrub top.

"Get a drink," Larry said. "Join us. Dance."

"I will in a minute," Joyce said. She went in the kitchen, poured herself a glass of wine and went out to the terrace. It was warm and clear, Karen Carpenter's voice blaring from outdoor speakers. To the left, fifty feet away, was the pool. Party guests were frolicking in the water and a naked guy was jumping on the diving board, his *thing* swinging up and down.

*

Hess drove to the house that was on the water, twenty minutes from Pompano, north on A1A. This was the address in Joyce's address book, cousin Larry on Lake Drive. He had phoned earlier asking for her, saying he was from the real-estate company, and was told she was napping. "Please do not disturb her," Hess had said to the man with a Spanish accent who answered the phone.

He went back to Max Hoffman's house, parked on the driveway, got out of the car and Lois Grant was standing there.

"I finally caught you," she said smiling. And then the smile faded. "You're not Max, who are you?"

"A friend from Cleveland. Max invited me to come down and get some sun while he's away."

"I wondered. I've called and called. I thought maybe something happened to him. Maybe he had a heart attack."

"No, Max is fine," Hess said. "Visiting relatives in Berlin." That seemed to satisfy her.

"I'm Lois Grant, by the way."

"I know all about you," Hess said. "Max speaks very highly of you."

Lois Grant smiled. "Does he? Nice meeting you, Mr . . ."

"Emile Landau. And nice meeting you, Lois."

*

After dinner, grilled hog snapper, French fries and two bottles of Lowenbrau, sitting at the counter at the Reef Grill, Hess drove back to Lake Drive in Boca. The street was lined with cars. It was difficult to find a place to park.

Hess moved to the house, looked in the front window and

saw men stripped down to their underwear, dancing with each other in some kind of bacchanalian ritual. Hess was disgusted yet fascinated.

On the water side of the house he heard voices, laughing and shouts, and saw nude men chasing each other around the pool. He went back the other way across the front of the house and around the side. There was a long deck built off the rear of the house that extended all the way to the pool. Joyce Cantor was leaning on the railing, looking out at the water ten feet above him.

Hess had been thinking how unlucky he was coming on the night of a party but now realized it was an advantage. He pulled the .38 out of his pocket. With all the noise who would hear the gunshot? A boat zoomed by and he turned and glanced at it and when he looked back Joyce was gone.

The music stopped at 12.28. Hess, sitting on rocks under the terrace, heard the partying homosexuals leaving the house, getting in their cars. He heard horns honking and music and tires squealing. The first-floor lights went off at 1.17, the second-floor lights at 2.15. He moved up the waterside stairs to the terrace. There was a sliding glass door that led to the kitchen. He pulled and it opened, moved into the kitchen, scanning counters lined with bottles and glasses and platters of hors d'oeuvres.

He glanced into the salon and saw a figure moving across the empty room. Hess retreated through the kitchen into the pantry. In the dim light he saw a naked man open the refrigerator and drink from a juice carton, return it and close the door. The naked man walked out of the kitchen.

It was 2.42 a.m. when Hess moved up the winding staircase. He saw what he assumed were three bedrooms, all the doors closed. The Jewess had to be sleeping in one of them. Hess opened the first door. Looked into a big white room with a wall of white drapes closed against the lake on one side. There was a man asleep in the bed, his bald head sticking out of the covers, turned facing the drapes. What surprised him was the naked man coming out of the bathroom. They surprised each other. "Who the hell're you?" He saw the gun, moved back in the bathroom. Hess shot him, walked out and closed the door.

\*

Joyce was in the woods at the edge of the pit, her back to the firing squad, looking down at the pile of bodies dead and dying. She heard the loud reports of gunfire and saw women falling on both sides of her, waiting for the impact of the bullet.

Joyce opened her eyes, saw moonlight slice across the room where the drapes weren't closed all the way. Heard gunfire in the house. She got up, opened the sliding door and went out to the balcony, heard the door to the bedroom open behind her. Ran down to the far end, heard someone on the balcony behind her, opened the sliding door to Larry's room and went in. Larry was asleep. Marty was on the floor in the bathroom. She ran out of the room, saw Armand on his stomach on the landing outside her bedroom.

Joyce ran down the stairs, heart bouncing in her chest, made it to the bottom when she heard a gunshot, and felt something sting her shoulder. Ran out of the house to the empty lot next door that was overgrown with sea grape, got down on the ground. Her shoulder ached, she rubbed it and felt something wet and sticky on her arm.

Joyce heard him pushing through the heavy foliage, saw a foot in a Docksider, looked up through the leaves at a face in a baseball cap, trying to keep pressure on her shoulder that was now throbbing with pain, trying to stop the bleeding. She heard him crashing through the sea grape and then he was gone. Joyce got up, dizzy, thought she might pass out. Saw glimpses of him walking to a car that was parked on the side of the road about thirty feet away. She moved behind the wall of foliage, saw him get in the car and saw the lights go on and read the license number.

# Twenty-three

The man who had followed Colette from the train station was sitting in a paneled VW bus, the kind tradesmen drove, parked across the street from her building. Colette zoomed in on his face with her telephoto lens. It was Franz Stigler, the MC from the Blackshirt rally. She hoped he was better at electrical wiring than he was at spying.

Hess had obviously been in contact with Stigler, told him to follow her. And although Hess was a wanted criminal, he evidently still held sway with the Blackshirts. Stigler looked to be alone although the rear of the van could have been filled with armed thugs.

Colette was leaving and wouldn't be back for a while. She didn't know what to do with the Van Gogh, couldn't take it with her, so she hid it in her bedroom closet. Packed a bag and carried it to the front door.

She went into the kitchen, opened a drawer and took out a cook's knife, touched the sharp edge with her thumb and sheathed the knife in a deep side pocket of her overcoat.

Colette walked out of her apartment, carried the suitcase down to her car, which was parked behind Stigler's van. She could see his face in the van's side mirror, watching her. She opened the car door, folded the seat forward against the steering wheel, lifted the suitcase in the backseat and pulled the front seat into the driving position. She kept the door open and moved toward Stigler's van, crouched next to the rear wheel and drove the cook's knife into the tire. There was a *whoosh* of air as the tire deflated, rubber resting on wheel rim.

The driver's door flew open. Stigler came charging. "What are you doing?"

Colette ran back to her car, got in, closed the door and locked it as Stigler, in a rage, banged on the window, yanked on the door handle. But Colette was already rolling, Stigler running next to the car, and then he was in the rearview mirror, receding fast.

\*

Colette had received Anke Kruger's address from Gunter at *Der Spiegel.* Anke's relationship with Ernst Hess had raised her profile in the tabloid press. Colette waited in front of Anke's apartment building and hoped she wasn't as obvious as Franz Stigler, or she would never get the information she needed.

She had been waiting for a couple hours when a taxi drove up to the apartment building. Leggy Anke got out with two shopping bags. Colette raced across the street and intercepted her on the sidewalk. "Anke."

She was taller than Colette and prettier, long blonde hair and high cheekbones.

"Do I know you?"

"My name is Colette Rizik."

"You're the journalist. You have a lot of nerve coming here. I have nothing to say to you." Anke moved away from Colette as if she had been rigged with high explosives.

"Ernst Hess stole paintings during the war," Colette said, following her to the door.

"I am going to call the police."

"No you're not," Colette said. "You don't want to get involved, have your picture in the paper for helping a war criminal."

"I'm not helping Ernst. I haven't seen or talked to him for weeks."

"Tell me what you know."

Anke unlocked the door, pushed it open with her hip and shoulder, glanced back at Colette and said, "Okay, you can come in."

The apartment building was big and solid, pre-war, old-world. It had six floors. Anke's apartment was a corner unit on the fifth. They sat in trim black leather chairs in the salon, Anke clearly uneasy, meeting with the enemy, obvious tension between them.

"I don't believe what you wrote about him."

"You think I made it up? All of the facts are documented. Hess is a murderer."

"Ernst is a good man, kind and generous."

"Tell that to the six hundred Jews he murdered." That seemed to take the wind out of her protests. "The photos from the article are from Hess' apartment. His mementos. Can you imagine murdering innocent people and keeping photos to relive the memory?"

"You don't know that."

"There are two witnesses, survivors who were there."

"I still don't believe it."

"Well you're the only one who doesn't." She brought a photo

187

of the painting out of her bag and handed it to Anke. Colette had gone to the library and verified that it was a Van Gogh titled *The Painter on the Road to Tarascon*. "What do you know about this?"

Anke studied the image. "Nothing." And handed it back to Colette. "I've never seen it before."

"Hess must have stolen it during the war."

"How do you know it belongs to Ernst? The Nazis confiscated thousands of paintings and works of art from occupied countries."

"Where are the other paintings?"

"I only know about one. It was a Dürer Ernst sold to an art broker in New York City. I was with him."

"Who's the broker?"

"I can't remember his name. He had a gallery on Park Avenue."

"Did Hess say where he got it?"

"No, and I didn't ask. There was no reason to. Ernst is wealthy."

"Did you travel with him?"

"What do you mean?"

"Where did he take you?"

"A lot of places. Paris, Berlin, Vienna, Gstaad, and one time, a villa in Nice."

Neither Colette nor her colleagues at *Der Spiegel* had been able to find any record that Hess owned property other than the apartment in Munich and the estate in Schleissheim. "Where is the villa?"

"In the hills northwest of the city. It was owned by someone else."

"Do you remember the address?"

"No. Ernst brought me there one time years ago."

"Did Hess mention the name of the owner?"

"I think it was Victor." Anke paused, thinking. "No, not Victor. Vincent. Vincent Chartier."

"Did you meet him?"

"No. I saw the name on a bill for electricity or water, I don't remember. I said, 'Ernst, who is Vincent Chartier?' And he said, 'The man who owns the villa.' And I said, 'How do you know him?' He said, 'Monsieur Chartier is a friend.'"

"And that was it? You never discussed it again?"

"There was no reason to."

"Does Ernst Hess speak French?"

"Yes, fluently."

# Twenty-four

"Can you give us a minute?" Harry asked the nurse, a 250-pound black woman who wasn't happy to see him in Joyce's room, even though Conlin had cleared it with the hospital.

"You a relative?"

"Yeah," Harry said. After all they'd been through together he felt related to her.

"Okay, but be quick. This patient needs her bed rest." The nurse gave Harry a dirty look and walked out of the room.

"Harry, it was Hess," Joyce said in a tiny voice that was barely audible next to the whooshing, thumping machines behind her bed.

Harry held her hand. "You saw him?"

"And I got his license number." She whispered it and Harry said it back to her and she tried to nod.

"Did you tell the police?"

"I don't think so," Joyce said, lids heavy, eyes glazed. She was drugged, out of it. "Harry, I'm afraid. Hess is going to find out I'm still alive. He's going to come back and finish me."

"The Nazis couldn't kill you in the woods that day outside Dachau, and Hess couldn't do it last night."

"I've used up two lives at least. How many more do I get?"

"As many as you need. Don't worry. The police are taking

this seriously. There'll be a cop outside your door twenty four-hours a day."

"Harry, you always make me feel better. What are you going to do?"

"Get out of here before that nurse comes back and beats me up."

*

Conlin had phoned his hotel room, woke him up at 6.15, told Harry what had happened. Joyce was in critical but stable condition, lucky to be alive.

Now, they were down the hall in an empty hospital waiting room. Conlin said, "If it's the same guy, and we think it is, he's popped seven. Two inches to the left, Ms Cantor would've been eight. I've got to believe you're on his short list along with the colored guy." Conlin paused, holding Harry in his gaze. "We know he's not an auto-parts salesman named Gerd Klaus. Who is he?"

"His name's Ernst Hess, a Nazi wanted for crimes against humanity."

"I saw him on the news. Why didn't you tell me this when he killed the security guard and the realtor?"

"I thought he was dead. That was the end of it."

"You're the one who shot him, aren't you? That seemed obvious when I found out you're licenced to carry a firearm."

"It was either him or me."

"What's your connection with the Nazi?"

"Hess and his men killed six hundred Jews in the woods

outside Dachau in 1943. Joyce and I were there, buried in a mass grave. We crawled out and escaped."

"You know where he's at, don't you? Planning to go over with the Mag, draw on him again. But that isn't going to happen. We're going to arrest him."

"I have no idea where he is, but I've got his license number. L50 56E."

"Probably stole the car. Wait here. I'll be back in a minute."

Conlin walked out of the waiting room and went down the hall to the nurses' station. Harry could see him talking and gesturing. One of the nurses handed him a phone.

Conlin came back ten minutes later. "Car belongs to Max Hoffman, lives in Pompano Beach. That sound familiar?"

"Never heard of him."

"Address on NE 5th Street. Know where that's at?"

*

Harry waited down the street in Conlin's car while the SWATs went in and secured the house. No one was home. And Max's car, a 1970 Chrysler New Yorker, was missing. After the SWATs had gone Harry and Conlin were on the driveway next to the house. Harry saw a woman coming toward them from next door.

"Hello, I'm Lois Grant, I live right there. Is there a problem? Did something happen to Max's cousin?"

Conlin said, "Who are you talking about?"

"Emile. He's been staying here while Max is in Germany, visiting relatives."

Conlin said, "Did Max tell you he was going?"

"No, that's the strange part. He never said a word."

Harry said, "How well do you know him?"

"We're buddies. I make him cookies and cobbler, we have dinner together, go to the track."

Conlin said, "Would he leave town without telling you?"

"I wouldn't have thought so but he did."

And maybe he didn't, Harry was thinking. "When's the last time you saw him?"

"It's been almost a week."

Conlin unfolded an eight-and-a-half-by-eleven piece of paper and handed it to Lois. Her eyes lit up. "That's him."

It was the passport photograph of Hess.

"He looks just like Max," Lois said.

A Pompano Beach police officer approached Conlin and told him they had found Max Hoffman's Chrysler in long-term parking at the Fort Lauderdale airport.

Conlin glanced at Harry. "You know him. Where do you think he's going?"

"No clue," Harry said. "But I'll bet anything he's traveling as Max Hoffman." He paused. "I'd get the manifest for every flight that took off from Lauderdale today."

*

Instinct told Cordell to leave the sunshine state even before he saw High-Step's body in the morgue. High had been shot fourteen times, the Colombians sending a message. He had stopped by High's crib was crime-scene tape in the shape of an X over the front door, and more tape that said *Don't cross this line* strung behind the house, some windows blown out, bullet holes in the ones that were still there.

Cordell drove to the Coconut Grove police station, asked the desk sergeant what happened to Carlos Bass, lives over on Bonita Avenue. He made a call and a Detective McBride came out, nice-looking white girl about thirty-five, took him to a room like the rooms he'd been taken to at the police station in Detroit. Asked him did he want something to drink, coffee, glass of water. He said, no thanks.

They sat across from each other at a conference table, couple ashtrays filled with cigarette butts, lingering smell of smoke, clock on the wall.

"How do you know Mr Bass?"

"He lived on my same block in Detroit. High said, 'You ever come down to Miami, stop by.' So that's what I done."

"Why do you call him High, he use drugs?"

"Name's High-Step. On account of one leg's shorter than the other, wore a special shoe. Go to the morgue, see that for yourself. Got nothin' to do with drugs."

"What was Mr Bass' line of work?"

"I don't know," Cordell said, looking right at her.

"That's the way it's going to be, huh?"

"What do you want me to say?"

"Carlos Bass, or whatever you call him, had twenty-five handguns in his house, .45s and .38s, not to mention four brand-new M16s. You don't think he sold guns, do you?"

"No idea. Haven't seen High in years."

"So you said. I'm going to take a wild guess and say Carlos pissed off the wrong people, or someone new to the neighborhood wanted to eliminate the competition. You think that's possible, Mr Sims?"

"I suppose."

Cordell got out of there and went to his car. Now he had to get out of Florida. He raced back to his apartment, sat in the parking lot, looking around, nervous, expecting Colombians with guns to appear. He got out of the car, reached back, felt the nickel-plate in the waistband of his claret-colored pants under his shirt. At the apartment door he drew the .45 and went in. They'd cleaned him out: the money he hid in the floorboard in the kitchen, the weed, even his clothes. Took everything.

Cordell got in the car, backed out of the space and saw them in the rearview, two dark-haired guys in blousy island shirts, getting out of a white Chevy sedan, guns in their hands, moving toward him.

Cordell put it in gear, revved the high-performance engine, popped the clutch and laid ten feet of rubber, went left on the main road, nailed it and lost them. Ten minutes later he pulled up in front of the Breakers, white clean-cut valet in a golf shirt giving him a look like—what you doing here? Hired help parks in back.

"Keep it close. Won't be too long," Cordell said, handing him the keys.

He called Harry from the lobby and they met outside, the beach bar, sat at a table under an umbrella, Cordell checking out two girls in bikinis coming up from the beach. They ordered drinks, a beer for Harry and Courvoisier and Coke for Cordell. He told Harry about High-Step and the Colombians, Harry listening without expression.

"I asked you to do me a favor—keep an eye on Joyce. And you go kill four Colombians. Unbelievable."

"High was the trigger. I didn't know what he was gonna do. I thought he was gonna talk to them that's all. I had nothin' to do with it."

"You know how dumb that sounds? You can't keep making excuses," Harry said, sounding like his honky father.

A waiter brought their drinks. Harry stopped talking, waiting for the guy to leave.

"You're in the big leagues now, accessory to murder," Harry said. "Congratulations, you're moving up in the world."

"Harry, what do you say to a black man in a suit and tie?" Cordell paused. "'Will the defendant please rise?'"

Harry didn't react. "I see you're taking the situation seriously."

Cordell was takin' the Colombians seriously. "Let me run it by you again. I didn't go to Miami with the intention of killin' anyone, okay? You with me so far?" Cordell took a big drink and got a boozy blast of Courvoisier, like an oil slick floatin' on the top. "I was getting the money back they stole from me."

"You went in there with a machine gun."

Cordell decided not to say anything else. Harry was right. Every time he opened his mouth, sounded like he was makin' excuses. But there weren't any. Happened the way it happened, and if Harry didn't believe him, what could he say?

Harry took a drink of beer, put the bottle back on the table. "What're you going to do about it?"

"Do about it? Not sure what you're sayin'."

"You should go to the police. Tell them what happened."

"You mean like you did Harry, shot the three Blackshirts."

196

"That was different. It was self-defense."

"What do you think happened with us? They pulled first."

*

Harry went back to his room at 6.30. There was a message from Stark: *Call me. It's important. I don't care what time it is.*

He sat at the desk, looking out at the dark ocean, picked up the phone, dialed Stark's home number, heard Stark say hello.

"What's so important?"

"Harry, we've got trouble. The Germans want to extradite you for that triple homicide in Munich."

"Somebody found the bodies, huh? Well, we knew this might happen. How'd you find out?"

"US Attorney. Evidently they've got ballistics confirmation, and as you know they've got the murder weapon."

"Let's say they're successful, how long before I'm sent over?"

"I have to believe the extradition request will be denied. So you're okay unless you go back to Germany."

# Twenty-five

Hess went to baggage claim, pulled Max's suitcase off the carousel and carried it to the men's room. He sat on the toilet in a locked stall with the suitcase across his legs, opened it, felt through the layers of clothes, brought out the .38 and slipped it in an outside pocket of Max Hoffman's blazer.

He locked the suitcase in a locker, walked outside to the taxi queue and took a cab to 681 Park Avenue at 68th Street. Hess had come here six months earlier with the Dürer, left it on consignment with Jürgen Mauer, a former gallery owner from Berlin Hess had done business with over the years. Mauer knew wealthy private collectors who would be interested in an original Dürer. The arrangement was: Mauer would sell it and take twenty-five per cent. The artwork, charcoal and colored chalk on paper, was estimated at $250,000, maybe a little more.

Several weeks later the Dürer was sold to a Japanese millionaire for $270,000. Hess had received $50,000 in cash, the first installment. Mauer had owed him an additional $152,500, the bulk of the sale, and had been holding out for months, but now he needed it.

Hess sat in a cafe next to the gallery, drinking coffee, waiting, watching for Mauer. A little past 1.00 p.m., the art broker, wearing a black overcoat, came out of the gallery, walking north on Park Avenue. Hess got up and went after him, catching

Mauer at 59th Street. He could hear the sounds of the city around him. "You move fast for an old man."

Mauer glanced at him in the Cleveland Indians cap and kept walking. Hess caught up to him again, coming up on his left. "I keep expecting the money but it does not come." This time Hess removed the cap and smiled.

"Herr Hess, forgive me. I did not recognize you."

"Where is my money?"

"The buyer has not yet paid in full."

"That's not what you told me. The buyer agreed to pay after the painting had been authenticated. Does that sound familiar?"

"Why would I cheat you?"

"You thought you could get away with it." Word had undoubtedly spread. Mauer knew Hess was a fugitive war criminal and wasn't expecting to be stopped by him on the streets of New York.

"I have additional master works for sale." Hess threw out the bait and Mauer went for it.

"Additional works by Dürer?"

"Picasso, Chagall, Matisse, Klee and others."

"Oh my." The potential commission on such a collection took his breath away. "How many do you have?"

"We can discuss that when you pay me."

"Come to the gallery this evening. Can you be there at seven?"

*

Hess checked into a room at the Pierre Hotel on East 61st

Street. He was Max Hoffman from Pompano Beach, Florida by way of Cleveland. Told the reception clerk American Airlines had lost his luggage. He went up to his room that had a view of Central Park, sipped a Macallan's and watched television, NBC *Nightly News* already in progress, staring in disbelief at a black-and-white photograph of himself in a Nazi uniform, posing in front of a pit filled with dead Jews, while the anchorman narrated.

"Ernst Hess, German entrepreneur, politician and former Nazi, is being sought by German authorities as a war criminal for crimes against humanity." The camera cut to shots of Hess posing with his men smiling, holding bottles of schnapps, dead bodies in the background. Another one of him at a Christian Social Union meeting, and photographs of his estate in Schleissheim and his apartment in Munich. There was a $250,000 reward for information leading to his arrest and conviction.

Hess turned off the television, thinking about meeting Mauer at his gallery, seeing police there to arrest him and Mauer collecting the reward. He booked a flight to Munich on Pan Am, walked out of the room, took the elevator down to the lobby, looking around. He walked outside, it was getting dark and the hotel was lit up. He took a cab to the airport.

*

The German customs inspector was behind the glass partition, staring at something, or was it an act? Keep the tired passengers waiting for no reason.

The customs man finally looked up, no expression, and Hess slid Max Hoffman's passport to him through the opening. The customs man opened it and compared the photograph to the man standing in front of him. He flipped through it and stamped one of the blank pages. "Welcome to Germany, Mr Hoffman."

Hess took a taxi to the Bayerischer Hof, the hotel where Harry Levin had stayed, on Promenadeplatz, happy to be back on familiar turf.

At 4.00, after a nap, shower and a plate of bratwurst and sauerkraut, Hess, wearing Max Hoffman's blazer, khakis and Cleveland Indians cap, met Franz Stigler at the Hofgarten. Hess, with a 35-mm camera on a strap around his neck, was the quintessential American tourist. Franz walked right by and didn't recognize him. "Franz, where are you going?" Hess said, breath condensing in the cold air.

Stigler stopped, turned, eyeing him curiously. Ernst removed the cap.

"Herr Hess?"

"Where is the journalist?"

They were alone in the colonnade. Stigler frowned. "I don't know."

"You don't know?"

"I saw her leave the apartment."

"Why didn't you follow her?"

"She punctured one of my tires."

Hess couldn't believe what he was hearing. "Where's the painting?"

"I'm coming to that. Do you remember Riemenschneider? I introduced you at the rally. He's a locksmith."

"Just tell me, do you have the painting, or not?"

"It's in the van."

"What about the weapon?"

Stigler reached into his overcoat pocket.

"Not here."

They walked to the parking area. There were only two vehicles, Hess' sedan and Stigler's van. It was 4.30, heavy cloud cover making it seem later. Stigler opened the rear doors. Hess saw the Van Gogh on the metal floor, leaning against the inside wall amid the clutter of tools and equipment. He could feel his blood pressure rise. "This is how you treat a master work of art?"

"I'm sorry. I had no idea, Herr Hess. I didn't think it was anything special. I couldn't understand why you'd want it."

Hess tried to calm himself, looking at the positive side. The painting had been returned to him. Now Stigler took a Walther PPK out of his pocket and gave it to him along with a suppressor and a box of cartridges. Hess handed him an envelope. While Stigler counted the money Hess ejected the magazine—it was fully loaded—and screwed the suppressor on the end of the barrel. When Stigler looked up, Hess was pointing the gun at him. "I think it's the perfect pistol. Small, lightweight, balanced. Did you know the Führer shot and killed himself with a weapon just like it?"

"Herr Hess, please. I have a wife and two children."

Hess smiled and slid the Walther in the side pocket of his sport jacket. "Franz, I'm not going to shoot you. I need you."

*

When he got back to the hotel Hess had the painting packaged and crated and asked the concierge to have it shipped to an address in Nice, France in the morning. He went up to his room and called *Der Spiegel* in Berlin and asked for Gunter.

"Which one?" the operator said.

"Colette Rizik's editor."

"Stein. I'll put you through."

"Hello."

"Is this Gunter Stein?"

"Yes, who's calling?"

"Harry Levin, a friend of Colette's."

"She's told me so much I feel like I know you. What did you think of the article?"

"Well written, provocative, first-rate journalism."

"I agree. Colette writes with the flair of a novelist."

"Do you know where she is? I've been calling her apartment for two days."

"She thought she was being followed, didn't feel safe. So she's staying with a friend. I'll give you the number."

Next, Hess dialed Huber, a Munich detective whose father had served with him during the war. Huber wasn't a neo-Nazi, but had given Hess information about Blackshirts the police were targeting.

Against Hess' explicit instructions, Huber had released Harry Levin from custody and had him deported a month earlier. Hess couldn't believe it. Huber's rationale: he didn't want Levin, a Holocaust survivor, prosecuted and incarcerated in Germany. It would have attracted too much attention, and quite possibly have implicated Hess himself.

*

When Huber returned to his desk the phone was ringing. He picked it up and said, "Huber."

"I need an address," a man's voice said.

It was difficult to hear in the big room filled with desks and detectives talking. He pushed his left ear closed with his index finger. "Who is this?"

"You know who it is."

Now he did. "I can't help you. Every law-enforcement agency in the country is looking for you."

"Do you want to be next on their list?"

This was typical Hess, using threats to get what he wanted. "You don't have anything on me."

"Are you sure about that?"

"No one will go near you. You're finished."

"Do you know who you're talking to?"

"A war criminal, a wanted man." Huber was stunned by the man's arrogance. He had never trusted Hess but had always been respectful of him because of his political position and his connections. "All right. But this is the last time. Where are you staying? How can I reach you?"

"I'll reach you."

An hour later Hess called back.

"The address is 60 Schellingstrasse." It was a street near the university. The apartment was registered to a Dieter Ritmeier, a Nazi expert and author of a book condemning the Third Reich. What would Hess want with Ritmeier? Unless it was revenge.

*

Hess drove to the university neighborhood, looking at young attractive girls carrying backpacks, trying not to run off the road. He parked on Schellingstrasse just down the street from number 60. It was a beautiful turn-of-the-century building. There was a restaurant on the ground floor, and four floors, likely four residences, above it.

Hess got out and crossed the street when he saw a police car drive by. Ritmeier was on the third floor. The door to the building was locked, but he could see a small lobby with mailboxes on one wall and an elevator straight ahead.

Back in the car Hess trained the binoculars on the third-floor windows, holding for a few seconds on each, but didn't see anyone. He didn't have the patience for surveillance work. He would have Stigler handle it.

*

Gerhard Braun's estate was in Baden-Württemberg outside Stuttgart. Hess parked in the circular drive, went to the door and rang the bell. The door opened. Martin, Braun's butler and bodyguard, was looking at him quizzically in the Max Hoffman disguise. He removed the baseball cap with his left hand and smiled.

"Herr Hess," Martin said, obviously surprised. "It has been a long time. Won't you come in?"

Hess stepped into the foyer, drew the silenced Walther from his right sport-coat pocket and shot Martin, shell casing *pinging* on the tile floor. He closed the door and moved along the long hall, hearing music, Wagner's 'Ride of the Valkyries', coming from Gerhard's study.

Braun was leaning back, arms conducting an imaginary orchestra, the music building as Hess entered the room and approached the desk.

"What is that you're wearing?"

"A baseball cap."

"I can see that. Quite out of character, wouldn't you say?"

"Gerhard, you look surprised to see me."

"I didn't recognize you."

"Well, now that you have?"

"I thought the odds were with Zeller. He was ex-Stasi. But then you have always defied the odds, haven't you, Ernst?"

"Zeller made a couple mistakes," Hess said. "And all it takes is one."

"I liked his confidence. You should have heard him. Guaranteed the day he would have you, almost guaranteed the time. It was impressive."

"But he didn't deliver."

"How did you get him to talk?"

"I explained my point of view in a compelling way. In the end he was anxious to tell me everything. Even suggested phoning you and saying I was dead."

"After the article appeared—guilty or not—you were finished. It reminds people of the war. It makes us look bad."

"And I thought it was because you wanted the paintings."

"That was part of it. The trouble you're in, I didn't think you would be able to sell them."

"The trouble I'm in, I need money. All my accounts are frozen."

"That's what happens when you're a war criminal. It happened to me after the Allied invasion."

"What the Americans confiscated they returned, as I recall."

"Only thirty per cent, but more than I expected. How about something to drink? Whisky, a glass of beer." Braun pressed a button on the side of his desk. Hess heard a buzzer sound in the hall.

"If you're looking for Martin, he's indisposed." Hess glanced at a Van Gogh on the wall to his left. "Where did you get that?"

"Hermann Göring. I traded a Raphael for the *Park at Arles* and the *Portrait of Dr Gachet*. You may remember, Van Gogh's paintings were considered degenerate art by the Führer. Göring was afraid Hitler would find out he had them in his collection."

"I doubt that. Göring probably thought the Raphael was more valuable."

Braun opened a humidor on the desktop, took out a cigar, clipped the end off with a cutter and lit it, blowing out puffs of smoke. "Where will you go? I imagine you still have contacts in South America."

"I was thinking about the Côte d'Azur. Did I ever tell you I own a villa in Nice?"

"I don't think so."

Braun's right hand slid off the desk and disappeared from view.

"Well, if that's all, Gerhard, I'd better be going." Hess knew what would happen next. He gripped the Walther behind his back and aimed it at Braun just as Braun's right hand appeared holding a Luger, but not in time. Hess fired, hit him in the center of his chest. Gerhard's body was blown back against the chair and slumped forward on the desktop.

# Twenty-six

Joyce was recovering faster than expected and had been moved to a private room with twenty-four-hour police protection, although Conlin said he could only justify it for a couple more days since they were pretty sure Hess had left the state.

Harry went to the hospital to say goodbye.

"I can't thank you enough."

"I'd like to stay but I have to get back to work. If you ever need me just pick up the phone."

"No, I'll whistle, Harry. Remember?"

"Sure." That's what he'd said to Joyce at the Frankels', thinking of the movie *To Have and Have Not*, the night Hess had surprised them.

"Say goodbye to Cordell for me."

"He feels bad about what happened."

"He should never have been put in that position. I'm not his responsibility. I'm not yours, either." Joyce took a breath. "You think this is the end of it, Harry?" She looked at him as if she could read his mind. "You don't, do you?"

"I know he's gone. Left in a hurry. According to Conlin, Hess alias Max Hoffman flew to New York City. His name was listed on the American Airlines manifest." They knew it wasn't the real Max Hoffman. Police had discovered his body buried in the garden behind his house, sniffed out by a German shepherd from the K-9 unit. But he didn't think Joyce had to hear that. "Joyce, he's wanted in Germany and now he's wanted here. I think he'll just disappear."

"Harry, you always say the right thing."

*

Harry had paid for a room for Cordell at the Breakers, and bought him a plane ticket back to Detroit. With the Colombians after him Cordell was anxious to get out of town. They flew Eastern Airlines first class to Detroit, Cordell excited, up front with the high rollers, drinkin' champagne before the plane took off and Courvoisier and Coke after it did. "Man, you do it right, Harry."

"What are you going to do when we get back?"

"I don't know."

"Where're you going to stay?"

"I could sleep in your basement."

"How about the guest room?"

Cordell nodded. "What are the neighbors gonna say, you got a colored guy stayin' with you?"

"You think I care what the neighbors say?" Harry paused. "How about a job? Try playing it straight for a change. You might like it. Nobody'll be coming after you with a gun."

"You makin' conversation or makin' an offer?"

"Know how to work a guillotine shear?"

"Yeah. Sure, Harry. Doesn't everyone?"

"How about a grapple hook?"

"Got any jobs you need done indoors, sittin' at a desk?"

"Become an expert at everything, one day you can buy me out."

"That's just what I want to do—own a scrap yard."

\*

Harry walked in the kitchen, put his suitcase on the floor, Cordell standing in the doorway, duffel balanced on his shoulder. "Your room's at the top of the stairs to the left. You'll like the floral motif."

Cordell moved down the hall and disappeared.

Harry went to the phone and checked his messages. There were forty-two. He fast-forwarded through them, erasing the sales calls and political pitches, until he heard Colette's voice. "Harry, I'm staying at a friend's. Call me as soon as you can. I'll explain everything." Colette took a breath. "Harry, I love you."

She'd never said it before, nor had he, and it made him happy, it made him want to see her and hold her. Harry dialed the operator, gave her the phone number in Munich. It rang a dozen times and he hung up. He'd try her again later.

# Twenty-seven

"That's her," Stigler said to Riemenschneider, sitting next to him in the front seat of his work van. He watched the blonde, in a cap and raincoat, come out of the apartment building and move down the street in a cold steady drizzle. People were walking under umbrellas and traffic was heavy. He could see a blur of headlights and taillights through the wet glass. Bauman was sitting on a toolbox in the back of the van.

"Will you turn on the heat? It's freezing back here."

Franz started the engine, turned up the heat. Riemenschneider got out and took off after Colette. Franz waited a few minutes then made a U-turn and cruised to the end of the block. He saw the big man standing in the square waving at them. Franz pulled over and rolled down the window.

"She went into a restaurant," Riemenschneider said.

"We'll wait."

Fifteen minutes later Franz saw Colette Rizik approaching, coming toward him through the haze, crossing the deserted square, rain still coming down. When she was right in front of him he said, "Excuse me, do you know the time?"

She was carrying a white plastic carryout bag, stopped, looked at her watch and said, "Eight thirty-eight."

Franz could see Riemenschneider's wide bulk in silhouette

coming behind her. "I had to get a new tire after what you did. Cost me forty Deutschmarks."

Colette swung the carryout bag at him and started to run.

Riemenschneider, surprisingly quick for his size, had closed in fast, grabbed her in his powerful arms, lifted her off the ground, Colette screaming, and Baumann coming behind Riemenschneider wrapped duct tape over her mouth and around her head, and taped her hands behind her back.

*

Colette opened her eyes and looked around. She was in a small room with an adjoining bath. They had removed the duct tape, but her wrists were cuffed to a chain that was bolted to the wood plank floor. She got up and looked out the window. The room was on the second floor of a house surrounded by woods. She went into the bathroom and splashed cold water on her face, dried herself, went back and sat on the edge of the bed.

Sometime later, the door opened. Colette saw Franz Stigler's head look in. "She's awake."

Ernst Hess came in and stood next to the bed.

"That day I came to your apartment dressed as a postman, I have been wondering, what gave me away?"

"Your shoes."

"No one noticed but you. But that's your business, isn't it? Observing, remembering details." Hess smiled. "That's what saved you. If you hadn't noticed my shoes, you would have been shot, and I'm guessing the article never would have appeared."

"I mailed the photographs to Berlin after I escaped."

"My point exactly. Was it fate? Was it luck?"

"I don't know, but you're the last person I would have expected. Why would you risk coming back?"

"There was some unfinished business. Now that I have *you* I can reel in Harry."

"He's not going to come back here. He'll be arrested and you know it."

"You think that's going to stop him?"

"I would worry more about myself if I were you. The reward is up to half a million dollars. Somebody is going to recognize you and call the police. Keep an eye on Franz and his buddies. How much do you think an electrician earns in a year? One phone call and he's rich."

Hess moved to the door, opened it. "Franz, come in here."

Stigler shuffled in the room, standing at the foot of the bed. He seemed nervous in Hess' presence.

"Fraulein Rizik thinks you are going to turn me in to the authorities and collect the ransom."

"I would never do that," Stigler said, giving Colette a dirty look.

"Franz, how much money do you earn in a year?"

Stigler shrugged. "Forty-five thousand marks."

"The reward is one million, seven hundred and forty thousand. Maybe Fraulein Rizik is right."

Hess winked at Colette, and Stigler looked helpless, caught in this hypothetical scenario.

"Herr Hess, I can assure you, I would never . . ."

Hess grinned, enjoying the game. He liked to make people squirm. "It's okay, Franz. I am just pulling your leg."

Stigler seemed to regain his composure.

"But if I hear anything . . ." Hess let it hang, patting Stigler on the back and grinning again. "Let Fraulein Rizik stretch her legs and have something to eat. I will be back later."

*

Hess had seen her come out of the beauty salon and started after her. Leopoldstrasse was crowded with shoppers, women mostly, carrying shopping bags, keeping the Munich economy going. "I am sorry I missed your birthday," Hess said when he caught up to Anke. She glanced at him, shrugged him off and kept moving. He grabbed her arm. "It's me."

Now he saw a glimmer of recognition on her face. "Ernst?"

Anke was stunning as always, long blonde hair and plump red lips, long legs in knee-high black boots, long fingers with bright red nails, the smell of her perfume engulfing him.

"Keep walking. Go to your car." He had followed her from the apartment he had rented for her, paying a year in advance.

"Ernst, what are you doing here? The police are looking for you. It is very dangerous."

"If you didn't recognize me no one else will."

They walked another sixty meters and got in Anke's Mercedes sedan, Hess' Christmas present to her the year before. He sat in the front passenger seat and took off the cap. Anke leaned over the console, wrapped her long arms around his neck and kissed him on the mouth. "I've been worried sick about you, Ernst. Why didn't you call?"

"I assumed the police had tapped your phone." Hess was conscious of the pedestrians walking past the car and the traffic on Leopoldstrasse.

Anke was nervous, head moving, eyes darting around. "Ernst, where have you been?"

"You don't seem happy to see me."

"Yes, of course I am, but I am afraid." Anke paused. "Where are you staying?"

"With you, I thought."

"The police could be watching me. You'll be arrested and I will too." Anke pulled away from him and sat sideways in the seat.

"Who has been asking about me?"

"First a man with the federal police. That was more than a week ago."

"Describe him."

"Tall, six three, long dark hair."

Hess pictured Zeller. "Who else?"

"Yesterday, the journalist who wrote the article about you was waiting outside my building. Have you seen it?"

Hess nodded.

"I didn't believe a word."

"What did she want?"

"She said you stole paintings during the war, and asked if I knew where they were. I told her the only one I knew about was the Dürer."

Hess couldn't believe it. "Why would you tell her that?"

"You sold a painting. Why does it matter?"

"What else did she ask?"

"Did you own property other than the estate in Schleissheim and the apartment in Munich."

"And what did you say?"

Anke was nervous now. "I said you had taken me to a villa in France one time, but it wasn't yours."

"You didn't." Hess could feel himself getting angry. "You told her it was in Nice?"

"But not where. She would have no idea how to find it. I don't even remember where it is."

"I can't believe this."

"Ernst, I'm sorry."

"Start the car."

"Where are we going?"

*

The room was dark. Hess glanced at the clock on the table next to him. It was 5.32 a.m. Anke was on her side of the bed, a bare shoulder sticking out of the covers, Hess recalling their lustful night. After drinking two bottles of champagne, Anke had been her old self again.

He slid out of bed, pulled the heavy floor-to-ceiling drapes apart and saw the dark shape of the Neues Rathaus rising up in the distance. He dressed in Max Hoffman's worn khakis, long-sleeved plaid shirt, sport coat and baseball cap.

Light was breaking as Hess walked out of the apartment building, breath smoking in the crisp fall air. He felt relaxed and at home, seeing the city he loved for perhaps the last time.

Marienplatz was quiet and empty at this early hour. He stopped for coffee with a shot of schnapps at a cafe, then lingering, having a second cup. When he came out Altstadt was starting to come alive. He smoked a cigarette, watching trucks pulling up, workers delivering food and beer to the restaurants.

It was a short walk back to the hotel. Hess was on Salvat-orplatz coming up on the Bayerischer when he saw the police cars, three of them parked in front of the hotel, lights flashing. He went to a newsstand across the street. Saw Huber step out of one of the cars and enter the hotel.

Hess glanced at the newspapers on display and froze. There was his photograph on the front page of the *Süddeutsche Zeitung*. The headline said: FUGITIVE WAR CRIMINAL ERNST HESS SEEN IN MUNICH.

He scanned the article that said Ernst Hess had been posit-ively identified in southern Florida and was a suspect in several murders. US authorities believed Hess had murdered an Amer-ican citizen, assumed his identity and returned to Munich. Now he had a better idea what had happened. Conlin, the Florida detective, had contacted the Munich police. Why didn't Huber tell him?

Hess bought the newspaper, folded it under his arm and walked to Karlsplatz. There was a phone booth in the Stachus. He telephoned Stigler.

# Twenty-eight

"Harry, it's the German girl," Phyllis said on the intercom. "Should I tell her you're busy? Just kidding."

Phyllis transferred the call. Harry picked up the phone. "Hello."

"Harry, they've got me." It was Colette, voice sounding strange, distant.

"Fraulein Rizik is understandably upset," Hess said, coming on the line. "She's not herself. You better come and help her, Harry. You're the only hope she has."

"Let me talk to her."

"You can talk when you see her. You've got forty-two hours. Someone will meet you at Frauenplatz, behind the church—the day after tomorrow, four p.m."

Harry started to say something but Hess had already hung up.

\*

Cordell said, "Harry, you're fuckin' with me, right? You're not goin' back 'cause you can't. Remember those two days you spent in the prison in Munich, goin' out of your mind? Now add like twenty years."

"More than that," Harry said.

218

They were in Harry's kitchen, sipping drinks at the island counter.

"Okay, so you're not crazy."

"I don't know."

"Harry, let me understand something, okay? You're gonna give yourself up for Colette, is that right?"

"It's a challenge. Hess is saying: you want her, let's see how good you are. Come and get her."

"He knows the police are gonna be after you?"

"They're after him too. That makes it more interesting."

"Like a game, huh?" Cordell sipped the Courvoisier and Coke. "Don't see how you can win though."

"I don't have a choice."

"Then you better have a plan and a good one. Where we gonna fly into? And don't say Munich."

"I was thinking Innsbruck. Go through customs in Austria, rent a car, drive north through the Bavarian Alps."

"That's what I'm talkin' about, Harry," Cordell said, smiling now.

"You can't go back either, remember?" Cordell had been implicated on Harry's gun possession charge by the Munich police. Now he could conceivably be prosecuted as an accessory to murder.

"I'm goin' and that's it. Now what exactly did the Nazi say?"

*

Harry called a travel agent and booked two flights to Innsbruck, Austria by way of London. It was 4:45 p.m. They were leaving in three hours.

"What kind of gun do you want?" Harry said to Cordell. "If we're going to do this we better be armed."

"A .45 in nickel-plate be my first choice. And a rifle, Harry, something accurate at distance."

"Where'd you learn to shoot?"

"The army, where you think?"

"You any good?"

"I can hit the target ninety-five per cent of the time from three hundred meters."

"That may come in handy."

"What I was thinking."

Next, Harry called Fedor Berman, a Holocaust survivor and private detective who had supplied the .38 Colt he'd used to defend himself against the Blackshirts, the gun Detective Huber had. Harry told Berman he needed the guns right away and Berman said, no problem. "What are you hunting, Herr Levin, big game?"

"The biggest. I'll see you tomorrow."

Harry carried his suitcase upstairs, unpacked and repacked with warm clothes for Bavaria in November. He thought about Colette, hoping Hess would keep her alive till he got there. Harry didn't question what he was doing. In his mind there was no other way. This time he would face Hess and finish it.

Cordell came downstairs, duffel bag over his shoulder, wearing the winter green leisure suit, a comb sticking out of his Afro. "Okay, Harry, let's go?"

"I think you should wear something a little more subdued. On this trip we want to blend in, not attract attention."

"What do you suggest?"

"I'd leave the leisure suits here. Dress more conservative."

"Harry, I don't have anything conservative."

"Or we can pick something up in Munich if you like."

"Tried that, you may recall."

"Yeah, and you fit right in."

"Fit right in on the set of *Heidi* maybe—with Shirley Temple and grandfather."

"I've got some clothes that might work."

"This ought to be good."

Harry took him up to his bedroom, opened the closet, took out a white dress shirt on a hanger and handed it to him. Cordell took off the leisure suit jacket, folded it over the back of a chair, unbuttoned the animals-rampant polyester, slid out of it. Harry handed him a pair of black pants, a light blue shirt with a button-down collar and a camel sweater. Try it on. I'll see you in a few minutes."

Cordell was checking himself out in the full-length mirror when Harry came back in the room.

"You look good."

"I look like you with an Afro. Brothers see me like this they gonna kick me out the tribe."

"The comb in your hair's a nice touch."

Cordell pulled it out and slid it in the right side pocket. "How's that? I pass inspection?"

# Twenty-nine

They landed at Gatwick airport outside London the next morning at 7.56. Had an hour wait and then a two-hour flight to Innsbruck, Austria, arriving at 11.03 a.m. Collected their luggage and went through customs. Harry rented a Mercedes-Benz sedan with tire chains.

The sun was up high and the road was snow-covered, the snow so bright it was blinding. They'd climb a steep mountain grade and fly down the other side, Harry trying to pass slow-moving trucks. Then the clouds rolled in and it started to snow, Harry watching the windshield fog up and the wipers thump back and forth, headlight beams coming the opposite way out of the grey gloom, holding the steering wheel with two hands.

They crossed the border into Germany, Harry nervous, thinking he was going to be arrested as a sleepy-eyed border guard glanced at their passports and took them into a little shack.

"What's up with that?" Cordell looked worried now.

"I don't know. Maybe he's making a copy."

"So they're gonna know we're here."

"But they've got to find us."

The guard came back and handed Harry the passports.

They drove on to Munich, arriving at 12.57 p.m. Harry was

exhausted. He'd only slept a couple hours on the transatlantic flight, and not at all on the flight to Innsbruck.

They met Berman at the Bavaria statue at Theresienwiese, the Oktoberfest grounds deserted now in early November. Berman got out of his car, smoking a pipe, looking dapper in a Loden sport jacket and Tyrolean hat. Harry introduced him to Cordell and they shook hands. Berman opened his trunk and brought out a box that he handed to Harry. "The weapons you requested, with appropriate cartridges." He went back to his trunk and took out the rifle wrapped in brown paper. "Who would like this?"

Harry nodded at Cordell and Berman handed him the rifle. "A silenced Mauser, eight millimeter, seven point nine to be exact, fitted with a scope." Berman paused. "You have returned, Herr Levin, and you need a lot of guns. I hope everything is okay."

"Now it is," Harry said.

*

They drove to a secluded area north of the city, parked in an empty lot next to an abandoned building. Cordell unwrapped the rifle. There were four five-round stripper clips taped to the stock. He loaded the rifle, screwed the silencer on the end of the barrel, adjusted the scope and got out of the car. Cordell brought the stock to his shoulder, worked the bolt, fed a round into the chamber, aiming at a chemical barrel about a hundred yards away. He squeezed the trigger, heard a *pfft* sound, felt the rifle buck and hit the center stripe he was aiming for.

Harry opened the box, looking at a Smith & Wesson .38

with a rubber grip, a matte black .45 Colt Commander, and a box of cartridges for each gun. Harry opened the cylinder and slid in five .38 cartridges, snapped it closed and put the hammer on the empty chamber.

*

Harry parked down the street from Martz's house. They needed a place to spend the night. Staying in a hotel was way too risky. Their passports would have been registered with the police and Harry would be on his way to jail.

Harry had no idea if the house had been sold, rented or what. He got out and walked to the front door, looked in the front window. Martz's furniture was still there. He rang the bell. No one came. Harry walked around the side of the house. Tried the door, expecting it to be locked, but it wasn't.

He went through the kitchen into the dining room, checked the salon and Martz's study. Everything looked the same as it did the night Martz and Lisa were murdered.

Harry turned the light on and walked down the stairs into the cellar, thinking about the night he'd found Martz and Lisa naked and dead on the floor. Hess had shot both of them in the back of the head and positioned their bodies next to each other. The chalk outlines of their bodies and bloodstains were still there.

*

"I think we're okay," Harry said, opening the front passenger door of the Mercedes. They brought in their suitcases and the guns. Harry was tired. He carried his things upstairs, stretched out on Martz's bed and fell asleep.

When he woke up it was dark. Harry got up and went downstairs. Cordell was asleep on a couch in the salon. Harry shook him. Cordell opened his eyes and yawned. "What's up?"

"Hungry? I'll go pick something up. What do you feel like?"

"What do I feel like, Harry? I feel like gumbo with lots of okra. But what am I gonna get?"

"Roast chicken or bratwurst, or how about Chinese?"

"Yeah, okay, I could go for something Chinesey. You know ribs, sweet-and-sour chicken, egg rolls."

"You got it. You can take a shower upstairs in Lisa's room, but let's keep the lights off. I don't want any neighbors calling the police."

Harry picked up the food and they ate by candlelight in the kitchen, neither talking while they polished off three entrees and four egg rolls. When Cordell finished he said, "Nervous about tomorrow?"

"Not yet."

"Well I'm gonna be there watchin' your back."

"I appreciate it."

"Remember coming to the hospital with the bolt cutter? You didn't show up when you did I wouldn't be here." Cordell stacked the empty takeout containers and threw them in the trash.

"Better get some sleep," Harry said.

"Don't take credit for anything, do you? Just get the job done."

"We'll see."

Harry opened his eyes looking at the clock. It was 5.05 a.m. He was thinking about Colette, picturing her coming in the hotel restaurant the day they met, every eye in the room on her as she sat at his table, Harry hoping she was single and available before he even met her. Today was the day. He'd meet someone at Frauenplatz. Harry would go with him and trade himself for Colette. But he had a surprise for them.

At first light he woke Cordell.

It was cold and clear, light traffic as they drove to Frauenplatz, seeing the orange roof and onion-dome towers of the Frauenkirche looming in the distance.

"You gonna tell me what we're doin'?"

"Planning our moves."

"What's that mean?"

"I'll show you."

Harry parked on Löwengrube and got out of the car, looking at the long rectangular side of the Frauenkirche. They walked to the square at the rear of the church, deserted now, but it would be crowded when they returned at four that afternoon. There was a fountain but the water was turned off. There were restaurants and shops in the buildings on the opposite side of the square.

Cordell said, "You really think they're gonna bring Colette?"

"They better or it's over." Harry paused. "They're going to want me to go with them and I will, but where're you going to be? How're you going to follow me?"

"I don't know."

"They could come from any direction," Harry said. "Take

me out to any of the streets around here, car pulls up, we get in. They've scoped the place out. They've got a plan, and we have to figure out what it is."

Harry and Cordell walked around Frauenkirche, Harry looking for something that made sense. "I think their car's going to be here," Harry said, pointing to a side street to the west of the church. "It's the closest, most direct way in and out."

"What if you're wrong?"

# Thirty

Huber was getting ready to go home when he received a wire from customs and immigration, saying that Harry Levin had crossed the Austrian border into Germany at a remote station somewhere north of Innsbruck. It seemed incomprehensible. Why would Levin, knowing the charges facing him, risk returning to Germany?

Huber had admired the man, a Holocaust survivor who stood up for himself. He had even believed Levin's allegations against Ernst Hess, believed the arrogant former Nazi had murdered Jews during the war. So, of course he was sympathetic when Levin was arrested in the young Jewish couple's apartment. Arrested not for murder, but for carrying a concealed weapon—still a serious charge.

Huber had stuck his neck out, put his reputation on the line when he stood up for Levin, had him released from prison and deported. A few weeks later Huber felt like a fool when a hunter discovered three badly decomposed bodies in the forest outside Munich, and ballistics confirmed they had all been shot with the same weapon, an unregistered revolver the police had taken off Harry Levin.

Huber knew Levin had not checked into a hotel or his department would have a record of his passport. So where would he stay? Levin's friend, the journalist Colette Rizik, had an apartment on Wagnerstrasse, and that's where Huber had gone, but no one was there.

Next he checked Martz, the murdered Jew's house and found takeout containers in a trash bin in the kitchen, a duffel bag full of clothes on the floor in one of the bedrooms, and an open suitcase in the other. People were staying there, and Huber had no doubt it was Harry Levin. He had the house watched but so far Levin had not returned.

Back at his desk, Huber received an anonymous phone call about Ernst Hess.

"I know where he is," the man said.

"Who is this?"

"Who I am is not important. But what I can give you is."

After the newspaper article had appeared, Hess was a hot topic again. "Come to police headquarters and we'll talk."

"It's not safe. Hess has friends everywhere."

"You choose the place."

"English Gardens this afternoon at one."

This is what Huber had been waiting for, hoping for, a connection to Hess, a way to find and arrest him. They had almost had him at the Bayerischer Hof. Conlin, the American detective, had given him accurate intelligence about Hess murdering and assuming the identity of an American citizen named Max Hoffman. Hoffman's passport had been registered with the police. That's how Huber knew he was staying at the hotel. They had found his clothes and passport in the room. Huber had leaked the story to a reporter at *Süddeutsche Zeitung*.

Arresting Hess would be a real coup. It would make his career. Whatever influence Hess had had with the police was eroding fast. From what Huber had heard, Hess had even lost standing with the Blackshirts.

*

Huber was in the English Gardens at the agreed time, at the agreed place. It was too cold to sit. He moved around, paced and rubbed his gloved hands together trying to stay warm. There were a couple tourists taking pictures of the Chinese Tower. Huber saw a thin, nervous-looking guy, maybe thirty-five, approach and knew he was his man.

"Detective Huber?"

"And you are?"

"That's not important at the moment."

"Where is Hess?"

"I don't know. But I know where he'll be this evening."

"How many men does he have?"

"Six."

"It's hard to believe there are six Germans naïve enough to still believe in him."

"It's difficult to say no."

Huber could relate. With sheer force of will Hess made you do things you didn't want to do. But now he was an outcast.

"Did you bring the money?"

"It doesn't work that way. When we have Hess in custody we'll talk about the reward. Tell me your name?"

"Franz Stigler."

"Where will Hess be this evening?"

# Thirty-one

Colette had been in the room for two days. In addition to Hess and Stigler she had seen six others. There were the two who had accompanied Stigler when she had been kidnapped that first night. One of the men, Riemenschneider, was huge and powerfully built. He had picked her up and carried her to the van like she was a stuffed animal.

There were the two that brought her meals. Colette had had the most contact with them. She would hear them come up the stairs with the tray and return later to take it away. One of the men, Willi, was small, shorter than she was, polite and nervous around her.

'Fraulein, how was your dinner? Are you finished? May I take your plate?'

Colette didn't think he was going to make it as a hate-mongerer, he was too nice.

Stefan was just the opposite, confident and belligerent. He had muscular tattooed arms on display in black sleeveless or denim shirts, calling her a traitor, a Jew-lover for turning against Ernst Hess, a true German, a hero.

There were two more Blackshirts she had seen smoking cigarettes in front of the house, but she didn't know their names. She had overheard them talking about meeting Harry at Frauenplatz. If she could escape she could be there before them.

Colette had tried to loosen the bolt in the floor, even bending one of the forks, but couldn't budge it. Then she thought of another way out.

On the morning of the third day Stefan had surprised her, saying, "Do you enjoy candy?"

Colette thought he was trying to be nice and said, "I have a weakness for chocolate."

He picked up the tray and walked out of the room.

Just after noon Colette heard footsteps on the stairs and a key slide in the lock. The door opened. Stefan walked in and placed the lunch tray on top of the dresser, and came toward her, tossing a chocolate bar on the bed.

"You remembered." Colette smiled.

"Now, what're you going to do for me?" Stefan took a small black semiautomatic out of a back jean pocket and placed it next to the tray. He came over, stood in front of her and unzipped his jeans. "Get on your knees."

Colette lifted her hands and said, "It will be better if you take these off."

He selected a small silver key from the ring hanging from his belt, unlocked the cuffs and dropped them on the floor. She looked up at him, unbuckled his belt, opened the top of the jeans and tried to pull them down but they were too tight.

He pushed the jeans over his hips and grabbed a fistfull of Colette's hair. Now the fabric was loose and she pulled them down, bunching at his ankles, keys jiggling, and got a whiff of him, the sour stench of unwashed man.

He had to sit on the bed to get out of the black combat boots. This is what Colette was hoping for, pictured it going this way, get the man thinking with his weenie. She made her move, got up, went to the dresser, grabbed the pistol. Stefan stood up, tried to take a step and fell, rolled on his back and pulled up his jeans. When Colette racked the pistol, he stopped moving, looked up at her. "Cuff yourself and get on the bed."

Stefan grinned. "You're never going to get out of here. Give me the gun before you get hurt."

Colette bent her knees slightly, holding the gun with two hands, barrel pointed at Stefan's head. He sat up, reached for the handcuffs and clamped them on his wrists.

"Give me the key."

He unhooked the key from the ring and tossed it on the floor at her feet. Colette crouched and picked it up, never taking her eyes off him.

"How many are in the house?"

"You'll find out."

"Get over on the other side of the bed."

He did without saying anything. Colette opened the door and went down the stairs. Figured she had a few seconds to get out of the house, moved past two Blackshirts sitting in the salon, reading the newspaper. Heard Stefan open the bedroom door, yelling from upstairs. "She's getting away. Stop her."

Colette ran to the front door, opened it and took off. Heard the explosive discharge of a gunshot, glanced over her shoulder and saw two Blackshirts running after her. The tree line was thirty meters. Twenty-five. Twenty. She was almost there when the big sedan skidded to a stop in front of her. Two more jumped out and charged toward her. Colette aimed the pistol at them, but now the others had caught up and surrounded her.

Franz Stigler said, "Are you going to shoot us all?"

At 3.30 they put her in the back seat of an Audi sedan sandwiched between Stefan and the big man, Riemenschneider, a hood over her head. Where were they taking her? She felt the bumps on the dirt road that went through the woods, and then a smooth ride followed by stop-and-go traffic, the sounds of a city around her. When they were parked the hood was lifted off her head, eyes squinting in the bright afternoon sun. They were in the shadow of the Frauenkirche. Colette saw Harry walking toward the car with Franz Stigler. Her eyes met his and then the car was moving. Stefan pulled the hood over her head. Everything was over in a few seconds.

\*

"You see, Herr Levin, Fraulein Rizik is alive and well."

Stigler steered Harry to another sedan parked just down the street and frisked him, moving his hands under Harry's arms, behind his back and between and down his legs.

"Okay."

Stigler opened the front passenger door and Harry got in next to the Blackshirt driver, who glanced at him but didn't say anything. There was a second Blackshirt behind the driver, and Stigler got in behind Harry. They took off. Harry saw his rental car at the end of the street, but no sign of Cordell and now he was concerned.

"Lean forward, Herr Levin, and place your hands behind your back."

Stigler cuffed him.

They drove through Altstadt, heading west, and a few minutes later were on the highway to Dachau. Harry glanced in the side mirror, didn't see a car in sight. Where the hell was Cordell?

*

Two Blackshirts brought Harry into the house, removed the handcuffs, escorted him upstairs, unlocked the door and pushed him in the room. Colette was sitting on the bed. She got up and Harry put his arms around her. She looked at him and started to cry. He brushed the tears away and kissed her.

"Harry, what are you doing here?"

"You think I was just going to let them take you?"

"You shouldn't have come."

"I didn't have a choice." Harry noticed Colette's cheek was swollen, looked like she'd tried to hide it with makeup. "What'd they do to you?"

"I tried to get away. One of them didn't like it."

"Point him out."

"What are you going to do, Harry, beat him up?"

He didn't say anything but that's what he was thinking. Colette sat on the side of the bed and he sat next to her.

"They're going to shoot us, Harry, and bury us in the woods."

"I'm going to get you out of here."

"How're you going to do that?"

"Cordell's out there." Harry hoped he was. "He'll make a move when the time is right."

"What do we have to trade if he isn't?"

# Thirty-two

Cordell ducked down as the car passed by and went left at the first street. He followed, hanging back through the city, losing them in heavy traffic, nervous all of a sudden, thinkin' they were gone. He sped up, driving like crazy, cutting between cars, people honking at him, Cordell thinking they must've turned somewhere back there. Then he saw them up ahead getting on the highway and let out a breath.

He followed for ten minutes and lost sight of them again. Floored it and got up to 140 kph, the Benz solid as a bank vault, drove two kilometers, didn't see 'em, now thinkin' they couldn't've got this far. He pulled over, did a U-turn and drove back, looking for a road, a place to turn. Drove about a kilometer, saw it on the left, dirt road or someone's driveway cutting through the woods. He turned and went half a kilometer and came to a clearing. There was a house in the distance.

He put it in reverse, backed off the road into the woods. It was getting dark. Cordell reached under the seat, grabbed the .45 and slid it in his right coat pocket. Harry's .38 was in his left. He got out, popped the trunk, picked up the Mauser and slung it over his shoulder. He walked uphill through the trees.

He could see the house now, two floors, walls made of plaster with wood beams. The two cars he'd seen at Frauenplatz were parked in front. Cordell unslung the rifle, rested the barrel on a branch that had cracked and fallen but was still attached to the tree. He brought the stock to his shoulder, adjusted the scope and moved the rifle across the front of the house, left to right, could see someone in the left upstairs window, a shape back in the room that could've been Colette. There was a group in the lower window on the right: Harry and four others.

Cordell couldn't cross the open ground to the house without being seen, so he doubled back to where the car was at, crossed the dirt road, went up through the woods and approached the house from the back. There was a garage behind it, a van in one of the stalls. Two Blackshirts came out, smoking cigarettes, Cordell put the crosshairs of the scope on one then the other. The Blackshirts smoked and talked, flicked their butts toward the tree line and went back inside. The sun was over the trees now and lights were on in the house.

He saw them bring Harry in a room with a long table and sit him down with Hess and another guy, three Blackshirts standing around the room, holding guns. One of the cars that was in front came around the house, high beams on lighting up a section of woods, and parked next to the garage. Two Blackshirts came out the back door of the house with Colette, holding her arms. The driver got out and popped the trunk. The Blackshirts took Colette to the back of the car and tried to force her in. A guy with tatted-up arms grabbed her hair.

Cordell brought the Mauser up, put the crosshairs on his head, pulled the trigger and felt the rifle buck, and blew the guy off his feet. The Blackshirts drew their guns, looking around, and pushed Colette back toward the house. Cordell shot the one on the left. The man dropped and didn't move. The other one pushed Colette through the door into the house.

Cordell could see everyone in the dining room turn to look at Colette and the Blackshirt coming back in. He scoped one of the guards and fired but the guy moved, and now everyone was scrambling, trying to get out of the room.

# Thirty-three

They brought Harry and Colette into the salon, and sat them next to each other on the couch. Someone had turned out the inside lights and turned on floodlights that lit up the area behind the house. The only light in the room was the glowing flame in the fireplace. Stigler stood at the side window, looking out into the yard. Hess nodded at two Blackshirts holding submachine guns. "Get him," and they went out the front door.

Now Hess glanced at Harry. "How is Joyce?" Asking like she was a friend.

"The last time I saw her she was in critical condition, not expected to live," Harry said, exaggerating her condition. "Detective Conlin would like to talk to you about it. But I guess he's going to have to get in line, isn't he? You've gotten very popular."

"That leaves you, Harry, the sole survivor. And my feeling is you're not going to be with us much longer."

"How'd you make it all the way to the Bahamas? I checked you, you didn't have a pulse."

"God knew my work wasn't finished and brought me back."

"It wasn't divine intervention, if that's what you're saying. It was luck. The bullet missed your main arteries by a fraction of an inch. A piece of wreckage drifted by, you grabbed it and kept yourself afloat. The current took you most of the way, and a Bahamian fisherman did the rest."

"You have all the answers, don't you?" Hess pointed the Walther at him. "Who's out there?"

Harry looked at him but didn't say anything. Hess moved to Colette and placed the barrel of the pistol against her temple, finger on the trigger, and glanced at Harry. "What happens now is up to you."

"Cordell Sims."

"I had forgotten about him. Tell the Negro to drop his weapon and come out where we can see him."

"Would you?"

"Either he comes out or you can say goodbye to Fraulein Rizik. And you're next on the list."

Two Blackshirts took Harry down a hallway to the kitchen and opened the door, the men behind him not taking any chances, holding him in the doorway.

"Cordell, they want me to tell you to put your gun down and come out or they're going to shoot Colette. And watch out. There are two coming through the woods."

The Blackshirts pulled Harry in, closed the door and beat him to the floor with their fists while he tried to cover up.

*

Cordell wanted to say, yo, Harry, ask the motherfucker how dumb he thinks I am. He couldn't see anything in the house now with all the spotlights pointed at the woods. But he heard them coming toward him from opposite directions, twigs snapping, feet on wet leaves. Hard not to make noise.

He laid the Mauser on the ground, pulled the .45 and moved deeper into the woods, crouching, using a big tree for cover. Cordell heard him before he saw him, motherfucker walked by the tree, Cordell spun to his right, shot him through the middle of his body, the .45 loud like an explosion. The man went down, finger on the trigger of the machine gun, firing a wild burst.

Another machine-gun burst came from the opposite direction, rounds chewing up everything close to him, Cordell on the ground, down as low as he could. The second Blackshirt came toward him, ejected a magazine, popped in a fresh one and that's when Cordell shot him. After the ringing in his ears stopped he stood still, listening, didn't hear anything. Walked over and squatted next to the second Blackshirt, touched his neck, felt for a pulse the way they'd showed him in the army. Dude was all the way gone.

Cordell picked up the machine gun. Ejected the magazine, got a fresh one out of the man's knapsack, jammed it home, and racked it. Want to even the odds? This was the way to do it. Cordell came out of the woods behind the garage, moved along the far side wall, peeked around lookin' at the house. The car was still in the driveway, motor runnin'.

*

When the shooting started Hess told Stigler to put Harry and Colette in the cellar. He would take out the Negro and then deal with them. Stigler led them to the kitchen, opened a trap door in the floor and told them to climb down. Harry went first, then helped Colette, lifting her to the dirt floor. He put his arms around her and held her close. "I've got my money on Cordell. But maybe we can find a way out of here."

When his eyes adjusted he could see shelves against the far wall and cured meats hanging from the ceiling. Across the room there were double doors that led to the outside, and a workbench in the corner. It reminded him of being in the farmhouse cellar the morning after he'd escaped from the pit when Hess and his men were on the Jew hunt.

Harry heard footsteps and voices above them, and the distant report of a gun followed by sporadic machine-gun fire. He moved to the workbench, ran his hands over the tools, feeling the familiar shapes of a sledgehammer and a crowbar. He picked up the crowbar and wedged the sharp end between the cellar doors and pulled as hard as he could. The wood creaked and groaned.

*

Cordell crossed the yard to the house, crouched along the side to the front and looked in the window. It was dark, he couldn't see anything. Holding the machine gun with his right hand he opened the front door with his left. Stepped over the threshold and two Blackshirts came at him, firing. Cordell squeezed the trigger, spraying them with a long automatic burst until the magazine was empty and they were on the floor. Cordell reloaded and walked into the dining room. The car that had been sitting on the driveway near the garage was speeding away.

He went upstairs, checked the bedrooms, nobody there. Looked out a front window, saw the car disappear in the woods.

He went back to the kitchen. "Yo, Harry, where you at?"

"Down here," said a faint voice. And he heard some banging under the floor.

He opened the trap door, looked down, saw Harry lookin' up at him.

"Where are they?"

"All dead or gone."

Colette came up the ladder first and Cordell took her hands and lifted her up to the floor, Harry right behind her.

"You okay?" He handed Harry the .38. "You may need this."

"What about Hess?"

"I think he was in the car, took off in a hurry."

Harry, looking through the doorway that led to the living room, said, "You hear that?"

Yeah, Cordell heard it—some kind of rumbling sound. He went in the living room, looked out, saw cars, lights off, spread out across the lawn coming toward the house. "Police."

They went out the back door and disappeared in the woods, Cordell leading the way, moving just inside the tree line. He could see armed cops in fatigues surrounding the house, and Detective Huber with a megaphone telling Hess to come out with his hands up.

They made their way down the hill to the dirt road, found Harry's rental car, moved a few branches out of the way and got in, Harry behind the wheel, Colette next to him, Cordell in back. Harry drove out of the woods onto the dirt road. They were almost at the highway when Cordell saw the police car.

"See him, Harry?"

"Yeah, I see him. Take it easy."

"What you think I'm gonna do?"

"I don't know, but don't shoot him."

Cordell popped the plastic cover off and unscrewed the dome light. He saw the cop get out of the car as they approached. "Be cool, Harry. I'll handle it."

When they were rolling to a stop Cordell opened the right passenger door and slid out, crouching next to the car. Moved around, squatting at the rear bumper, saw the cop, gun drawn, standing at the driver's door, window down, yellin' somethin' in German.

The cop opened the door, Harry got out, leaned against the side of the car, palms on the edge of the roof. The cop kicked Harry's feet apart, holstered his weapon, and brought Harry's wrists together, tryin' to handcuff him. Cordell moved toward the cop, aiming the .45, took his gun and keys, led him to his car and cuffed him to the steering wheel.

*

Stigler turned onto the highway and had gone maybe one hundred meters when they passed six police cars, lights flashing, coming the other way. Hess looked in the side mirror and saw them slowing down, turning into the woods where they had just driven out. "Who told the police?"

"I have no idea," Stigler said.

Hess studied his face, believing that you could read an expression, see when a man was lying, his face giving him away with a nervous twitch or blink. But Stigler's face was like granite in the dim light. Who else could it have been? The men Stigler commanded were low-IQ laborers. They were brawn, good at carrying out orders but not at making decisions. Hess was sure it was Stigler, the electrician, looking for a way to better his life, and he was also sure Fraulein Rizik had given him the idea. She had been causing trouble, that was obvious, but interesting how prescient her accusation turned out to be.

A few kilometers down the road Hess said, "Franz, pull over, I have to take a leak."

Stigler slowed down and stopped the car on the side of the road. "Do you mind if I join you? My bladder feels like it is going to explode."

Inside the tree line, Hess pulled the Walther and shot Stigler while he was relieving himself.

Hess changed into a dark green electrician's uniform he had taken earlier from Stigler's van, hiding it in the trunk of the sedan. The shirt was too small and the trousers were too long. The cap fit well. He drove to a gaststätte on the outskirts of the city for a beer and something to eat, sat at a table in the loud crowded room, men lining the bar, hoisting mugs, smoke from cigarettes swirling up to the wood beams, the scene so comfortable and familiar, so quintessentially Bavarian. No one gave him a second look in his new disguise. He ate weisswurst and a pretzel, drank his beer, paid the bill and walked out to the parking lot.

# Thirty-four

"They're gonna be lookin' for us and we're gonna be easy to spot," Cordell said. "Police know what we look like, know what kinda car we're drivin'. Probably sent our pictures to immigration. Where we goin'?"

"France," Harry said, holding the Mercedes steady on the dark highway, heading west to Baden-Württemburg.

"What about Austria, isn't it a lot closer?"

"We think Hess might be going to Nice," Colette said. "He has a friend who owns a villa outside the city."

"You're not wanted in France, are you, Harry?"

"I don't think so. We'll cross over somewhere along the Rhine," Harry said, glancing at Colette. "Do you know a place?"

"Kehl. It's across the river from Strasbourg."

"Never been to France," Cordell said.

"Listen, I appreciate everything you've done. But you don't have to come with us to Nice. If I was you I'd take a train to Paris and catch a plane back to Detroit."

"I got nothin' to go home to. You don't mind, I'll hang with y'all for a while longer. You never know, you may need some help."

"We don't even know if we are going to find Hess," Colette said. "And if we do, who is he going to have with him? No offense, Harry, I think we need Cordell."

Harry wasn't trying to get rid of him. "All right, come with us."

*

Harry stopped for gas on the way to Ettlingen, bought a cup of coffee and a map of Baden-Württemburg, opened it at a table in the cafe and drew a circle around Kehl. The guy who worked in the gas station thought it was about 160 kilometers.

When he went back to the car Cordell was asleep in the front seat, and Colette was stretched out in back, snoring. Cordell opened his eyes one time and said, "Yo, Harry, where we at?"

"Just passed Rastatt."

"Oh yeah? Rastatt, huh?" Then his eyes closed and he was snoring in cadence with Colette, Harry thinking they were a lot of fun to travel with.

He arrived in Kehl a little before 2.00 a.m., drove south through town and west toward the river. He could see the lights of Strasbourg in the distance. Getting a hotel would attract too much attention, so Harry parked in a municipal lot near the Rhinepromenade, turned off the car, rolled the seat back and closed his eyes.

*

In daylight Strasbourg looked enormous spread out across the river. Harry could see the spire of a church rising above medieval buildings. He woke up Colette and Cordell and drove through Kehl. Approaching the bridge to Alsace-Lorraine,

Harry saw German police stopping cars, checking IDs and pulled over. "Got any ideas?" he said to Colette.

"Go back to the docks," Colette said. "We'll take a sightseeing cruise into Strasbourg. The ship stops in the old town and you have a couple of hours to see the city."

\*

Harry bought three tickets for the Kehl–Strasbourg Scenic Cruise. They were on the top deck, sitting in chairs—every seat taken—getting ready to leave when Harry saw the police car creeping through the parking lot past rows of cars, stopping behind his Mercedes rental. He felt a vibration as the engines started. Two cops got out and looked inside his car. One of them said something to the other and pointed at the boat. Deck stewards released the mooring lines.

"Harry, they're coming this way," Colette said.

"Stay calm and stay down." Saying it as much to himself as Colette and Cordell. What happened from here was out of their control.

The cops were moving through the parking lot almost to the dock when the ship started to move, engines laboring then picking up speed, chugging up river.

They cruised north past Strasbourg, passing ships and barges and spectacular views on both sides of the river. Thirty minutes later they crossed over to the French side and came back, taking a canal into the city, docking in the old town. Harry, Colette and Cordell got off the ship with the other passengers and showed their passports to immigration officials.

Harry rented a Peugeot sedan at Hertz, got in behind the

wheel and unfolded a map of France, tracing a line with his finger straight down from Strasbourg to Nice. They'd have to go through Switzerland and the western edge of Italy. Harry didn't like it. He wanted to stay in France, avoid any more foreign borders.

He plotted a course that took them through Mulhouse, Besançon, and Lyons straight south to Avignon, Aix-en-Provence, and then east along the Côte d'Azur. Harry drove eight hours to Aix. Colette directed him to Les Deux Garçons, a brasserie on the Cours Mirabeau. It felt good to get out of the car.

They crossed the street and went in the restaurant. Harry ordered sole *meunière*; Colette, *fruits de mer*, and Cordell, fillet of beef. They drank a bottle of Côtes du Rhône and ate without saying much, had profiteroles and coffee for dessert, and got back in the car.

Cordell took it the rest of the way, found a radio station in Marseille that played Motown, singing along with Stevie Wonder and the Temptations.

"Harry, check this out," Cordell excited as they passed through Cannes, the city lit up and alive on one side of the car, the Mediterranean on the other—pleasure yachts outlined in lights, anchored in the harbor. "I might like this better than Palm Beach and there ain't no Colombians tryin' to blow my head off."

"Just Germans."

Traffic was heavy in Nice, people on the street partying, Cordell taking it all in, eyes lit up again. "Might like it here even better."

Harry directed Cordell to the Hôtel Negresco on the promenade des Anglais, woke Colette up, gave the Peugeot to the valet and checked in, getting a two-bedroom suite at 12.20 p.m., three people and no luggage.

# Thirty-five

In the morning, Hess went to a men's shop and tried on clothes. He purchased three white dress shirts, grey trousers, a tweed sport jacket and a black overcoat, the salesman looking at him quizzically. "I've waited on you before, if I'm not mistaken."

"I have never been in your shop, but I can assure you I will return."

Even in the electrician's uniform, the salesman thought he knew him.

Hess also purchased socks, underwear, shoes, a belt and a fedora, paid in cash and walked out carrying the new clothes in a shopping bag. He signaled a passing taxi. He noticed a newspaper on the front passenger seat as he opened the door and sat in the back and told the driver take him to his daughter Katya's school in Oberschleissheim, arriving at 2.53, cars lining the street on both sides, mothers standing in groups in front of the building.

"Here you are," the driver said.

"I am waiting for someone."

The driver seemed annoyed. Hess, in the rear seat, could see the man's eyes watching him in the rearview mirror. He put the window down and smoked a cigarette, seeing schoolgirls in their plaid skirts and blazers coming out of the building. He saw Katya, his only child and the only person he loved, with two friends, laughing, enjoying themselves. Katya was a lot like him, she had the same sense of humor, and the same intolerance for fools. Hess was sorry he had to leave her, regretted that he wouldn't see her grow up. But he knew that like him, she was self-sufficient. When Katya put her mind to something she did it. This was his last opportunity to see her for a long time, maybe ever.

Hess removed the cap, rubbed his forehead and noticed the driver looking at him again, eyes in the rearview mirror.

"Take me to the railway station."

"You look familiar. Do I know you?"

"I don't think so."

On the way to the station, Hess saw the man glance at the passenger seat, reach over and unfold the newspaper. The driver looked over his shoulder. "Excuse me, I have to stop and make a phone call. I'll deduct it from the fare."

They were driving through the village of Schleissheim. He pulled over to the curb next to a small park with a fountain in the center and a bench occupied by an elderly couple in hats, gloves and overcoats. There was a phone booth at the entrance to the park. "I have a train to catch."

"I'll just be a minute."

Hess drew the silenced Walther and shot the driver twice through the seatback, the man falling against the steering wheel. He reached between the seats and grabbed the newspaper and saw his face on the front page. He pulled the man away from the wheel, tilting his body sideways across the seats. The train station was at the far end of town. He got out, glanced at the couple on the bench and started walking.

Hess changed in the men's room in the terminal. The train to Stuttgart arrived at 5.27. He kept to himself, hiding under the fedora and behind a newspaper in a nearly empty second-class car. He disembarked and boarded the 6.12 train to Karls-ruhe, across the Rhine from Alsace. It was a quick trip, only about forty kilometers. Again, no one looked at him except the conductor asking for his ticket and that exchange was fast and impersonal.

Hess took a tram into the city, walked around and checked into a small hotel. He was a businessman from Essen on his way to Geneva. He had dinner and two superb glasses of Mosel-Saar at a bistro in Ludwig Square, then he walked back to the hotel, retired to his room and went to bed early.

In the morning he checked out and took a cab to the port. There were dozens of ships and barges being loaded with heavy equipment. He went to the docks and rented a twenty-foot boat with an outboard engine, paid forty Deutschmarks for two hours and set out, heading down river trailing a barge, looking across at Alsace-Lorraine on the other side. The Rhine was crowded, boats going in both directions, faster boats passing him. He stayed on the tail of the barge for an hour under a perfect blue sky, autumn sun warming the chill out of him, and by eleven o'clock he was hot and removed the over-coat.

When the river traffic lessened he crossed over to the French side and took a series of canals into a village. Hess steered to a dock, got out and tied up the boat. The village was small. There was no taxi service or rail line. Hess offered money to a truck driver for a ride to Besançon. From there he took a train to Nice.

*

Hess opened the sliding door and walked out to the terrace, looking out at homes dotting the hills. He could see Nice in the distance and beyond it the bright blue Mediterranean. He sat at the table drinking coffee, sun coming up over the hills behind him. There was a slight chill in the air, the temperature about sixteen degrees.

The Van Gogh had arrived before he did and was waiting on the desk in his office. He removed it from the crate and carefully unwrapped the canvas, the painting beautifully intact. He had taken it up to his bedroom, leaned it against the wall on top of his dresser.

The sliding door opened. Hess glanced over his shoulder at Marie-Noëlle Despas, the housekeeper born on Christmas Day, coming out with a tray. She served him a croissant stuffed with ham and cheese, pain au chocolat from a bakery just down the road, and more coffee.

"Anything else I can bring you, *monsieur*?"

Hess shook his head and watched her walk back in the house, a stocky farm girl with heavy legs and small breasts, and yet there was something sexy about her. He was sure she was having an affair with the gardener, Claude D'Amore. Hess had seen Marie-Noëlle sneak out of his cottage down the hill at first light. He hadn't been able to sleep and had been standing on the deck outside his second-floor bedroom. Marie-Noëlle was married to a truck driver who was on the road for days at a time, and Hess could only imagine she was lonely.

Hess had purchased the villa, La Citronneraie, on August 22, 1948, when property in Nice was relatively inexpensive. Between construction projects he would retreat here to drink wine and relax.

He was certain he could live here indefinitely without attracting attention. His only problem was money. His account at Société Générale was down to 1,700 francs, and the *taxe foncière* was due in less than one week. Of the money he had withdrawn from Max Hoffman's Florida bank account only $9,870 remained. Sooner or later he would have to sell one of the paintings, and it would take time to find a qualified buyer.

Hess showered and dressed, wearing an ascot and a sport jacket. He had a Renault in the garage, a basic car that wouldn't attract attention, and drove to Galerie Broussard on avenue de l'Hermitage in Monaco. Hess was acquainted with M. Broussard, the owner, who had been with the French Resistance. Mention the war and Broussard would talk about the Nazis plundering art from galleries, museums and private collections. He had lost dozens of paintings from his gallery, which had been in Nice, moving to Monaco after the war.

Hess had stopped by the gallery over the years, planting the seed that he had masterworks by Picasso, Klee and Matisse in his collection that might one day be for sale. "Please keep us in mind," Broussard had said.

He was thinking about selling the Van Gogh that was in his bedroom. Present *The Painter on the Road to Tarascon* to Broussard and observe his reaction.

Hess was studying a Chagall, remembering his fellow Nazis

had described Chagall's art as full of: "green, purple and red Jews shooting out of the earth, fiddling on violins, flying through the air . . . representing an assault on Western civilization."

Hess saw Broussard coming toward him. "M. Chartier, it has been too long. I see the Chagall has caught your eye. This is one of my favorites. You can feel the emotion." Broussard paused, out of breath. He was overweight and walking across the gallery floor had exhausted him. "Picasso once said, 'When Matisse dies Chagall will be the only one who knows color.'"

"It is magnificent," Hess said. "But I am here to sell, not to buy."

"What are you selling?"

"A Van Gogh."

Broussard blinked with excitement. He rubbed the tip of his long Gallic nose. "When can I see it?"

"I will bring the painting to you."

"At least tell me the title if you wouldn't mind." Broussard could hardly contain his excitement.

"I'll surprise you."

"I can't wait. How about tomorrow morning? Will that be convenient?"

*

Hess drove back to Nice and had lunch at a restaurant overlooking the harbor. Ordered a bottle of Puligny-Montrachet and a bowl of mussels to start, followed by grilled sea bass, enjoying a leisurely lunch, watching the pleasure boats motor in and out.

On his way to the villa Hess stopped at a cafe on boulevard Gambetta for coffee, sitting outside, the sun on his face, drinking the bitter double espresso in three sips, feeling that surge of caffeinated energy. He paid for the coffee and walked down the street, stopped in a wine shop and bought a Chablis for the cheese, and two bottles of Bonnes-Mares, thinking an earthy Nuits would be perfect with the coq au vin Marie-Noëlle was preparing.

# Thirty-six

Harry checked the phone book. The only name close to Vincent Chartier was V. Chartier in Antibes, a quaint little town down the coast. The address was a small house just out of town. The owner was a stylish fifty-year-old woman named Vivienne Chartier. She didn't know a man named Vincent Chartier in Nice. All of her relatives were from Aix-en-Provence and Marseille.

She invited them in for coffee and pastries, Harry thinking this older broad was surprisingly attractive. Colette picked up the vibe and gave him a look that said she did too and he'd better watch himself.

After coffee and conversation with Mme Chartier they drove back to the hotel to get Cordell. He'd left a note in the room saying he was going to walk the beach, scope the topless sunbathers, Harry thinking at sixty-two degrees the locals were going to be wearing parkas, not bikinis.

The concierge had given Harry the name of a high-end real-estate broker who might be able to help them. His office was just down the street. They went there and met M. Gascon, a plump effeminate man with a little mustache who had been selling properties on the Côte d'Azur since the end of the war.

"*Mademoiselle* is trying to locate her estranged uncle," Harry said, referring to Colette. "Her aunt died recently and no one has heard from Vincent Chartier, Uncle Vince, for quite some time. His name is not in the phone book. How do we find him?"

"The property is registered in the uncle's name?"

"As far as we know," Colette said.

Gascon looked at her quizzically. "The system of land registration in France is *cadastre*. It is maintained by the French public land registry under the auspices of the tax authority, the Direction Générale des Finances Publiques."

Gascon might as well have been speaking Chinese for all Harry could understand.

"To find the owner of a specific plot, you must consult the *matrice cadastrale*. You go to the local land registry, the Centre des Impôts Fonciers."

Harry said, "Is it in Nice?"

"Yes, of course, Nice. On rue Joseph Cadei."

\*

They took a taxi to the office, waited an hour for the only clerk who spoke English. Gilles, a young longhaired Frenchman, escorted them to an office and sat across a table from them. Harry explained who they were and what they wanted.

"What proof do you have that M. Chartier is your uncle? How do I know you are related to this man? Do you have a passport? A birth certificate?"

Harry could see they weren't going to get anywhere with this guy unless he took a chance. "I have something better than a passport." He slid a wad of francs across the table. The clerk stared at the money, Harry wondering what he was thinking.

There was a long silence and then the clerk picked up the bills and put them in his pocket.

*

Harry said, "Where is the corniche des Oliviers? I don't see it."

The concierge studied the map that was open on the mahogany hotel counter and pointed to an area north of the city. "You do not see the street name because it is not there. But here you see route de St Pierre de Féric?" The concierge traced the road with his index finger.

Colette leaned in close.

"This road becomes the one you look for." The concierge pointed again to show Harry. "Right here, past the church."

Harry looked at the maze of winding roads. "How do we get up there?"

"You see boulevard Gambetta?" The concierge pointed to a heavier line on the map that went straight up from the Mediterranean. "Take this to boulevard du Tzarewitch, go left and follow this." He highlighted the route in red marker.

Harry thanked the man and gave him a ten-franc note and folded up the map. He and Colette sat on a couch in the lobby that was always crowded, always full of people walking around.

Harry said, "Are you ready?"

"What are we going to do?"

"Drive up and find the villa."

"And then what? Are you going to ring the bell?"

"I haven't gotten that far."

Colette frowned.

"If you don't want to come—"

"I want to, I'm just nervous, wondering what's going to happen."

"Probably nothing. First we have to find it. Then we'll decide what to do. How does that sound?"

"Okay, Harry. I'll be your navigator."

The valet brought the Peugeot and Harry drove along the promenade des Anglais, past the joggers and walkers and blue-and-white beach chairs lined up facing the water. "This is it," Colette said, the map spread open in her lap. "Turn right."

Now they were on boulevard Gambetta passing shops and cafes, markets and bakeries. He went left where Colette told him to turn and they climbed a steep incline in a residential neighborhood. He went left again and then right on avenue du Dauphiné, climbing higher into the hills on a narrow winding road that didn't look wide enough for two cars. Driving alongside a brick wall about five feet high added to his feeling of claustrophobia. Harry saw a bus approaching and got over as far as he could. The bus passed inches away. Harry let out a breath. They went around a blind 180-degree turn and through a one-lane brick tunnel, halting at a stop sign at the top of a hill. Harry looked at Colette. "You have any idea where we are?"

"Harry, this is it, this is the road, turn right," Colette said, looking up from the map.

He turned and they drove up a steeper stretch of road. Out the right side he could look down the valley and see the city of Nice spread out stretching all the way to the Mediterranean. They were on route de St Pierre de Féric. Harry saw a church on the left, and according to the concierge, the road now turned into corniche des Oliviers. Fifty yards further on, Colette pointed to her right and said, "There, Harry."

He hit the brake and saw number 26 on a black metal gate, the entrance to the villa. Driving by he could see the top floor set behind a six-foot wall made of stone. Harry wanted to stop but there was no place to pull over. He looked in the rearview mirror and saw a truck bearing down on them and sped up. Just ahead they came to a small cafe on the left and pulled in.

"Harry, I can't believe we've found him."

They'd been lucky to say the least, lucky Anke Kruger had remembered the name Vincent Chartier, and lucky they'd been able to trace the property through tax records. But it didn't prove Hess was living there, and if he wasn't there, where was he?

Harry convinced Colette to drop him on the road near the villa.

"I want to go with you."

"You can't. There's no other way to get close. Give me twenty minutes, I'll meet you at the cafe."

"I have a bad feeling about this. I think we should come back with Cordell."

"I just want to see what the place looks like. If I'm lucky Hess will be sitting outside reading a book. I'm not going to take any chances."

Harry got out of the Peugeot just north of the villa at 26 corniche des Oliviers, using the wall for cover. He walked to the entrance. Looking through an opening in the gate he could see the villa, built on the side of a hill on two levels. The upper level was where you entered. The lower level opened to a deck with lounges and a long dinner table and chairs on one side and a swimming pool on the other side.

Harry saw a stocky woman wearing a wide-brimmed hat,

cape and scarf come out of the house and walk toward a Fiat parked on the driveway just inside the gate. Harry moved north along the outside wall, walking on the road. He saw a car approaching and turned his back. He heard the gate open and saw the Fiat drive out heading south, and on impulse, he ran back and slipped through the gate as it was closing and ducked behind the garage.

From this vantage point, he could see across the valley, clouds resting on higher hills in the distance. Looking south he could see the red tiled roofs of Nice and beyond it the Mediterranean. Stone stairs led to another level of the property. There was a small shed or cottage at the bottom of the slope. Harry went down to the pool deck. The afternoon sun was slanting through the sliding glass doors and he could see into the house. It was a big room with a lot of furniture, and no one appeared to be in it. A wall overflowing with flowering plants ran north parallel to the villa. A man in a work shirt was trimming a palm tree on the far side of the property.

Harry went back up to the garage and followed the stone walk—looking down at the pool—to the main entrance, assumed the door was locked but it wasn't. He opened it and stepped into a small marble entryway. Stood listening, but heard nothing. There were two bedrooms on his left. There were stairs that went up and stairs that went down. He went down into an office that had a desk, chair and typewriter. He could see the gardener through the window, wiping his brow and then drinking water out of a bottle.

He sat and opened drawers and found envelopes addressed to Vincent Chartier, a phone bill that listed calls—though nothing long-distance from Germany or the US. He found a water bill, tax bills, bank statements. Okay, so Vince lived here, but he already knew that or assumed it. What was his connection, if any, to Hess?

Harry moved along a hallway that led to the back of the villa, kitchen on the left, wine bottles, fruit and baguettes on the counter, food in the refrigerator. The salon was next, with glass doors that went out to the pool. The gardener walked by, crossed the deck and took the steps to the lower level.

Harry went back upstairs to the main floor, and up to the master bedroom that took up the entire second floor. There was a bed and dresser, chairs and a table, and a sliding door that led to another deck with a view of the entrance gate, garage, and directly below him, the pool

He checked the closet, men's clothes on hangers. There was a bright-colored painting on top of the dresser, leaning against the wall. He checked the drawers, moved his hand under handkerchiefs that were neatly folded, felt something and brought out a passport. It was a deep red color and said *République française* in gold type over a gold crest. Harry opened it, looking at a photograph of Ernst Hess, a younger version, taken many years before. Over the photo it said *Vincent Paul Chartier*.

He heard something, looked out the glass door and saw the electric gate opening. The woman in the Fiat had returned, pulling into the short driveway. Harry put the passport back, closed the drawer, ran down the stairs to the front door, opened it and looked toward the driveway. The woman in the hat had a grocery bag in her hand and was leaning over the wall, talking to someone—probably the gardener. Her hat tipped forward and she fit it back on her head.

Harry went out the front door and unlocked a wrought-iron

gate in the outer wall, opened it and walked out to the road, his back to traffic, cars zipping by, looking over his shoulder.

Colette was in the cafe parking lot behind the wheel of the Peugeot. Harry got in and looked at her. "Hess is Chartier. I saw his passport."

"Oh my God. Thinking it is one thing, Harry. Knowing it is something else."

Now they had to decide what to do with him.

# Thirty-seven

"It smells wonderful in here," Hess said, walking in the kitchen, putting the paper bag on the countertop and taking out the three bottles of wine. "Nothing like the smell of sautéed onions and garlic."

"Someone was in the house," Marie-Noëlle said, slicing mushrooms on a cutting board. "I was returning from the market." She put the knife down. "Claude was cleaning the pool. I stopped to talk to him."

"Who was it?"

"I have never seen him before." Marie-Noëlle's face was perspiring. She dabbed her cheeks and forehead with a dishtowel.

"Did you ask what he wanted?"

"No, *monsieur*. It happened quickly. I saw something out of the corner of my eye. And when I looked again the man was moving to the wall, and then through the gate to the street."

"You did not follow him?"

"No, *monsieur*. I wanted to see if anything had been stolen."

"Was he carrying anything?"

"I could not see."

"You checked the house. Is anything missing?"

"I do not think so."

"What did this man look like? Describe him."

"He had dark hair. Not tall. Not heavy. I did not see his face."

"Was he a laborer?" Maybe a man looking for work.

"I cannot be sure. I am sorry, M. Chartier. I looked over and saw him, the man surprised me."

Hess thought there might be a reasonable explanation. The man had been hunting and came up from the valley chasing after his game. "Was he carrying a rifle?"

"I do not know, *monsieur*."

More likely the intruder had been walking from villa to villa looking for work. No one could possibly know Hess was in Nice. Anke had been to the villa two years ago, but she didn't know he owned it, and he doubted she would have any idea how to find it. Anke was pretty but not particularly bright.

Hess went out to the pool. Claude was skimming leaves off the surface of the water. The gardener noticed him and said, "*Bonjour, monsieur.*"

"Let me ask you something. Have you seen anyone on the property today?"

"No, *monsieur*." He rubbed the reddish-brown stubble on his jaw. "Mme Despas asked me. I didn't see anyone."

Claude was sleeping with her but always referred to Marie-Noëlle in a formal way.

"Keep your eyes open and your shotgun close."

"Is there a problem, *monsieur*?"

"If the man returns."

Hess went back inside. He thought about the painting, ran up to the bedroom: there it was on top of the dresser where he had left it. So evidently the intruder was not an art aficionado. He thought about the passport, checked the drawer; it was there. The villa was owned by Vincent Chartier, Hess' French alias. He had a forged French passport and French driver's license, and spoke the language fluently. No one but Anke knew about the villa, and no one but Leon Halip knew that Vincent Chartier was Ernst Hess. All of the bills, *taxe d'habitation* and *taxe foncière*, electric, water and telephone, were paid by Marie-Noëlle from an account at Société Générale. Hess had opened the account with cash, making periodic deposits to maintain enough to cover expenses. The bank statements were mailed to the villa. There was no paper trail that connected it to Hess.

He went to the cellar, staring at the crates that had not been opened since he had purchased the villa, and inventoried the paintings in his head. He had another Van Gogh: *Still Life: Vase with Five Sunflowers*, a Chagall, two Matisses, a Kandinsky, a Klee and several dozen lesser works. He and Braun had taken them from what remained of Hans Frank's collection at the end of the war, and divided them. Many had 'ERR' stamped on the back, confirming they had been stolen by the Einsatzstab Reichsleiter Rosenberg, most likely from private collections and museums in France and the Netherlands, and had ended up in Frank's collection at the palace of Count Potocki, his residence in Krzeszowice.

Frank had been Hitler's legal adviser and had been appointed governor general of occupied Poland. Hess had met Hans Frank over the years and they had become friends. Both were avid chess players and ardent anti-Semites. Hess and Arno Rausch had visited Frank on their way out of Poland in early January 1945. When they had arrived at the palace, Frank's men were filling trucks with his collection of confiscated art. Frank was shipping everything to his estate in Tegernsee in southern Bavaria.

After dinner Hess walked Marie-Noëlle to her car. She was wearing the dark brimmed hat, red scarf and green cape, her trademark apparel. He thought she looked like a bullfighter. Hess said good night, opened the electric gate and watched her drive out. He went back to the house, locked the doors, turned off the lights and went upstairs. He loaded the Benelli shotgun and laid it on the bed, barrel pointing at the sliding door on the other side of the room. The Walther was on the table next to him—less than an arm's length away. The drapes were open. He could see a three-quarter moon and the lights of Nice in the distance.

# Thirty-eight

"I think we should follow him," Harry said, looking out at lights on the promenade, the night sky and the Mediterranean dark behind it. They were sipping evening cocktails in their suite at the Negresco. "See what he's up to. Make sure he's at the villa before we go after him."

Cordell said, "Look for a place to grab him."

· "The way Mossad kidnapped Adolf Eichmann in Buenos Aires," Colette said. "Took him out when he got off the bus, returning home from work, kept him in a house in the city for a week. To get him out of Argentina they drugged him and dressed him in an El Al uniform, saying he'd had too much to drink as they boarded a plane bound for Israel. The Israelis were surprised how cooperative Eichmann was. It was as if he was expecting them."

"That's what I'm sayin', grab him off the street." Cordell sipped his drink.

"There's that bakery just down the hill from the villa," Harry said. "We can wait there till he drives by. I agree with Cordell, it might be easier to surprise him."

Colette said, "What will we do with him?"

"Take him out. What do you think?"

"I think we should bring him to the police."

Cordell glanced at her. "What're they going to do?"

"Arrest him."

"As far as they know he's a French citizen named Vincent Chartier," Harry said. "You think they're going to take our word over his? They're going to let him go, and he's going to disappear again."

"Harry, we have proof he's a war criminal. You're the survivor. Tell them your story."

"What do I have that proves I'm a survivor? And what do I have that connects me to Hess?" Harry paused, sipped his whisky. "Hess has a French passport. According to the tax records he's owned property in Nice since '48. He's a solid citizen."

*

They were parked on corniche des Oliviers at eight the next morning in front of the bakery, car facing down hill, Cordell behind the wheel, Colette next to him and Harry in back, training binoculars on every driver and passenger in every car that passed them in a steady stream of traffic. The small parking lot was crowded. He saw the dark-haired woman from Hess' villa come out of the bakery carrying two baguettes and a white bag of pastries. She got in the Fiat and drove back up the hill.

By ten there was hardly any traffic, just an occasional car or truck passing by. Looking through the rear window Harry could see a dark sedan come over the hill. He waited till it was about fifty yards away, raised the binoculars, put them on the grill, it was a Renault, put them on the windshield, sun glinting off making it difficult to see in. Tried to focus on the driver's face but the car was moving too fast. He adjusted the viewfinder, pulling back as the car closed in on them, held on the driver's face till he was sure. "There he is."

Colette turned in her seat.

Cordell started the car, glanced in the side mirror. "I see him."

The Renault sped by. Cordell started the Peugeot and took off after it. They followed Hess down the steep winding roads to boulevard Gambetta and all the way to the promenade des Anglais, then around the harbor and up the coast.

"Where you think he's goin'?"

"Maybe he knows we're on to him, he's leaving the country. The Italian border's right up here. Head down the Riviera, re-invent himself in Rapallo."

A few minutes later they were in Monaco, Harry looking at the marina filled with pleasure boats and yachts, and highrise apartment buildings built around the harbor. Hess turned and they followed him into the city that reminded Harry of Palm Beach with its wide boulevards, palm trees and Greco-Roman architecture.

Hess parked in front of Galerie Broussard, got out, closed the door, moved to the trunk, opened it and took out a rectangular package wrapped in brown paper. Harry pictured the painting he saw on the dresser in Hess' room and now it made sense. "That's the painting you found in the locker, I'll bet."

Colette said, "*The Painter on the Road to Tarascon* by Van Gogh."

"Describe it."

"It's a self portrait—Van Gogh on the road, carrying artist's supplies—showing himself as an alienated outsider."

"The painting in Hess' villa was signed *Vincent*."

"That's how Van Gogh signed his paintings. Harry, you saw it and didn't say anything?"

"It didn't occur to me till now."

*

Hess was thinking about the value of the painting as he walked into the gallery. Based on what he knew, and he was no expert, the Van Gogh would sell for somewhere between five and seven million dollars. The sale would be confidential and discreet. Absolutely no publicity. No one except Broussard would know his identity. The money would be paid to Broussard, and Broussard would deduct his fee and send the balance to Hess. He would deposit the money in his account at Société Générale, and at the appropriate time, transfer the money to his Swiss account. When he needed additional funds he would sell another painting.

Broussard saw Hess enter the gallery and came right over. "*Bonjour*, Monsieur Chartier. I see you have brought the painting. How exciting. Shall we unveil it in my office?"

Hess followed Broussard across the gallery floor to a hallway that led to offices. Broussard's was big and open, simple chrome-and-glass desk, black leather chairs, a wall of bookshelves. The only thing that looked out of place was a chrome easel set up on the floor next to the desk.

Hess unwrapped the painting. Broussard took the discarded paper from him, folded it and placed it on the desk. Hess set the painting on the easel and now Broussard came over and stood close, smiling.

"*The Painter on the Road to Tarascon*." Broussard's grin faded and he held Hess in his gaze. "It is impossible. This painting was destroyed when the Allies bombed Magdeburg, setting fire to the Kaiser Friedrich Museum. Where on earth did you get it?"

"I can't tell you anything about how the painting came into my possession. The sale has to be completely confidential. The buyer can't know who I am."

"But M. Chartier, this is a missing masterpiece. There is a story behind it, a mystique that will add to its value. Prospective buyers will want to know, not to mention the art world."

"What is it worth?"

"I can't say with certainty. We will have to establish a selling price based on what other paintings by Van Gogh have sold for." Broussard turned to the painting. "But this, I can assure you, will command a very high price. I would think eight to ten million dollars. What were you expecting?"

"Somewhere in that range."

"I assume you have a bill of sale from the original owner, gallery or auction house."

"I'm afraid not."

"M. Chartier, we cannot in good conscience trust its authenticity unless you have authentication credentials. Van Gogh has been forged more frequently than any other modern artist. Before we can establish a price the painting has to be authenticated. So you won't mind leaving it with me?"

"Authenticated? You can see it is original. Look at the signature."

"Signatures can be forged."

"Maybe I should take it to another gallery," Hess said, even though he had had a similar experience selling the Dürer to the broker in New York. That had had to be X-rayed to prove its nature and origin.

"They will tell you the same thing. Without authentication you will not be able to sell the painting."

"Do you know someone? I want to make this happen quickly. I will be leaving France soon for an extended vacation."

"The only person in Nice who can give an absolutely trustworthy and acceptable attribution is M. Givry. He is an art expert who intimately understands Van Gogh. M. Givry worked at the Van Gogh Museum in Amsterdam, and he has curated exhibitions of his paintings at museums around the world. Let me see what I can do. Please make yourself comfortable." Broussard waved his arm indicating the leather couch. "May I offer you coffee?"

Hess shook his head and sat on the couch. Broussard moved to the desk, took an address book out of a drawer, opened it and made a phone call.

*

Hess walked out of the gallery. He didn't have the patience to sit in Broussard's office and wait until the expert arrived and authenticated the painting. Hess noticed a silver Peugeot parked across the street, morning sun reflecting off the sheet metal, making it difficult to see if anyone was in it. He had passed a car just like it on corniche des Oliviers on his way to Nice. Was he being followed, or was he suspicious because Marie-Noëlle had seen a man on the property?

Hess walked to a cafe down the street, sat outside, feeling the warmth of the sun, and drank two cups of *café americain*, discreetly staring at two well-dressed, good-looking ladies a few tables away.

When he returned to the gallery an hour later the Peugeot was gone, confirming that his jittery nerves and paranoia were an overreaction. Broussard was in his office, talking to a dapper little man wearing a dark suit and bow tie.

"M. Chartier, let me present our foremost Van Gogh expert, M. Givry."

The little man stared at Hess, making no attempt to shake hands.

"Have you finished the authentication?"

Broussard said, "I am afraid we have bad news."

"This painting is a forgery," Givry said. "The technique is all wrong. Van Gogh lathered his colors roughly on the canvas."

"How do I know this is the painting I brought?"

"M. Chartier," Broussard said, plump cheeks turning red. "We have been selling art for fifty years. I can assure you . . ."

Givry, too, looked nervous, rubbing his hands, eyes darting around.

Hess had taken the painting from Hans Frank. How could it be a fake? The Dürer was from the same collection and it had been authenticated. "I should phone the police and have you arrested."

Broussard, offended now, moved to his desk, picked up the telephone receiver and glanced at Hess. "Here you are. Make your call, but it will not change anything. This was not painted by Vincent Van Gogh."

Hess lifted the canvas off the easel and walked out of the office. He sat in the car, thinking about Hans Frank and the paintings, now wondering if the others had been forged.

After the war Hess had visited Frank's estate. Hans had been uncharacteristically uneasy, pacing while they talked. "The Allies are closing in," Hans had said. "They are going to arrest me."

"Why don't you leave Germany?"

"There is no place I can go." He handed Hess a map. "I need you to move the paintings to a secure location. I'll contact you when I have been released from prison."

Frank was arrested a few days later. He was taken to Nuremburg, tried and found guilty of war crimes and crimes against humanity. He was hanged on October 16, 1946.

Hess found the cave and what remained of Frank's art collection and contacted Gerhard Braun. Hess needed a way to move the paintings and Braun had trucks. They agreed to split everything fifty–fifty.

# Thirty-nine

"Harry, you see him lookin' over here? Why's he lookin' at us?"

Hess had come out of the gallery and was staring at them. "It's the car. I think he's looking at the Peugeot."

But then Hess turned and walked down the street to a sidewalk cafe and sat at a table.

Cordell made a U-turn. Harry said, "What're you doing?"

"Gettin' outta here. Don't you know nothin' about surveillance? Man seen the car, we got to be more careful. When I worked for Chilly, see, we'd have to watch out for the police. They come to the projects in beat-up old cars, cops dressed for the street. They'd park, smoke cigarettes, lookin' around, waitin' for somethin' to go down, couldn't've been more obvious."

Colette said, "What did you do?"

"Wait till they took off, or came back another time."

"But you got busted, you told me."

"Yeah, but it had nothin' to do with that. I was suckered by a cop dressed like he was homeless, livin' in a refrigerator carton. Man was a stone actor."

Cordell took the first left, made another U-turn and parked on the street with a clean angle on Hess' car and the gallery entrance. No way Hess'd be able to see them.

"How do you like me now?" Cordell said, glancing at Harry.

"Not bad."

"There he is," Colette said.

Harry saw Hess come out of the gallery, carrying a painting. He put it in the trunk, got in the car and pulled out, going right toward Monte Carlo.

Colette said, "What do you think he is doing with the painting?"

"Trying to sell it," Harry said. "His German assets are frozen. I think he needs money."

"It has to be worth a fortune," Colette said. "I looked it up in the library. It was looted by the Nazis and supposedly lost during the war, destroyed in a museum fire."

Harry saw Hess heading back to the harbor and then turning right toward Nice.

*

Instead of turning right on boulevard Gambetta, Hess drove through Nice, going west, just driving, the Peugeot still behind him, seeing it in the rearview and side mirrors. At Antibes he turned off the highway and drove into town. It was midday and congested. He parked in an angled space on the street, picked the pistol up off the passenger seat and slid it in his pocket.

Hess went into a restaurant. Standing just inside the door he could see the Peugeot double-parked behind the Renault, stopping traffic, horns honking. He walked past the maître d' into the crowded dining room, heard the loud din of voices, saw waiters carrying trays of food, moving about. He walked through the dining room into the stainless-steel kitchen, hearing the sharp clatter of plates and utensils, line cooks working, eyes on him but no one questioning his being there or trying to stop him, and then he was outside, walking along the alley behind the restaurant. He made a series of turns taking him blocks from the main street where he had parked. There was a taxi sitting in front of a small hotel. Hess got in and told the driver to take him to Nice.

The taxi dropped him at a cafe back on boulevard Gambetta. Hess phoned Marie-Noëlle to pick him up. He sat at a table inside, drank an espresso in two swallows, watching the street. The Fiat pulled up a few minutes later. He went outside and got in, looking around for a silver Peugeot.

"*Monsieur*, where is your car?"

"Antibes."

She pulled away from the curb and made a U-turn, window down, left hand on the steering wheel, holding a cigarette between her index and middle fingers, shifting with her right. Hess felt claustrophobic in the small interior, his shoulder and Marie-Noëlle's almost touching.

"What happened, if you don't mind my asking?" She brought the cigarette to her mouth, blowing out smoke, and made a left turn. He was conscious of her earthy smell mixing with the cigarette smoke and diesel exhaust.

"Mechanical trouble."

"Is the garage picking it up?"

Hess nodded. "Have you seen anyone else on the property?"

"No, *monsieur*."

"Or cars parked outside the gate?"

"No, *monsieur*." She dropped the cigarette out the open window.

"Any hunters?" On occasion Hess had seen villagers in the hills, hunting rabbits and quail.

"No, *monsieur*, no one."

They rode the rest of the way in silence. Marie-Noëlle lit another cigarette, kept it hanging in her mouth as she drove the winding roads to the villa, shifting and down-shifting, the cigarette ash breaking off, falling in her lap, Marie-Noëlle brushing it on the floor.

Back at the villa, Hess contacted a service garage in the village just up the hill, and arranged to have his Renault towed there. Then he went to his bedroom and stood on the deck with binoculars scanning the hills and valley behind his property, and felt foolish when he saw Claude, the gardener, look up at him from trimming palm trees by the pool.

He went inside and took a thick wad of money out of his jacket pocket, counting the bills on the bed. $9,635 and 2,200 francs. He owned the villa free and clear, but selling it would take time. He would have to meet with realtors. And he owned twelve expressionist paintings and a couple dozen others that were, depending on their authenticity, worth either a fortune or nothing. But selling the paintings—going through an auction house or a gallery—would probably take even longer than selling the villa. He knew it was time to leave.

*

At 4.30 the manager of the service garage phoned to tell Hess his car had been towed to the lot but there was no way to check its functions without the ignition key. Hess said he would bring the key in the morning.

He waited until he was sure the garage was closed before he went to find Marie-Noëlle. She was folding clothes in the laundry room on the lower level.

"I need your help with something."

"Yes, of course, *monsieur*. What can I do for you?"

"Drive me to pick up the car. They have it at the garage."

"*Monsieur*, are you sure? I can take Claude if you would rather not."

# Forty

Cordell had parked on the street in Antibes. Harry saw Hess walk into the restaurant at 12.10, and now all they could do was wait. At 2.40 Harry was getting concerned. He glanced at Colette and Cordell and said, "What do you think?"

"The French take their time eating but this is ridiculous," Colette said.

"Maybe he's not in there," Harry said. "Slipped out, we didn't see him, or went out the back."

"What I was sayin' earlier. Dude might've made us and took off."

Colette glanced at Harry. "And leave the painting, a priceless work of art?"

"Unless it isn't," Harry said. "I'm going in."

Harry got out of the car, waited for traffic to clear and crossed the street. Looked in Hess' car. Nothing. He went into the restaurant and scanned the dining room. Only half a dozen tables were occupied and Hess wasn't at any of them. He checked the men's room. It was empty. He walked out and went around the block. There was an alley behind the restaurant. Hess could've walked through and come out here. But why?

Harry went back to the car. Cordell was on the sidewalk smoking a Davidoff. "Let me guess. Isn't there, is he?"

"Where'd he go and why'd he leave his car?" Harry said, and saw Cordell focussed on something across the street.

"Harry, check it out."

Harry turned and saw the tow truck parked behind Hess' Renault.

Colette rolled the back window down. "Maybe this explains it."

"Maybe." But Harry didn't think so. "If Hess had car trouble he would've called a tow truck right away and stayed there." Leaving the painting was another thing that didn't make sense. He watched the tow truck lift the back end of Hess' Renault.

They followed it to Nice and up the winding roads into the hills, past Hess' villa to a garage on the outskirts of the village. They waited in a wooded area across the street from the garage until dark.

"Harry, we know where the man lives, what're we doin' here?"

Colette offered to go to the village and get food and coffee.

"Let's just give it a few more minutes," Harry said.

And then he saw the Fiat drive in, the housekeeper in the spaghetti-western hat behind the wheel, and someone sitting next to her.

*

It was dark when they arrived in the village, the shops lit up. People picking up food on their way home from work, coming out of the bakery carrying baguettes, coming out of the butcher shop with cuts of meat wrapped in brown paper. Trucks and automobiles parked and double-parked, *monsieur* alert, looking about.

Marie-Noëlle pulled into the lot and put the car in neutral. The bay doors were closed, the lights off. *Monsieur*'s Renault was parked on the side of the building.

"I think it is not going to work today, *monsieur*. I can bring you back in the morning."

"Where do you live?"

"Just down there." She pointed north. "Half a kilometer."

"Is your husband at home?"

"No, *monsieur*. Henri is delivering parts to Flins, gone for three days."

"Show me your house."

Marie-Noëlle glanced at him, wondering if he was serious.

"You have worked for me ten years. I want to see where you live."

She was nervous now, riding with her boss to an empty house. They were alone in the villa much of the time and he had never made a pass at her. So what was this all about?

"How long have you been sleeping with Claude?"

Marie-Noëlle could feel herself blushing. How did he know that? They had been so careful. "*Monsieur*, I get lonely."

"It's all right. I understand. But Claude? I think you can do better."

*Monsieur* sounded as if he was offering himself. But why now? And why her? She was thinking about the German model he had brought to the villa one time, tall and beautiful. She turned off the main road, *monsieur* staring at her legs working the pedals.

"There it is," she said, slowing down, pointing to her small stone house, embarrassed, but this was where she lived. "*Monsieur*, have you seen enough? I can take you back."

"Let's go in."

"Ah, *monsieur*. I don't know."

"You don't know what? We are friends, aren't we?"

Marie-Noëlle didn't see it that way. He owned the villa, and she worked for him. What was going on?

She drove to the house, parking near the side entrance, her heart pounding now. She opened the door, waited for him to get out and come around the car. She unlocked and opened the door to the house, and they went in. It was completely dark. Marie turned a lamp on in the salon, removed her hat, hung it on a hook and fussed with her hair, self-conscious about the way she looked.

"Are you going to give me the grand tour?"

"*Monsieur*, there are only four rooms. Come this way."

Hess followed her into the kitchen that had a wide stone fireplace against one wall, a small refrigerator and a simple wooden table in the center of the room.

"May I offer you something, cognac, Pernod?" She didn't have anything up to his standards, but had to ask.

"A little Pernod would be nice."

\*

Hess didn't believe in coincidence. He had to be sure. He didn't see the silver Peugeot when they had passed through the village. He didn't see it when they drove to the garage, or to Marie-Noëlle's house. But when they came out a little after eight there it was parked on the street between two cars.

They were turning onto the main road, Hess looking in the side mirror, when he saw the Peugeot's lights pop on, and the car swing out and follow them. Marie-Noëlle was driving, a lipstick-stained cigarette butt clamped between her teeth, window open halfway, cold air blowing in. He had thrown down a quick glass of Pernod at her house as she sat across the table from him, nervous, keeping her distance. Then she had offered to drive him back to the villa.

# Forty-one

Colette pulled over. Harry and Cordell got out and crossed the road and stood at the wall in front of Hess' villa. No car had passed by for several minutes. Cordell hoisted him up and Harry grabbed the tile cap, went over the top of the wall and dropped down in the garden twenty feet from the front door. Harry crouched, listening, heard a dog barking in the distance.

He drew the .38 from his coat pocket and took the stairs down to the lower level. He moved along the back of the villa, looking in windows, passing a dark bedroom, an office with a desk light on. He passed the kitchen, saw a pot on the stove top, a plate and wine glass set on the counter. He kept moving, glanced at the pool, crossed the deck and looked through the sliding doors. The TV was on in the salon. There were signs of life but no one was in any of the rooms. He turned and looked at the houses scattered through the dark hills, and down the valley at the city of Nice, lit up but subdued by cloud cover.

Harry went along the house, back the way he'd come. Halfway up the stairs, he heard a door close and footsteps on the pea-gravel path that led to the cars. Went up, moved along the side of the villa to the front and saw the housekeeper in hat and cape, carrying a small suitcase to the Fiat.

Harry went to the front door, glanced to his right. The housekeeper was in the car. He heard it start and saw the lights go on and the gate open. But then she got out and went in the garage. Harry opened the door, stepped into the small foyer, closed it and went up the stairs to Hess' bedroom. It was dark. He crossed the room, looked out the sliding door and saw the Fiat in the driveway.

He went downstairs, gripping the .38, moved through the office into the hall, heard voices in the salon and then something else, a sound like someone moaning. He opened a door and there was the housekeeper tied to a chair in the laundry room, a rag stuffed in her mouth. He pulled it out. Hess was wearing her hat and cape. Hess was in the Fiat getting away.

"Where is Chartier going?"

"I don't know, *monsieur*."

\*

Claude was bringing a bag of trash up from his cottage to put in the bin in the garage, hoping to see Marie-Noëlle. He had been thinking about her all day. He had kissed her when she came out to bring him a glass of water. He couldn't resist, even though she had told him no demonstrations of affection unless *monsieur* was away. He didn't like it when she was in the villa alone with Chartier. *Monsieur* was a man, and Claude didn't trust any man in Marie-Noëlle's company.

Now he was coming up the stairs and saw something out of the corner of his eye and ducked down. A figure moving along the back wall of the house, a man looking in the windows. Was this the one *monsieur* had been talking about? It was very strange. Where did he come from? How did he get on the property?

Claude ran down the stairs to the cottage, went in and lifted the shotgun off the hooks above the fireplace. The gun was hot from the fire. He broke it open, loaded two shells and snapped it closed. Claude's hands were shaking. He was a gardener, not a gendarme, but he had to protect Marie-Noëlle.

*

Harry heard him, looked over his shoulder and saw the gardener holding a shotgun, the man probably thinking he had tied her up. Harry rested the .38 on top of the washing machine.

The housekeeper said, "*Dépose le fusil, Claude.*"

The gardener looked at her but didn't say anything.

"*Claude, laisse-le tomber.*"

The gardener lowered the barrel as Cordell came down the hall from the salon with the .45 in his hand. The gardener raised the shotgun and aimed it at him.

"*Claude, je suis hors de danger, laisse tomber le fusil.*"

The gardener crouched, resting his shotgun on the floor, and moved past Harry to the housekeeper, putting his arms around her.

Harry wanted to tell the woman what was going on but this wasn't the time. He picked up the .38 and he and Cordell ran upstairs, went out the front door and through the wrought-iron gate. The Peugeot was across the road, lights on, Colette behind the wheel. Harry got in front next to her, Cordell in back.

"Hess is in the Fiat," Harry said.

"Are you sure?"

"I saw him pull out," Cordell said. "Thought it was the French lady."

"He's headed toward Nice," Colette said. She gripped the steering wheel and accelerated, high beams trying to light the dark narrow road, the Peugeot going downhill, picking up speed.

*

Hess got out of the Fiat and went into the garage. There were boxes of shotgun shells on a metal shelf against the back wall. He opened a box and grabbed a handful, stuffed them in his pocket and returned to the Fiat.

The gate was open. He backed out and spun the front end around, pointing toward Nice. He turned, glanced up the road and saw the Peugeot parked about twenty meters away. Hess reached behind him, lifted the shotgun off the rear seat and angled it, barrel first on the passenger-side floor, stock resting against the seatback. He put the Fiat in gear and started down the hill, stone wall flanking the road on the left, glancing in the rearview mirror, expecting to see headlights, but no one was following him.

There was an opening in the wall at avenue du Dauphiné. He turned left, went thirty meters, pulled off the road, and turned off the engine. There were lights on in the houses dotting the valley. Hess got out with the shotgun, walked back to the intersection and looked up the dark road, using the edge of the wall for cover, and waited.

There was a flicker of light at the top of the hill, and then headlights appeared coming down the road. He assumed it was the Peugeot, pulled back the twin hammers on the shotgun. The car, a Citroën, paused at the stop sign and continued on. Now another light appeared at the top of the hill. Hess held the shotgun across his body and walked down avenue du Dauphiné about twenty meters. The Peugeot stopped at the stop sign. He was in the middle of the road when it turned left and came toward him.

Hess brought the stock to his shoulder, aimed between the headlights, squeezed the first trigger and the shotgun kicked and boomed, blowing out the radiator. Now he aimed just above the headlights, fired at the windshield and stepped out of the way as the car came at him, rolling to a stop down the road. He cracked open the shotgun, ejected the spent casings, reloaded and snapped the gun closed.

*

The punctured radiator made a high-pitched whine, and smoke was coming from the engine compartment, swirling over the headlights. The second blast had blown a hole through the center of the windshield, spraying the interior with pieces of glass. Colette seemed dazed but was otherwise okay. She grabbed his hand and squeezed it. He looked in the backseat.

Cordell was leaning against the door behind her. There was blood spatter on the seat and on the rear window, which was pocked with holes.

"Cordell, you all right?"

"I'm hit, man."

Harry said, "How bad?"

"I don't know."

Harry looked through the side window and saw Hess with the shotgun, moving toward the car. He reached in his coat pocket and drew the revolver. "Get down, he's coming back."

Colette glanced at him and turned her body, knees on the floor, face flat on the seat bottom. Cordell slid off the rear seat onto the floor. Through the side window Harry saw Hess approaching, getting close. He opened the door and went down on his knees. Heard the blast and felt the concussion, glass from the driver's-side window spraying over him. When he looked again Hess was coming around the front of the car, visible for a second in the headlight beam.

Harry raised the Colt and fired but Hess kept coming, firing the shotgun, blowing out the right side of the windshield. Harry, on his knees, fired another round, but Hess had disappeared. Harry got up and saw him limping along the side of the road.

Harry went after him, got to Hess as he was pulling away, aimed for the left rear tire and squeezed the trigger. The Fiat fishtailed, went off the road and rolled a couple times down the hill into a thicket, headlight beams angled out of the shrubs. Harry climbed down, crouched and pointed his gun. The front passenger door was open, dome light illuminating the interior. He could see blood on the seats. Hess was gone, but he was hurt.

Harry stood behind the Fiat and listened, heard the wind and the rustling of branches. He had one round left in the .38. He looked over the car into the darkness and started down the hill.

*

Hess had been shot in the soft tissue just above his right hip. The bullet had gone through him. He could feel blood leaking out of the exit wound, his shirt and trousers wet with it. He wasn't wearing a seatbelt, and had gripped the steering wheel when the Fiat started to roll, and when he couldn't hold on any longer, let go and bounced around the interior till the car got tangled in dense shrubs and came to a stop.

He had moved down the hill about seventy meters below the car, leaning against a tree trunk, holding the Walther, waiting for Harry Levin. Shoot him when he had the chance. He could see the headlights above him, and feel a breeze come up from the valley. He was looking down at the lights in houses scattered through the hills, the city of Nice to his right hidden from view.

*

Harry took his time, zigzagging down the hill using trees and overgrown shrubs for cover, feet in loafers sliding on the steep terrain. Visibility was better now, the heavy clouds had moved out and there was a three-quarter moon lighting up the landscape. He stopped and listened, heard twigs snap just below him, and crouched behind a broadleaf evergreen. He saw a figure move down the hill, then disappear behind a tree.

Hess appeared again maybe fifteen feet away, limping, looking unsteady. Harry closed in, raised the .38 and aimed the barrel between Hess' shoulders. "Take another step, you're dead." He couldn't tell if Hess was holding a gun but had to assume he was.

"That's what you said to me the last time. In the kitchen

294

in Palm Beach, remember?" Hess paused. "You shot me again. That's twice I owe you."

"I'll try to do better next time. Toss the gun away from you, and put your hands up where I can see them."

"I'm not armed."

Harry didn't believe him.

Hess glanced over his shoulder at him. "Are you going to shoot me in the back?"

"Back or front, it doesn't matter."

Hess lowered his arms and turned, lost his footing and slid to the bottom of the hill. Harry watched him all the way and went after him, aiming the revolver, trying to keep his balance, telling himself again he had one round in the gun and to make it count.

When he got to the bottom of the hill, Hess was moving toward him, aiming a pistol. Hess fired and missed, fired again, the shots echoing around the hills. And now Harry, holding the .38 in two hands, aimed and squeezed the trigger. Hess went down on his knees, dropped the pistol and fell back.

Harry picked up the gun and stood over him, Hess' hands pressing on the wound in his chest, trying to stop the blood that was running between his fingers.

"You put another hole in me."

"That one's for my daughter."

"You think it's over? I'll be coming for you, Harry, but you won't know when or where."

"Not this time." He aimed Hess' gun at him, finger feeling the weight of the trigger. Hess tried to sit up and Harry pushed him back on the ground with his foot. Hess' eyes were open, staring up at him, but he wasn't moving. Harry crouched at his side, touched his neck and felt for a pulse.

*

Colette was waiting for Harry when he got to the top of the hill. She put her arms around his waist and hugged him. "I heard the gunshots. I didn't know."

"It's over. How's Cordell?"

"He needs a doctor."

They walked back to the Peugeot at the side of the road, headlights still on. Harry opened the rear door. Cordell was sitting up in the backseat.

"You got him, huh, Harry?"

"I got him."

"You sure?"

"You can go down there and see for yourself."

"I'll take your word for it."

"How're you feeling?"

"Not bad for being blasted with a shotgun."

"You're talking—that's a good sign."

"Got a lot more to say."

"I'll bet you do." Harry paused. "There's a restaurant down the road about a mile. I'm going to walk there, call a taxi and come back for you."

*

The concierge called a doctor, who came to the suite with his black bag. Cordell told him a hunter had shot him accidentally

296

while he was taking a walk up in the hills. "Man huntin' birds or somethin'."

The doctor looked at him quizzically. "What time was this?"

"Earlier this evenin', didn't know if I'd need medical attention."

"By the look of your wounds I think you make the right decision."

The doc led Cordell into the bathroom, cleaned him up, administered an anesthetic, and removed eight pellets from his right shoulder and arm, a couple requiring stitches, but he was okay.

When the doctor walked out of the suite Harry said, "I think we should leave, and the sooner the better. In the morning someone is going to see the Peugeot with the blown-out windshield and blood in the backseat and call the police. Then they're going to find the Fiat and the murdered body of Vincent Chartier. They'll go to the villa and talk to the housekeeper. She'll tell them what happened last night and describe Cordell and me." Harry paused. "I think it's a good time to go to Detroit."